HER HUSBAND'S HANDS AND OTHER STORIES

BOOKS BY ADAM-TROY CASTRO

Lost in Booth Nine: Silver Salamander

X-Men and Spider-Man:

Time's Arrow, Book 2: The Present (with Tom DeFalco)

Spider-Man: The Gathering of the Sinister Six

An Alien Darkness

A Desperate Decaying Darkness

Spider-Man: The Revenge of the Sinister Six

Spider-Man: The Secret of the Sinister Six

Vossoff and Nimmitz:

Just a Couple of Idiots Reupholstering Space and Time

Tangled Strings

With the Stars in their Eyes (with Jerry Oltion)

Emissaries from the Dead

The Shallow End of the Pool

The Third Claw of God

Gustav Gloom and the People Taker

Gustav Gloom and the Nightmare Vault

Gustav Gloom and the Four Terrors

Gustav Gloom and the Cryptic Carousel

HER HUSBAND'S HANDS AND OTHER STORIES

Adam-Troy Castro

PRIME BOOKS

HER HUSBAND'S HANDS AND OTHER STORIES

Hand stock photo by Deceptico, DeviantArt.com
Nanobot stock photo by Vladislav Ociacia,
ociacia.com, istockphoto.com
Cover design by Sherin Nicole.

Prime Books
www.prime-books.com

For more information, contact Prime Books:
prime@prime-books.com

ISBN: 978-1-60701-408-9

CONTENTS

INTRODUCTION

Back in 1968, I met one of my favorite people—Robert Bloch.

Yes, I know, this is supposed to be an introduction to Adam-Troy Castro's collection of stories. I'll get there, I promise. But first I want to talk about Robert Bloch.

Bloch is mostly known as the author of Psycho. He is also known for saying that he has the heart of a ten year old boy—in a jar on his desk.

But I remember Bloch as just an all-round good guy. He was one of the funniest and most charming men in the science fiction community, often in demand as a speaker and toastmaster at conventions. One of his best lines came from his sale of Psycho to Alfred Hitchcock—actually, not Hitchcock, but to a dummy company Hitch had set up so he wouldn't have to pay as much for the movie rights if his name were attached.

According to the story, Bloch only received $750 from that dummy company. So Robert Bloch went on to claim that he was the forerunner of the gay liberation movement, because he was the first man screwed by Alfred Hitchcock. (This is a joke I have since purloined and used with another producer's name inserted.)

But the reason I mention Bloch is because of another joke he once told from the podium. He said he was passing a room where he heard two male voices talking, one saying, "I'll put yours in mine if you'll put mine in yours." He assumed it was a gay liaison, but when he opened the door it was only two authors assembling anthologies, agreeing to publish each other's stories. (This was during the 70's, a time when many SF authors were also editing anthologies. I did five myself.)

That joke came immediately to mind when I sat down to type this introduction. Because Adam-Troy Castro and I are trading introductions. He wrote a generous introduction to my story collection, *In the Deadlands*, from BenBella Books, available on Amazon, and in return I am writing an introduction to this story collection. I'll put his in mine and he'll put mine in his. Robert Bloch can snicker all he wants, I'm still not taking a shower with him.

Let me step away from the homoerotic references and recontextualize all of the above as literary back-scratching (with everyone keeping their clothes on) and leap ahead to the subject at hand.

Adam-Troy Castro is a cherished friend. This in itself is remarkable because I am well-known as a cantankerous, reclusive, grumpy old curmudgeon. But Adam-Troy is one of the few people who can tell me that I'm full of shit and still remain a cherished friend, because when he says it, he's not only right—he's insightful.

(In 1995 at the Nebula Awards Banquet, held in some posh hotel in New York City, I was attempting to be modest, while holding a Nebula award under my arm. It is not possible to be modest with a Nebula trophy under your arm. Adam-Troy Castro stopped me from digging my big toe in the sand and saying, 'Aw, shucks,' and told me I was full of shit. He was right. I do not know how to savor a moment of acknowledgment. Fortunately, that kind of embarrassment does not happen often, so I haven't had to learn. But the important part of that story is that he was right.)

Since then, Adam and I have had few more occasions to break bread together—most memorably that marvelous Brazilian restaurant in Las Vegas, the one where the waiters continued slicing huge slabs of various animals onto our plates until I had to pull a sidearm to stop them because my gut had become so distended

I feared my ability to stand might be permanently impaired—but Adam and his wife Judi remain two of the most charming dinner companions this side of Paul DeFilippo and Deb. (This is shameless name-dropping on my part, but it's still true.)

Much more relevant is that Adam-Troy and I engage in almost daily exchanges online, often on Facebook, sometimes in private messages or emails, and once even by phone, I think. Usually, these conversations are serious, rigorous, and important enough to slow down and pay serious attention.

You really have to like someone to put up with them on a daily basis. Especially if you're not related to them. But this kind of mutual affection is something that feels unique to the community of science fiction writers. At least, in my not-too humble opinion.

In most other environments, particularly television and movies, writers often behave like bitchy little girls or FBI agents. The highest compliment any Hollywood writer can give any other is healthy disrespect. From there it's all downhill. The rest is a demonstration of backstabbing, frontstabbing, malicious name-calling, and lies. (Well, all writers are liars—the good ones get paid for it.) Hollywood writers will repeat the most abhorrible career-killing stories about other writers, all in pursuit of the illusory staff job or possible script assignment.

Try this experiment. Next time you're having lunch in any restaurant within shouting distance of a studio, ask your waiter how the screenplay is coming along. This will give you some idea of the level of desperation in that particular job market.

Contrast this with the science fiction community.

This is my experience. SF and fantasy writers not only respect each other, they admire each other. Get a group of these authors together and within fifteen minutes they'll be listing the writers who influenced them, the books they loved growing up, and the things they've learned from each other. Introduce two writers to each other at a convention and you're likely to hear simultaneous cries of, "I loved your book—" I am not making this up. I've been in the center of this transaction more times than I can remember, once even with a Pulitzer Prize winner. It's weird and embarrassing and joyous.

But even beyond that, even if a writer has not been able to keep up with the torrent of new novels pouring out of several thousand computers every month, science fiction and fantasy writers tend to have a genuine respect for each other—because only they know how hard it really is.

Take any other genre—romance, history, horror, detective, western, whatever—and the rules are already in place. The milieu is established, the resources for research are readily available, the format is understandable.

Not so, science fiction.

Science fiction requires world-building. Everything. It requires a level of research beyond anything required by any other genre. It demands the mutual skills of extrapolation and speculation. It demands awareness of sociology, anthropology, psychology, as well—because you're not only creating an environment, you're predicting how human beings will live and act and react to each other within that environment. And . . . the hardest part of all, it has to be believable. The author has to believe in it before the reader can.

The reason there are so many bad science fiction movies, TV shows, novels, and stories is that science fiction is *hard*—it's not about eye-candy, it's not about special effects, it's not about techno-babble, it's about that strange and terrible place where human beings are fundamentally challenged by the possibilities of the world that the author has constructed around them. This is what (most) science fiction writers know about themselves and each other—that any author who has that kind of grasp on the genre well enough to turn out a consistently competent effort is worthy of serious respect.

And that brings me—finally—to Adam-Troy Castro.

As I said above, we're friends. As I said above, we're trading introductions. But putting both of those things aside, it's still a privilege to write an introduction to this collection of stories—because Adam-Troy Castro is a damn good writer.

Actually, I need to be more specific than that. This man's virtues as a storyteller are considerable.

First, his sentences are easy to read.

This is one of the highest pieces of praise I can give to any writer. The true test of a writer's skill with language is to read his paragraphs aloud. If they flow easily from the tongue, they will flow easily in your mind as you read.

More than that, Adam-Troy Castro tells his stories with a seeming minimum of effort. He does not engage in gaudy constructions or labored trowelings of adjectives and metaphors. Instead, he lets the story grow as if it is occurring in front of your eyes. He glides through the narrative, creating magic with the simplest of tools, demonstrating the kind of linguistic muscle memory that only comes from ten thousand hours of sitting at the keyboard, paying meticulous attention to the words, the sentences, the paragraphs, and the way they all fit together—doing the authorial equivalent of "wax on, wax off."

In other words, Adam-Troy Castro sweats blood to make it look effortless. The result is a clean clear voice. *Readable.* Evocative. (And the rotten bastard makes it look easy!)

Why is this important? Because if the reader has to stop and decode the sentence he's not in the story, he's trapped in the writing. The job of the writer is to evoke the story so vividly that the reader forgets he's reading and rides the roller coaster as fast as he can, eagerly turning pages (or tapping the side of his ebook reader's screen) to find out what happens next.

But no matter how skillful any author might be at constructing sentences, he also has to make you believe in the story, and this is where Adam-Troy Castro really shines.

That's the second point.

You believe in the story because his characters believe in it. They are not standard issue archetypes dropped into their situations as much as they are grown from the worlds they inhabit.

His characters are genuine. They have histories. They have passions, fears, desires, and sorrows. They have feelings, they can hurt. As a writer, he cares about the people in his stories as if they are friends, family, acquaintances, enemies—and because Adam-Troy Castro cares, the reader cares too. Dip into any of these stories and as the characters come to life for you, you will care about them too.

That in itself should establish this man as a writer well worth your attention.

But his skill with language and character are merely the foundations on which he builds.

Adam-Troy Castro has something worthwhile to say in every story. He's using his stories to illuminate and explore the subtext of our world. He's commenting on the terrible traps that humanity has stumbled into, the things we do to each other, and the ethical dilemmas that bind us.

Adam-Troy Castro tells stories that *disturb.*

That's why he's worth reading. The status quo is the enemy. The writer's job is to be subversive, to awaken the reader, to annoy the reader, to make the reader uncomfortable, to stamp the reader with an indelible experience that will change the way he looks at the universe from that moment on. Adam-Troy Castro does that.

Dip into this collection with caution. Do not try to assimilate it all in one read. Notice the spread. Notice the dynamic range. These are thought-grenades. They are time-bombs shoved down your throat. They will lurk in your gut and explode at all the wrong moments.

Pay attention, dear reader. This man is doing what writers are supposed to do.

He's making a difference.

—David Gerrold

ARVIES

STATEMENT OF INTENT

This is the story of a mother, and a daughter, and the right to life, and the dignity of all living things, and of some souls granted great destinies at the moment of their conception, and of others damned to remain society's useful idiots.

CONTENTS

Expect cute plush animals and amniotic fluid and a more or less happy ending for everybody, though the definition of happiness may depend on the truncated emotional capacity of those unable to feel anything else. Some of the characters are rich and famous, others are underage, and one is legally dead, though you may like her the most of all.

APPEARANCE

We first encounter Molly June on her fifteenth deathday, when the monitors in charge of deciding such things declare her safe for passengers. Congratulating her on completing the only important stage of her development, they truck her in a padded skimmer to the arvie showroom where she is claimed, right away, by one of the Living.

The fast sale surprises nobody, not the servos that trained her into her current state of health and attractiveness, not the AI routines managing the showroom, and least of all Molly June, who has spent her infancy and early childhood having the ability to feel surprise, or anything beyond a vague contentment, scrubbed from her emotional palate. Crying, she'd learned while still capable of such things, brought punishment, while unconditional acceptance of anything the engineers saw fit to provide brought light and flower scent and warmth. By this point in her existence she'll greet anything short of an exploding bomb with no reaction deeper than vague concern. Her sale is a minor development by comparison: a happy development, reinforcing her feelings of dull satisfaction. Don't feel sorry for her. Her entire life, or more accurately death, is happy ending. All she has to do is spend the rest of it carrying a passenger.

VEHICLE SPECIFICATIONS

You think you need to know what Molly June looks like. You really don't, as it plays no role in her life. But as the information will assist you in feeling empathy for her, we will oblige anyway.

Molly June is a round-faced, button-nosed gamin, with pink lips and cheeks marked with permanent rose: her blonde hair framing her perfect face in parentheses of bouncy, luxurious curls. Her blue eyes, enlarged by years of genetic manipulation and corrective surgeries, are three times as large as the ones imperfect nature would have set in her face. Lemur-like, they dominate her features like a pair of pacific jewels, all moist and sad and adorable. They reveal none of her essential personality, which is not a great loss, as she's never been permitted to develop one.

Her body is another matter. It has been trained to perfection, with the kind of punishing daily regimen that can only be endured when the mind itself remains unaware of pain or exhaustion. She has worked with torn ligaments, with shattered joints, with disfiguring wounds. She has severed her spine and crushed her skull and has had both replaced, with the same ease her engineers have used, fourteen times, to replace her skin with a fresh version unmarked by scars or blemishes. What remains of her now is a wan amalgam of her own best-developed parts, most of them entirely natural, except for her womb, which is of course a plush, wired palace, far safer for its future occupant than the envelope of mere flesh would have provided. It can survive injuries capable of reducing Molly June to a smear.

In short, she is precisely what she should be, now that she's fifteen years past birth, and therefore, by all standards known to modern civilized society, Dead.

HEROINE

Jennifer Axioma-Singh has never been born and is therefore a significant distance away from being Dead.

She is, in every way, entirely typical. She has written operas, climbed mountains, enjoyed daredevil plunges from the upper atmosphere into vessels the size of teacups, finagled controlling stock in seventeen major multinationals, earned the hopeless devotion of any number of lovers, written her name in the sands of time, fought campaigns in a hundred conceptual wars, survived twenty regime changes, and on three occasions had herself turned off so she could spend a year or two mulling the purpose of existence while her bloodstream spiced her insights with all the most fashionable hallucinogens.

She has accomplished all of this from within various baths of amniotic fluid.

Jennifer has yet to even open her eyes, which have never been allowed to fully develop past the first trimester and which still, truth be told, resemble black marbles behind lids of translucent onionskin. This doesn't actually deprive her of vision, of course. At the time she claims Molly June as her arvie, she's been indulging her visual cortex for seventy long years, zipping back and forth across the solar system collecting all the tourist chits one earns for seeing all the wonders of modern-day humanity: from the scrimshaw carving her immediate ancestors made of Mars to the radiant face of Unborn Jesus shining from the artfully re-configured multicolored atmosphere of Saturn. She has gloried in the catalogue of beautiful sights provided by God and all the industrious living people before her.

Throughout all this she has been blessed with vision far greater than any we will ever know ourselves, since her umbilical interface allows her sights capable of frying merely organic eyes, and she's far too sophisticated a person to be satisfied with the banal limitations of the merely visual spectrum. Decades of life have provided Jennifer Axioma-Singh with more depth than that. And something else: a perverse need, stranger than anything she's ever done, and impossible to indulge without first installing herself in a healthy young arvie.

ANCESTRY

Jennifer Axioma-Singh has owned arvies before, each one customized from the moment of its death. She's owned males, females, neuters, and several sexes only developed in the past decade. She's had arvies designed for athletic prowess, arvies designed for erotic sensation, and arvies designed for survival in harsh environments. She's even had one arvie with hypersensitive pain receptors: that, during a cold and confused period of masochism.

The last one before this, who she still misses, and sometimes feels a little guilty about, was a lovely girl named Peggy Sue, with a metabolism six times baseline normal and a digestive tract capable of surviving about a hundred separate species of nonstop abuse. Peggy Sue could down mountains of exotic delicacies without ever feeling full or engaging her gag reflex, and enjoyed taste receptors directly plugged into her pleasure centers. The slightest sip of coconut juice could flood her system with tidal waves of endorphin-crazed ecstasy. The things chocolate could do to her were downright obscene.

Unfortunately, she was still vulnerable to the negative effects of unhealthy eating, and went through four liver transplants and six emergency transfusions in the first ten years of Jennifer's occupancy.

The cumulative medical effect of so many years of determined gluttony mattered little to Jennifer Axioma-Singh, since her own caloric intake was regulated by devices that prevented the worst of Peggy Sue's excessive consumption from causing any damage on her side of the uterine wall. Jennifer's umbilical cord passed only those compounds necessary for keeping her alive and healthy. All Jennifer felt, through her interface with Peggy Sue's own sensory spectrum, was the joy of eating; all she experienced was the sheer, overwhelming treasury of flavor.

And if Peggy Sue became obese and diabetic and jaundiced in the meantime—as she did, enduring her last few years as Jennifer's arvie as an immobile mountain of reeking flab, with barely enough strength to position her mouth for another bite—then that was inconsequential as well, because she had progressed beyond prenatal development and had therefore passed beyond that stage of life where human beings can truly be said to have a soul.

PHILOSOPHY

Life, true life, lasts only from the moment of conception to the moment of birth. Jennifer Axioma-Singh subscribes to this principle, and clings to it in the manner of any concerned citizen aware that the very foundations of her society depend on everybody continuing to believe it without question. But she is capable of forming attachments, no matter how irrational, and she therefore felt a frisson of guilt once she decided she'd had enough and the machines performed the Caesarian Section that delivered her from Peggy Sue's pliant womb. After all, Peggy Sue's reward for so many years of service, euthanasia, seemed so inadequate, given everything she'd provided.

But what else could have provided fair compensation, given the shape Peggy Sue was in by then? Surely not a last meal! Jennifer Axioma-Singh, who had not been able to think of any alternatives, brooded over the matter until she came to the same conclusion always reached by those enjoying lives of privilege, which is that such inequities are all for the best and that there wasn't all that much she could do about them, anyway. Her liberal compassion had been satisfied by the heartfelt promise to herself that if she ever bought an arvie again she would take care to act more responsibly.

And this is what she holds in mind, as the interim pod carries her into the gleaming white expanse of the very showroom where fifteen-year-old Molly June awaits a passenger.

INSTALLATION

Molly June's contentment is like the surface of a vast, pacific ocean, unstirred by tide or wind. The events of her life plunge into that mirrored surface without effect, raising nary a ripple or storm. It remains unmarked even now, as the anesthetician and obstetrician mechs emerge from their recesses to guide her always-unresisting form from the waiting room couch where she'd been left earlier this morning, to the operating theatre where she'll begin the useful stage of her existence. Speakers in the walls calm her further with an arrangement of melodious strings designed to override any unwanted emotional static.

It's all quite humane: for even as Molly June lies down and puts her head back and receives permission to close her eyes, she remains wholly at peace. Her heartbeat does jog, a little, just enough to be noted by the instruments, when the servos peel back the skin of her abdomen, but even that instinctive burst of fear fades with the absence of any identifiable pain. Her reaction to the invasive procedure fades to a mere theoretical interest, akin to what Jennifer herself would feel regarding gossip about people she doesn't know living in places where she's never been.

Molly June drifts, thinks of blue waters and bright sunlight, misses Jennifer's installation inside her, and only reacts to the massive change in her body after the incisions are closed and Jennifer has recovered enough to kick. Then her lips curl in a warm but vacant smile. She is happy. Arvies might be dead, in legal terms, but they still love their passengers.

AMBITION

Jennifer doesn't announce her intentions until two days later, after growing comfortable with her new living arrangements. At that time Molly June is stretched out on a lounge on a balcony overlooking a city once known as Paris but which has undergone perhaps a dozen other names of fleeting popularity since then; at this point it's called something that could be translated as Eternal Night, because its urban planners have noted that it looks best when its towers were against a backdrop of darkness and therefore arranged to free it from the sunlight that previously diluted its beauty for half of every day.

The balcony, a popular spot among visitors, is not connected to any actual building. It just sits, like an unanchored shelf, at a high altitude calculated to showcase the lights of the city at their most decadently glorious. The city itself is no longer inhabited, of course; it contains some mechanisms important for the maintenance of local weather patterns but otherwise exists only to confront the night sky with constellations of reflective light. Jennifer, experiencing its beauty through Molly June's eyes, and the bracing high-altitude wind through Molly June's skin, feels a connection with the place that goes beyond aesthetics. She finds it fateful, resonant, and romantic, the perfect location to begin the greatest adventure of a life that has already provided her with so many.

She cranes Molly June's neck to survey the hundreds of other arvies sharing this balcony with her: all young, all beautiful, all pretending happiness while their jaded passengers struggle to plan new experiences not yet grown dull from surfeit. She sees arvies drinking, arvies wrestling, arvies declaiming vapid poetry, arvies coupling in threes and fours; arvies colored in various shades, fitted to various shapes and sizes; pregnant females, and impregnated males, all sufficiently transparent, to a trained eye like Jennifer's, for the essential characters of their respective passengers to shine on through. They all glow from the light of a moon that is not *the* moon, as the original was removed some time ago, but a superb piece of stagecraft designed to accentuate the city below to its greatest possible effect.

Have any of these people ever contemplated a stunt as over-the-top creative as the one Jennifer has in mind? Jennifer thinks not. More, she is certain not. She feels pride, and her arvie Molly June laughs, with a joy that threatens to bring the unwanted curse of sunlight back to the city of lights. And for the first time she announces her intentions out loud, without even raising her voice, aware that any words emerging from Molly June's mouth are superfluous, so long as the truly necessary signal travels the network that conveys Jennifer's needs to the proper facilitating agencies. None of the other arvies on the balcony even hear Molly June speak. But those plugged in hear Jennifer speak the words destined to set off a whirlwind of controversy.

I want to give birth.

• • •

CLARIFICATION

It is impossible to understate the perversity of this request.

Nobody gives Birth.

Birth is a messy and unpleasant and distasteful process that ejects living creatures from their warm and sheltered environment into a harsh and unforgiving one that nobody wants to experience except from within the protection of wombs either organic or artificial.

Birth is the passage from Life, and all its infinite wonders, to another place inhabited only by those who have been forsaken. It's the terrible ending that modern civilization has forestalled indefinitely, allowing human beings to live within the womb without ever giving up the rich opportunities for experience and growth. It's sad, of course, that for Life to even be possible a large percentage of potential Citizens have to be permitted to pass through that terrible veil, into an existence where they're no good to anybody except as spare parts and manual laborers and arvies, but there are peasants in even the most enlightened societies, doing the hard work so the important people don't have to. The best any of us can do about that is appreciate their contribution while keeping them as complacent as possible.

The worst thing that could ever be said about Molly June's existence is that when the Nurseries measured her genetic potential, found it wanting, and decided she should approach Birth unimpeded, she was also humanely deprived of the neurological enhancements that allow first-trimester fetuses all the rewards and responsibilities of Citizenship. She never developed enough to fear the passage that awaited her, and never knew how sadly limited her existence would be. She spent her all-too-brief Life in utero ignorant of all the blessings that would forever be denied her, and has been kept safe and content and happy and drugged and stupid since birth.

After all, as a wise person once said, it takes a perfect vassal to make a perfect vessel. Nobody can say that there's anything wrong about that. But the dispossession of people like her, that makes the lives of people like Jennifer Axioma-Singh possible, remains a distasteful thing decent people just don't talk about.

Jennifer's hunger to experience birth from the point of view of a mother, grunting and sweating to expel another unfortunate like Molly June out of the only world that matters, into the world of cold slavery, thus strikes the vast majority as offensive, scandalous, unfeeling, selfish, and cruel. But since nobody has ever imagined a Citizen demented enough to want such a thing, nobody has ever thought to make it against the law. So the powers that be indulge Jennifer's perversity, while swiftly passing laws to ensure that nobody will ever be permitted such license ever again; and all the machinery of modern medicine is turned to the problem of just how to give her what she wants. And, before long, wearing Molly June as proxy, she gets knocked up.

IMPLANTATION

There is no need for any messy copulation. Sex, as conducted through arvies, still makes the world go round, prompting the usual number of bittersweet affairs, tempestuous breakups, turbulent love triangles, and silly love songs.

In her younger days, before the practice palled out of sheer repetition, Jennifer had worn out several arvies fucking like a bunny. But there has never been any danger of unwanted conception, at any time, not with the only possible source of motile sperm being the nurseries that manufacture it as needed without recourse to nasty antiquated testes. These days, zygotes and embryos are the province of the assembly line. Growing one inside an arvie, let alone one already occupied by a human being, presents all manner of bureaucratic difficulties involving the construction of new protocols and the rearranging of accepted paradigms and any amount of official eye-rolling, but once all that is said and done, the procedures turn out to be quite simple, and the surgeons have little difficulty providing Molly June with a second womb capable of growing Jennifer Axioma-Singh's daughter while Jennifer Axioma-Singh herself floats unchanging a few protected membranes away.

Unlike the womb that houses Jennifer, this one will not be wired in any way. Its occupant will not be able to influence Molly June's actions or enjoy the full spectrum of Molly June's senses. She will not understand, except in the most primitive, undeveloped way, what or where she is or how well she's being cared for. Literally next to Jennifer Axioma-Singh, she will be by all reasonable comparisons a mindless idiot. But she will live, and grow, for as long as it takes for this entire perverse whim of Jennifer's to fully play itself out.

GESTATION (I)

In the months that follow, Jennifer Axioma-Singh enjoys a novel form of celebrity. This is hardly anything new for her, of course, as she has been a celebrity several times before and if she lives her expected lifespan, expects to be one several times again. But in an otherwise unshockable world, she has never experienced, or even witnessed, that special, nearly extinct species of celebrity that comes from eliciting shock, and which was once best-known by the antiquated term, *notoriety.*

This, she glories in. This, she milks for every last angstrom. This, she surfs like an expert, submitting to countless interviews, constructing countless bon mots, pulling every string capable of scandalizing the public.

She says, "I don't see the reason for all the fuss."

She says, "People used to share wombs all the time."

She says, "It used to happen naturally, with multiple births: two or three or four or even seven of us, crowded together like grapes, sometimes absorbing each other's body parts like cute young cannibals."

She says, "I don't know whether to call what I'm doing pregnancy or performance art."

She says, "Don't you think Molly June looks special? Don't you think she glows?"

She says, "When the baby's born, I may call her Halo."

She says, "No, I don't see any problem with condemning her to Birth. If it's good enough for Molly June, it's good enough for my child."

And she says, "No, I don't care what anybody thinks. It's my arvie, after all."

And she fans the flames of outrage higher and higher, until public sympathies turn to the poor slumbering creature inside the sac of amniotic fluid, whose life and future have already been so cruelly decided. Is she truly limited enough to be condemned to Birth? Should she be stabilized and given her own chance at life, before she's expelled, sticky and foul, into the cold, harsh world inhabited only by arvies and machines? Or is Jennifer correct in maintaining the issue subject to a mother's whim?

Jennifer says, "All I know is that this is the most profound, most spiritually fulfilling, experience of my entire life." And so she faces the crowds, real or virtual, using Molly June's smile and Molly June's innocence, daring the analysts to count all the layers of irony.

GESTATION (II)

Molly June experiences the same few months in a fog of dazed, but happy confusion, aware that she's become the center of attention, but unable to comprehend exactly why. She knows that her lower back hurts and that her breasts have swelled and that her belly, flat and soft before, has inflated to several times its previous size; she knows that she sometimes feels something moving inside her, that she sometimes feels sick to her stomach, and that her eyes water more easily than they ever have before, but none of this disturbs the vast, becalmed surface of her being. It is all good, all the more reason for placid contentment.

Her only truly bad moments come in her dreams, when she sometimes finds herself standing on a gray, colorless field, facing another version of herself half her own size. The miniature Molly June stares at her from a distance that Molly June herself cannot cross, her eyes unblinking, her expression merciless. Tears glisten on both her cheeks. She points at Molly June and she enunciates a single word, incomprehensible in any language Molly June knows, and irrelevant to any life she's ever been allowed to live: "Mother."

The unfamiliar word makes Molly June feel warm and cold, all at once. In her dream she wets herself, trembling from the sudden warmth running down her thighs. She trembles, bowed by an incomprehensible need to apologize. When she wakes, she finds real tears still wet on her cheeks, and real pee soaking the mattress between her legs. It frightens her.

But those moments fade. Within seconds the calming agents are already flooding her bloodstream, overriding any internal storms, removing all possible sources of disquiet, making her once again the obedient arvie she's supposed to be. She smiles and coos as the servos tend to her bloated form, scrubbing her flesh and applying their emollients. Life is so good, she thinks. And if it's not, well, it's not like there's anything she can do about it, so why worry?

BIRTH (I)

Molly June goes into labor on a day corresponding to what we call Thursday, the insistent weight she has known for so long giving way to a series of contractions violent enough to reach her even through her cocoon of deliberately engineered apathy. She cries and moans and shrieks infuriated, inarticulate things that might have been curses had she ever been exposed to any, and she begs the shiny machines around her to take away the pain with the same efficiency that they've taken away everything else. She even begs her passenger—that is, the passenger she knows about, the one she's sensed seeing through her eyes and hearing through her ears and carrying out conversations with her mouth—she begs her passenger *for mercy.* She hasn't ever asked that mysterious godlike presence for anything, because it's never occurred to her that she might be entitled to anything, but she needs relief now, and she demands it, shrieks for it, can't understand why she isn't getting it.

The answer, which would be beyond her understanding even if provided, is that the wet, sordid physicality of the experience is the very point.

BIRTH (II)

Jennifer Axioma-Singh is fully plugged in to every cramp, every twitch, every pooled droplet of sweat. She experiences the beauty and the terror and the exhaustion and the certainty that this will never end. She finds it resonant and evocative and educational on levels lost to a mindless sack of meat like Molly June. And she comes to any number of profound revelations about the nature of life and death and the biological origins of the species and the odd, inexplicable attachment brood mares have always felt for the squalling sacks of flesh and bone their bodies have gone to so much trouble to expel.

CONCLUSIONS

It's like any other work, she thinks. Nobody ever spent months and months building a house only to burn it down the second they pounded in the last nail. You put that much effort into something and it belongs to you, forever, even if the end result is nothing but a tiny creature that eats and shits and makes demands on your time.

This still fails to explain why anybody would invite this kind of pain again, let alone the three or four or seven additional occasions common before the unborn reached their ascendancy. Oh, it's interesting enough to start with, but she gets the general idea long before the thirteenth hour rolls around and the market share for her real-time feed dwindles to the single digits. Long before that, the pain has given way to boredom. At the fifteenth hour she gives up entirely, turns off her inputs, and begins to catch up on her personal correspondence, missing the actual moment when Molly June's daughter, Jennifer's womb-mate and sister, is expelled head-first into a shiny silver tray, pink and bloody and screaming at the top of her lungs, sharing oxygen for the very first time, but, by every legal definition, Dead.

AFTERMATH (JENNIFER)

As per her expressed wishes, Jennifer Axioma-Singh is removed from Molly June and installed in a new arvie that very day. This one's a tall, lithe, gloriously beautiful creature with fiery eyes and thick, lush lips: her name's Bernadette Ann, she's been bred for endurance in extreme environments, and she'll soon be taking Jennifer Axioma-Singh on an extended solo hike across the restored continent of Antarctica.

Jennifer is so impatient to begin this journey that she never lays eyes on the child whose birth she has just experienced. There's no need. After all, she's never laid eyes on anything, not personally. And the pictures are available online, should she ever feel the need to see them. Not that she ever sees any reason for that to happen. The baby, itself, was never the issue here. Jennifer didn't want to be a mother. She just wanted to give birth. All that mattered to her, in the long run, was obtaining a few months of unique vicarious experience, precious in a lifetime likely to continue for as long as the servos still manufacture wombs and breed arvies. All that matters now is moving on. Because time marches onward, and there are never enough adventures to fill it.

AFTERMATH (MOLLY JUNE)

She's been used, and sullied, and rendered an unlikely candidate to attract additional passengers. She is therefore earmarked for compassionate disposal.

AFTERMATH (THE BABY)

The baby is, no pun intended, another issue. Her biological mother Jennifer Axioma-Singh has no interest in her, and her birth-mother Molly June is on her way to the furnace. A number of minor health problems, barely worth mentioning, render her unsuitable for a useful future as somebody's arvie. Born, and by that precise definition Dead, she could very well follow Molly June down the chute.

But she has a happier future ahead of her. It seems that her unusual gestation and birth have rendered her something of a collector's item, and there are any number of museums aching for a chance to add her to their permanent collections. Offers are weighed, and terms negotiated, until the ultimate agreement is signed, and she finds herself shipped to a freshly constructed habitat in a wildlife preserve in what used to be Ohio.

AFTERMATH (THE CHILD)

She spends her early life in an automated nursery with toys, teachers, and careful attention to her every physical need. At age five she's moved to a cage consisting of a two story house on four acres of nice green grass, beneath what looks like a blue sky dotted with fluffy white clouds. There's even a playground. She will never be allowed out, of course, because there's no place for her to go, but she does have human contact of a sort: a different arvie almost every day, inhabited for the occasion by a long line of Living who now think it might be fun to experience child-rearing for a while. Each one has a different face, each one calls her by a different name, and their treatment of her ranges all the way from compassionate to violently abusive.

Now eight, the little girl has long since given up on asking the good ones to stay, because she knows they won't. Nor does she continue to dream about what she'll do when she grows up, since it's also occurred to her that she'll never know anything but this life in this fishbowl. Her one consolation is wondering about her real mother: where she is now, what she looks like, whether she ever thinks about the child she left behind, and whether it would have been possible to hold on to her love, had it ever been offered, or even possible.

The questions remain the same, from day to day. But the answers are hers to imagine, and they change from minute to minute: as protean as her moods, or her dreams, or the reasons why she might have been condemned to this cruelest of all possible punishments.

HER HUSBAND'S HANDS

Her husband's hands came home on a Friday. Rebecca had received word of the attack, which had claimed the lives of seven other soldiers in his unit and reduced three others to similar, minimal fractions of themselves: One man missing above the waist, another missing below, a third neatly halved, like a bisected man on display in an anatomy lab.

The Veteran's Administration had told her it could have been worse. The notification officer had reminded her of Tatum, the neighbor's daughter so completely expunged by her own moment under fire that only a strip of skin and muscle remained: A section of her thigh, about the size and shape of a cigarette pack, returned to her parents in a box and now living in their upstairs room, where it made a living proofreading articles on the internet. That's no life, the notification officer said. But Bob, he pointed out, was a pair of perfect hands, amputated from the body at the wrists but still capable of accomplishing many great things. And there was always the cloning lottery. The chances were a couple of million to one, but it was something to hope for, and stranger things had happened.

Rebecca had asked her parents, and his, and the friends so anxious to see him, to stay away. It was a personal moment and she could not be sure that she would be able to take their solicitous platitudes. She waited at home wanting a cigarette as much as she'd ever wanted anything in her entire life and stared at the door until the knock came and the two smartly uniformed escorts brought what was left of her husband inside in a box with an American flag on it.

They opened the box and showed her Bob's hands, resting side by side on a white pillow. The left one lay palm-down, the right one palm-up. The one that was palm-up twitched and waggled fingers at Rebecca when it saw her. The new light-sensitive apertures at the fingertips blinked many times in what she could only assume was excitement. The fingernails had been manicured and buffed to a high sheen. Rebecca's eyes inevitably wandered to the wrists, which ended in thick silver bands, a lot like bracelets except for the flat bottoms where arms should have emerged. They, Rebecca knew, contained not just the life support—without which her husband's hands would just be graying meat—but also his most recent memory backup, without which everything he had ever been, and everything he had ever done, would now be gone.

She had not supposed that a pair of hands could be personal enough to be recognized, but she did recognize them. There was a crooked angle to one of the pinkies where he had once broken it catching a baseball and it had not healed back precisely right. And there was a scar on one of the knuckles where he had once cut himself, almost to the bone, on broken glass. She knew those hands as the same ones that once could make her shiver, when they were at the end of strong and comforting arms.

The fingers wagged some more, and the escort told her that her husband wanted to talk to her. She said that she did not know what to do. The younger of the two escorts presented her with a flat black pad with slots for fingers, turned it on, and placed it in the box where Bob's hands could get at it. As the text display came up, Bob's hands turned around, inserted fingertips into the pad's control slots and did . . . something, not exactly typing as she knew it from the familiar QWERTY keyboard but something very much like it, with subtle and practiced movements that over the next few seconds forced words and sentences onto the screen.

rebecca please don't be afraid, her husband's hands typed. *i know this is strange & frightening but it's still me. i can see you & i'm glad to be home. i love you. please i want you to kiss me*

There were few things Rebecca wanted to do less right now, but she knew her husband's hands would sense any further hesitation, and so she reached down and touched them. They disengaged from the black pad and let her pick them up, one hand in each of her own. They were as warm as she remembered, and heavier than she expected. A sick feeling rose in her throat as, driven by obligation, she gave each one a sweet kiss on the knuckles. Each one turned around in the hand that held it and twined its fingers through hers, a grip as tight and as complete as a hug would have been had fate decided to let him come home as a whole man.

One of the escorts said, "We'll leave you two alone now."

Rebecca couldn't help thinking: *What do you mean, you* two? *His hands are now two separate objects; don't you mean, you three? Or, since they don't add up to anything even close to the whole man, shouldn't you be using fractions? Telling me, we'll leave you one and a tenth alone now? Or whatever?* She thought all this but did not say it, as they donned their caps and told her to call if she needed anything, and left her alone grasping what had once been part, but not all, of the husband who only four years before had struck her eighteen-year-old self, sitting across from him in a college seminar, as the most beautiful man she'd ever seen.

For a long time she sat with him—with them—in silence. Sometimes, as she closed her eyes and waited for the reassuring squeezes that were as close as he could come to conversation without the typepad, she could almost fool herself into thinking those hands were connected to wrists that were connected to arms that joined at shoulders with a chest and a beating heart and lips and eyes and a man who could lie beside her and arouse her passions as well as her pity.

After a while, his left hand gently disengaged from her right and climbed up to her shoulder, squeezing that as well before crab-crawling to her face and finding the tear-tracks on the side of her cheek. It froze at the discovery, and she could not help feeling that she'd failed him, that she'd proven herself shallow, that she'd hurt him or what was left of him at the moment he needed to know that she was still capable of loving him.

Some time later his hands withdrew to the table so they could talk to her about the problems they now faced. The left one turned over on its back so the light-apertures on the fingertips could see her face, and the right one went to the typepad and told her that he knew how she felt, that this wasn't how he had envisioned their future either, and that if she gave him a chance he would still be the best husband to her that he possibly could. Her hesitation, her struggle to come up with words that would not be a mockery or a lie, spoke volumes, and may have broken whatever he now had for a heart. But after a long time she nodded, and it was a start.

He could not tell her anything about what had happened to him. The last backup before the attack that had destroyed the rest of him was only a week old, sparing him the memories of a hellish ordeal under fire, watching the rest of the unit fall away, one or two at a time, in pieces. He typed that he had at best an academic knowledge of what had been in that backup, as he said there were things even then that he chose not to remember, and had preferred to live the rest of his life arrested at an even earlier set of memories, recorded two months before that, and blessedly free of some experiences that would have crippled him even more than his current condition.

He typed that the war had been so terrible that he would have gotten rid of even more, had that been possible; there were certainly vets who backed up just as they were shipped out and came back as parts or wholes refusing to remember any of what they'd done, or had done to them, over there. Rather than recall a single day in-country they preferred to live a life where being strong and fit and whole and on a troop carrier getting their past coded into a database was followed, without so much as a single moment of transition, by being older and finished with their time and back, reduced to a sentient body part on a plate. But there'd been buddies, people in his unit, who had done things for him in that time during his hitch that he would never allow himself to forget, not even if he also had to remember visions out of hell. He typed that the little he could remember, he would never talk to her about.

After that, there was little to say; she made some lunch for herself and his hands sat on the table watching her eat, the palms held upward so the fingertips could see, giving the accidental but undeniable impression that they were being held upward in supplication.

Later, as the silence of the afternoon grew thick, the hands typed, *i still enjoy watching you eat.* It was something he had said before, as they'd circled each other performing the rituals that connect early attraction to couplehood; he had appreciated her meticulousness, the way she addressed a plate of food as much like a puzzle to be disassembled as a meal to be savored. She did not respond that once upon a time she'd loved watching him eat as well, the sheer joy he'd taken in the foods he loved, the unabashed and unapologetic gusto with which he'd torn into meals that were not good for him. It was, she knew, a gusto he could never show anymore, and that she'd never witness, again: Another of life's pleasures robbed from them, left on a bloody patch of dirt beneath a foreign sky. She could not help thinking of the all the meals to come, the breakfasts and lunches and dinners that for years unwritten would always be reminders of what had been and would never be again.

Conversation lagged. They watched television, the hands sitting on her lap or beside her on the couch showing pleasure or displeasure in the set's offerings with mimed commentary that at one point, an angry response to an anchorman's report on the war, included a silent, but vehement, middle finger. Rebecca answered some concerned phone calls from family and friends who wanted to know how the reunion was going, and told them that no, she and Bob were not ready to receive any visitors just yet. More hours of silence broken by intervals of halting conversation rendered necessarily brief by his limited skill at typing inevitably and to some extent horrifically led to dinner, where the discomfort of lunch was not only repeated but doubled by the awareness that all this was still only starting, that the silence of their meals would soon be a familiar ritual, for as long as the future still stretched.

There was only one sign of real trouble before bedtime. Bob's wandering right hand encountered a framed photograph of himself in uniform, on an end table next to the sofa. Rebecca happened to be watching as his hand hesitated, tapping the glass with a fingertip as if somehow hoping to be allowed back into the image's frozen moment of time. It looked like he knocked the photo over deliberately. She was almost a hundred percent sure.

That night she lay on her habitual side of the bed, the ceiling an empty white space offering no counsel. His right hand burrowed under the covers and settled at about waist level, while his left sat on his fresh pillow, preferring the sight of her to any warmth the blanket might have provided. When she turned off the lamp, the pinprick red lights of his left fingertips cast a scarlet glow over everything around them, making that pillowcase look a little like the aftermath of a hemorrhage. The fingers caught Rebecca looking at them and waggled; either a perversely jaunty hello, or a reminder from Bob that he could see her. She forced herself to lean over and kiss his palm, somehow fighting back an instinctive shudder when the fingers curled up to caress her cheeks.

Rebecca called Bob's hand by his name and told it she loved him.

Under the covers, his right hand crawled toward her left and wrapped its fingers around hers. She had already held that hand for hours, on and off, and would have preferred freedom for her own, now. But what could she say, really, knowing that to reject the touch now, in this most intimate of their shared places, on the very day he'd returned to her, would have amounted to rejecting him? She had to give him something. She had to pretend, if nothing else. So she squeezed him back and whispered a few loving words that sounded like fiction to her own ears and let him hold her with one hand while the other watched with eyes like pinprick wounds.

She slept, and in her dreams, Bob's hands had still returned to her, but without the nice sanitized bands that allowed them his memories and mind and hid the magnitude of the violence done to him behind polished silver. In her dreams his hands returned to her with the wounds ragged and raw, strips of torn and whitened skin trailing along behind them like tattered streamers. Each had a splintered and blackened wrist bone protruding from the amputation point, like a spear. The fingertips of these Bob remnants were blind and useless instruments, incapable of leading him anywhere except by touch; as they crawled across the polished kitchen floor in search of her, while she fought air as thick as Jell-O to stay just beyond their reach, they left a continuous gout of blood behind, more than mere hands could have possibly bled without becoming drained sacks of flesh. The kitchen became a frieze of twisted blood-trails, which only continued up her bare legs after the chase ended and she found herself standing as paralyzed as any dream-woman with her feet nailed to the floor, while the disembodied hands climbed her.

She might have screamed herself awake, but she couldn't breathe in the dream, as the air around her was not an atmosphere a woman could breathe, but a thicker substance that refused to pass her lips, no matter how deeply her chest labored or her ears thundered or how desperately she struggled to draw anything capable of sustaining her into her lungs.

Then she woke up and knew it was not a dream. He was strangling her. His hands had tightened around her throat, the two thumbs joining at her windpipe while his coarse and powerful fingers curled around the curve of her neck to meet, as if in terrible summit, at the back. Even as a man with more than hands he had always possessed a strong grip, and the hands that were all that remained of him seemed to add the strength of his arms and back as well, all dedicated to the deadly impossible task of compressing her throat to nothingness.

A woman being strangled by a complete man might have died clawing at his chest or grasping for his face or even going for the hands themselves, which would have possessed the advantage of being anchored to arms and shoulders. Rebecca had nothing to fight but the hands, and they provided a focus for her resistance. She reached for the sharpened pencil she kept beside the book of crossword puzzles that had been her only companion since Bob went to fight that goddamned stupid war, and jabbed at the back of his hands until his skin broke and his grip went soft and the two little pieces of Bob fell away, freeing her to breathe again.

She might have screamed and continued to stab her husband's hands until there was nothing left of them but torn flesh, but something in the way they now lay on the bed, ten glowing red lights staring up at her, halted her in a way that crazed or uncomprehending eyes might not have.

She flipped on her bedside lamp and regarded Bob's murderous hands in the glare of harsh light.

All things have faces even when they don't have faces; the human eye insists on putting faces on them. Even hands have faces, and expressions, that change depending on how the fingers are held in relation to the palm. Hands can look calm or agonized or desperate. They can look gentle and they can look brutish, sometimes while remaining the same hands. For no reason at all that made any sense to her, her husband's hands looked lost. She didn't understand, but she could sense that there was something she was failing to see, something she could almost see that was just outside of her field of vision.

Bob's right hand mimed a typing motion.

She was reluctant to leave them alone long enough to get the typepad. She had read too many stories about people who turned their back on monsters. But they made the motion again, insistently. She went to the other room, returned to see that her husband's hands remained where they had fallen, and, not trusting them to keep their distance, tossed the pad onto the bed.

He typed.

i am sorry so so sorry i would not hurt u for anything i was having a nightmare i have been having them for a while i didnt know it was you i was hurting pls understand pls forgive me pls

Rebecca was not ready to forgive him. "You could have killed me."

i know. it was not the man you married but the man who lived through hell over there. when i know where i am im all right. maybe we cant sleep in the same bed for a while. please understand. please

She wanted to die. But after long minutes standing there feeling her fury churn inside her she went to her husband and told him it was all right, that she would set up another place for him in another room, and that they would sleep apart but see each other in the morning. She kissed him on the knuckles and went to make his new bed, a pillow stuffed into an unused drawer of a bureau in another room. He allowed her to carry him there, without argument. And they parted, though the sound of frantic thumping continued in the night and she was reduced to lying sleepless, her eyes fixed on unseen bloody carnage in the darkness.

The VA man said that she should take Bob to the first available support group, and even specified a local chapter that was meeting the next day. They went. It amounted to five sectioned veterans and their spouses, sitting in an approximate circle on folding chairs that must have known happy occasions as well as sad: christenings, religious meetings, political rallies, maybe even amateur theatre productions, all dissipating in the air as soon as the chairs were put away and stacked and returned to the anonymity enjoyed by furniture. The idea that somebody might sit in the very same chair she sat in now, a day or a week from now, and sip fruit punch while discussing plans for the decoration of the school prom, seemed almost incomprehensible to her.

There were five fragmented veterans along with spouses and other family members at the meeting, some of them arguably better off than Bob, others so much more reduced that it was impossible to know whether to scream in horror at their predicament or giggle uncontrollably at its madness. There was a boy of twenty-two who had been in-country for less than a day before a bombing reduced him to a thin strip of face that included one (blind) eye, two cheeks, a nose, and part of his upper lip, all now mounted on the very same silver plate that kept him alive, which his mother had attached to a plaque suitable for mounting on a wall. Another was just a torso, devoid of limbs, genitalia, or head, and plugged at all the stumps by more silver interfaces. Another was a shapely woman with delicately sculpted nails, a short skirt designed to show off a killer pair of legs and a top designed to accentuate her cleavage. Her every move reeked of sexuality, which may have been the way she carried herself before being drafted or the way she now compensated for losing the front half of her head, which instead of a face or a jaw or a pair of eyes now displayed a plane of mirrored silver before her ears. A fourth had not been salvageable as anything but a mound of shredded internal organs but had been gotten to in time and was now completely enclosed in a silver box about the size of a briefcase, with a screen for communication and a handle for her grim husband's convenience.

The last was, like Bob, a pair of amputated hands. He was the one who made Rebecca want to run screaming, because his lovely blonde wife had dealt with the problem of maintaining a relationship with him by amputating her own hands and having his attached at the end of her own wrists. The silver memory disks marking the junction points on her arms would have resembled bracelets had his calloused, darker-skinned, hairier, and disproportionately larger paws not resembled cartoon gloves at the ends of her smooth, milk-white arms; and had her husband's hands not usurped much of the control of those arms, which now gesticulated in a perversely masculine manner as his loving wife described at length how much this measure had saved her marriage. More than once during the meeting, Rebecca caught those hands resting on the other woman's bare knees and caressing them, the arms stroking them back and forth with a lascivious energy that the other woman clearly recognized and appreciated but otherwise seemed wholly removed from. She could only wonder if that's what her own husband wanted, if that was something Bob could ever ask of her, and whether she could ever come to want it herself.

The man lugging around the briefcase told all the other spouses at the meeting that he considered them lucky. Their loved ones had returned to them as parts that could be touched, skin that gave off an undeniable if largely artificial warmth, flesh that evoked the memory of what had been even in those cases where it could manage little else. But his wife? He produced a picture of the woman she had been, a plump little chubby-cheeked thing with a premature double-chin, but a smile of genuine warmth and eyes that seemed to express substantial mirth at some hidden personal joke. He said that she could see him through the interface and even communicate with him through the typepad, but words had never been a major part of her, not even when she was whole; she had been more a creature of silent gestures, of accommodating smiles, of kind acts and expressive glances and sudden stormy silences. Now, he said, she was a sack of nonfunctioning organs containing just enough meat to qualify as alive. And though she would occasionally answer direct questions, she more often remained silent, telling him when pressed that she just wanted to be left alone, put on a shelf, and forgotten. It was getting harder and harder for him to argue otherwise. "My wife is dead," he told the group, and after a moment of shocked silence repeated himself, with something like stunned wonder, "My wife is dead. My wife is dead." The wife whose arms ended with her husband's hands just pawed herself.

Gallows humor intruded, as it always does among survivors of extreme loss, when the man who was just a strip of face said that he'd met a guy, back in the hospital, who had turned out to be nothing but an asshole. The wife of the torso said that she'd met one guy who was a real dick. Somebody else said that his lieutenant had always been a little shit and probably still was, and the variations only went downhill from there. There were a few little flights of fancy involving the prospect of sectioned people who had been reduced to nothing but their sexual organs and how their chances of making a living after the service were so much better than anyone else's, but by then the shocking jokes had started to trail off, replaced by uncomfortable silence.

The meeting broke up with ten minutes of internal business involving when the next one would be held and who was going to get the word out to others who might benefit by attending. Rebecca went to the table where the coffee and the cookies were laid out on a plastic tablecloth and stood there not wanting any of it but needing to do something other than return to a house and a life now dominated by silence, and found herself shaking until the woman with a flat silver mirror for a face came up behind her and, speaking through a voice synthesizer, said, "You're not alone." Rebecca broke down and accepted the hug, feeling the warmth of the other woman's arms but also keenly aware of the how cold the mirror felt against her own cheek. She wanted to tell the other woman, *of course I'm alone, and my husband's alone, and you're alone, and we're all alone; the very point of being in hell is that there's a gulf between us and all our efforts to bridge it for even a moment give us nothing but a respite and the illusion of comfort before those bridges retract and we're left to face the same problems from our own separate islands.* She wanted to say it, but of course she couldn't, not if it meant embracing despair in defiance of this sectioned woman's kindness, and so she wept herself blind and took the hug as the gift it was meant to be.

By Saturday night, the answering machine was filling up with calls from family and friends, eager to know how it was going and wanting to know when they could enjoy their own happy reunion. Following her husband's wishes, Rebecca called them all back to thank them but put them off, saying that there still adjustments to be made, and accommodations to be arranged. Again, many wanted to know if Bob was all right. She wondered how she could possibly be expected to answer that question but said, yes, he was all right. They asked her if she was all right and again she gave the answer they wanted, that yes, she was all right.

The two sat together, watching the latest reports from the war for a while, not reacting to the news that a hundred thousand more had been called up, and how this would not be enough; or, afterward, to the feel-good assurance, delivered by a smiling red-headed anchorwoman, that actual deaths that counted as deaths were at an all-time low. Bob's hands tapped at his pad, producing a string of lower-case profanities that Rebecca supposed were now his angry equivalent of embittered muttering.

She fingered the bruises on her neck and decided that maybe they shouldn't be watching this. She turned off the set with the remote and sat with him, feeling and tasting the oppressive silence as if it were the very air, rendered so thick that every moment felt like an eternity spent underwater.

Some time later, her husband's hands released hers and went to the typepad.

do you want me to leave or do you think there's any future for us

She didn't know. She didn't know but she thought of her husband in better times, that strong man, that smiling man, that occasionally petulant man, the man with the naughty streak who sometimes became the child who treated her as the authority figure who mischief needed to be hidden from. She remembered him pulling one form of foolishness or another, peering at her out of the corners of his eyes to see whether she thought it maddening or funny. She remembered the shape of his head in the middle of the night, when the lights were out and it was too dark to see him as anything but silhouette, when he was awake and looking at her, not knowing that she was awake and looking at him, this shadow of him that was to her every bit as revealing as his features viewed in the full light of day, because she knew him and could fill in the darkness. She remembered what it was like to let him know with a touch that she was awake too, and how sometimes that led to whispers and sometimes to more. She remembered his lips, his teeth, his touch, his gentleness, and his passion. She remembered sometimes not letting him know that she was awake, instead just continuing to feign sleep, and thinking that this was her man and her lover and her friend and someday the father of her children. She remembered, once, feeling so proud to have won him that her heart could have burst.

say something

She didn't know if there was anything to say. That was the thing. She didn't know but she was proud. She was proud and she didn't want to be the one to fail. She knew that it didn't speak well of her that this remained the chief motivating force in her current relationship with what had become of her husband, the stubborn refusal to be the one who failed; to be driven not so much by an instinctive, unquestioning need to support him in what he had become, but the drive to be the better one, the strong one, the one who did the right things and held on when it might have been easier to just be the bitch who gave up. Maybe, she thought, that was the way back; not through love, but a fierce, unyielding pride. Maybe if she could stoke that, the other would return. But how could she, when it was so much more than she could make herself give?

Bob's hands had gone back to typing.

becks, i lied

She looked at them, and perceived something ineffably tense about the way they sat against the typepad. "About what?"

whatever happens i need you to know that i remember more than i told you. its worse than the news reports say, its dirtier and bloodier and nowhere near as simple. it's the kind of place that makes you forget that theres any good anywhere in the world. its why so many of us choose to forget. but i backed myself up for the last time only two days before the attack. i remember everything terrible that happened to me over there, everything terrible i did. afterward when they downloaded me they gave me a choice of keeping it all or going back to some earlier recording. i almost threw out the whole damn war. but i decided to keep it all because i had to.

She stared. "Why?"

the only thing worth remembering about any of it was how much of it i spent wanting to return to you

That, at long last, destroyed her. For the first time since his return she gave in to her sense of loss and howled. She buried her face in her hands and didn't see her husband's hands disengage from the typepad or return to the couch. But she did feel the weight of them on her shoulders, the strength they still had when they squeezed her there, the gentleness they still showed as the index fingers brushed the tear-tracks from her cheeks.

She found his touch both familiar and alien in some ways, like he had never left; in others, like he was a stranger, returned from a war with nothing but gall and a vague resemblance to seduce the widow with dire lies of being the man who had left. She missed the weight of him, the solidity, the sound of his breath. And she still hated the cold feel of the metal attachments at the ends of his wrists, so much like chains. But for the first time she was able to feel the presence of the boy she had fallen in love with, the man she had married, the husband who had been with her at night. It was him; against all odds, at long last, it was him. And for the first time, irrationally, she wanted him.

She told him she needed a minute, and went to the bathroom, where she ran water over her face, damned her red nose and puffy eyes, and made herself presentable, or at least as presentable as she could. She knew that it was not the best time. She was terrified, a wreck. From what he'd typed, he wasn't much better. But there would never be a best time, not if she just kept waiting for it. In life, there were always thresholds that had to be crossed, whenever they could be, if only because that was the only way to get to whatever awaited on the other side.

When she had done everything that was possible she returned, kissed her husband's hands, and carried what was left of him to bed. After she undressed and got under the covers, his hands hesitated, with a sudden shyness that was almost possible to find endearing, then slipped under the covers themselves, and crawled through the darkness to her side, one heading north and the other heading south. The sheets rustled, and she allowed herself one last analytical thought: how lucky she was, after all, to have him come back as a pair of hands, and not as some useless strip of flesh in a sealed silver box. How very much they'd been left with.

She closed her eyes, grew warm, and let her husband love her.

OF A SWEET SLOW DANCE IN THE WAKE OF TEMPORARY DOGS

Before

1.

On the last night before the end of everything, the stars shine like a fortune in jewels, enriching all who walk the quaint cobblestoned streets of Enysbourg. It is a celebration night, like most nights in the capital city. The courtyard below my balcony is alive with light and music. Young people drink and laugh and dance. Gypsies in silk finery play bouncy tunes on harmonicas and mandolins. Many wave at me, shouting invitations to join them. One muscular young man with impossibly long legs and a face equipped with a permanent grin takes it upon himself to sprint the length of the courtyard only to somersault over the glittering fountain at its center. For a heartbeat out of time he seems to float, enchanted, over the water. Then I join his friends in applause as he belly-flops, drenching himself and the long-haired girls wading at the fountain's other rim. The girls are not upset but delighted. Their giggles tinkle like wind chimes as they splash across the fountain themselves, flinging curtains of silver water as their shiny black hair bobs back and forth in the night.

2.

Intoxicated from a mixture of the excellent local wine and the even better local weed, I consider joining them, perhaps the boring way via the stairs and perhaps via a great daredevil leap from the balcony. I am, after all, stripped to the waist. The ridiculous boxers I brought on the ship here could double as a bathing suit, and the way I feel right now I could not only make the fountain but also sail to the moon. But after a moment's consideration I decide not. That's the kind of grand theatrical gesture visitors to Enysbourg make on their first night, when they're still overwhelmed by its magic. I have been here nine nights. I have known the festivals that make every night in the capital city a fresh adventure. I have explored the hanging gardens, with all their deceptive challenges. I have climbed the towers of pearl, just down the coast. I have ridden stallions across Enysbourg's downs, and plunged at midnight into the warm waters of the eastern sea. I have tasted a hundred pleasures, and wallowed in a hundred more, and though far from sick of them, feel ready to take them at a more relaxed pace, partaking not as a starving man but as a connoisseur. I want to be less a stranger driven by lust, but a lover driven by passion.

So I just take a deep breath and bask in the air that wafts over the slanting tiled roofs: a perfume composed of equal parts sex and spice and the tang of the nearby ocean, all the more precious for being part of the last night before the end of everything. It occurs to me, not for the first time, that this might be the best moment of my life: a life that, back home, with its fast pace and its anonymous workplaces and climate-controlled, gleaming plastic everything, was so impoverished that it's amazing I have any remaining ability to recognize joy and transcendence at all. In Enysbourg such epiphanies seem to come several times a minute. The place seems determined to make me a poet, and if I don't watch out I might hunt down paper and pen and scrawl a few lines, struggling to capture the inexpressible in a cage of fool amateurish june-moon-and-spoon.

• • •

3.

The curtains behind me rustle, and a familiar presence leaves my darkened hotel room to join me on the balcony. I don't turn to greet her, but instead close my eyes as she wraps me in two soft arms redolent of wine and perfume and sex. Her hands meet at the center of my chest. She rests a chin on my shoulder and murmurs my name in the musical accent that marks every word spoken by every citizen of Enysbourg.

"Robert," she says, and there's something a little petulant about the way she stresses the first syllable, something adorable and mocking in the way she chides me for not paying enough attention to her.

By the time I register the feel of her bare breasts against my bare back, and realize in my besotted way that she's mad, she's insane, she's come out on the balcony in full view of everybody without first throwing on something to cover herself, the youths frolicking in the fountain have already spotted her and begun to serenade us with a chorus of delighted cheers. "Kiss her!" shouts a boy. "Come on!" begs a girl. "Let us see!" yells a third. "Don't go inside! Make love out here!" When I turn to kiss the woman behind me, I am cheered like a conqueror leading a triumphant army into Rome.

Her name is Caralys, and she is of course one of the flowers of Enysbourg: a rare beauty indeed, even in a country where beauty is everywhere. She is tall and lush, with dark eyes, skin the color of caramel, and a smile that seems to hint at secrets propriety won't let her mention. Her shiny black hair cascades down her back in waves, reflecting light even when everything around her seems to be dark.

I met her the day after my arrival, when I was just a dazed and exhausted tourist sitting alone in a café redolent with rich ground coffee. I wasn't just off the boat then, not really. I'd already enjoyed a long awkward night being swept up by one celebration after another, accepting embraces from strangers determined to become friends, and hearing my name, once given, become a chant of hearty congratulation from those applauding my successful escape from the land of everyday life. I had danced the whole night, cheered at the fires of dawn, wept for reasons that puzzled me still, and stumbled to bed where I enjoyed the dreamless bliss that comes from exhaustion. It was the best night I'd known in a long time. But I was a visitor still, reluctant to surrender even the invisible chains that shackled me; and even as I'd jerked myself awake with caffeine, I'd felt tired, surfeited, at odds.

I was so adrift that when Caralys sauntered in, her hair still tousled and cheeks still shining from the celebrations of the night before, her dress of many patches rustling about her ankles in a riot of multiple colors, I almost failed to notice her. But then she'd sat down opposite me and declared in the sternest of all possible tones that even foreigners, with all their worries, weren't allowed to wear grimaces like mine in Enysbourg. I blinked, almost believing her, because I'd heard words just like those the previous night, from a pair of fellow visitors who had caught me lost in a moment of similar repose. Then she tittered, first beneath her breath and then with unguarded amusement, not understanding my resistance to Enysbourg's charms, but still intrigued, she explained much later, by the great passion she saw imprisoned behind my gray, civilized mien. "You are my project," she said, in one expansive moment. "I am going to take a tamed man and make him a native of Enysbourg."

She may well succeed, for we have been in love since that first day, both with each other and with the land whose wonders she has been showing me ever since.

4.

We have fought only once, just yesterday, when in a thoughtless lapse I suggested that she return with me on the ship home. Her eyes flashed the exasperation she always showed at my moments of thoughtless naïveté: an irritation so grand that it bordered on contempt. She told me it was an arrogant idea, the kind only a foreigner could have. Why would she leave this place that has given her life? And why would I think so much of her to believe that she would? Was that all she was to me? A prize to be taken home, like a souvenir to impress my friends with my trip abroad? Didn't I see how diminished she would be, if I ever did that to her? "Would you blind me?" she demanded. "Would you amputate my limbs? Would you peel strips off my skin, slicing off piece after piece until there was nothing left of me but the parts that remained convenient to you? This is my country, Robert. My blood." And she was right, for she embodies Enysbourg, as much as the buildings themselves, and for her to abandon it would be a crime against both person and place. Both would be diminished, as much as I'll be diminished if I have to leave her behind.

5.

We leave the balcony and go back inside where, for a moment in the warm and sweet-smelling room, we come close to collapsing on the bed again, for what seems the thousandth time since we woke sore but passionate this morning. But this is the last night before the end of everything, when Enysbourg's wonders emerge in their sharpest relief. They are not to be missed just so we can keep to ourselves. And so she touches a finger to the tip of my nose and commands that it's time to go back into the world. I obey.

We dress. I wear an open vest over baggy trousers, with a great swooping slouch hat glorious in its vivid testimony to Enysbourg's power to make me play the willing fool. She wears a fringed blouse and another ankle-length skirt of many patches, slit to mid-thigh to expose a magnificent expanse of leg. Dozens of carved wooden bracelets, all loose enough to shift when she moves, clack like maracas along her forearms. Her lips are red, her flowered hair aglow with reflected light. Two curling locks meet in the center of her forehead, right above her eyes, like mischievous parentheses. Somewhere she wears bells.

Laughing, she leads me from the room, and down the narrow stairs, chattering away at our fellow guests as they march in twos and threes toward their own celebrations of this last night. We pass a man festooned with parrots, a woman with a face painted like an Italian landscape, a fire-eater, a juggler in a suit of carnival color, a cavorting clown-faced monkey who hands me a grape and accepts a small coin in payment. Lovers of all possible, and some impossible, gender combinations flash inebriated grins as they surrender their passions in darkened alcoves. Almost everybody we pass is singing or dancing or sharing dizzy, disbelieving embraces. Everytime I pause in sheer amazement at something I see, Caralys chuckles at my saucer-eyed disbelief, and pulls me along, whispering that none of this would be half as marvelous without me there to witness it.

Even the two fellow tourists we jostle, as we pass through the arched entranceway and into the raucous excitement of the street become part of the excitement, because I know them. They are the ones I met on that first lost day before Caralys, before I learned that Enysbourg was not just a vacation destination offered as brief reward for earning enough to redeem a year of dullness and conformity, but the repository of everything I'd ever missed in my flavorless excuse for a life. Jerry and Dee Martel are gray retirees from some awful industrial place where Dee had done something or other with decorating and Jerry had managed a firm that molded the plastic shells other companies used to enclose the guts of useful kitchen appliances. When they talk about their jobs now, as they did when they found me that first night, they shudder with the realization that such things swallowed so many years of finite lives. They were delivered when they vacationed in Enysbourg, choosing it at random among all the other oases of tamed exoticism the modern world maintains to make people forget how sterile and homogenous things have become. On arriving they'd discovered that it was not a tourist trap, not an overdeveloped sham, not a fraud, and not an excuse to sell plastic souvenirs that testify to nothing but the inane gullibility of the people who buy them, but the real thing, the special place, the haven that made them the people they had always been meant to be. They'd emigrated, in what Jerry said with a wink was their "alternative to senility."

"Was it a sacrifice for us?" Jerry asked, when we met. "Did it mean abandoning our security? Did it even mean embracing some hardships? Of course it did. It meant all those things and more. You may not think so, but then you're a baby; you haven't even been in Enysbourg long enough to know. But our lives back home were empty. They were nothing. At least here, life has a flavor. At least here, life is something to be treasured."

Living seven years later as natives, spending half their time in the capital and half their time out in the country exploring caves and fording rivers and performing songs they make up on the spot, they each look thirty years younger than their mere calendar ages: with Jerry lean and robust and tanned, Dee shorter and brighter and interested in everything. They remember me from nine days ago and embrace me like a son, exclaiming how marvelous I look, how relaxed I seem in comparison to the timid creature they met then. They want to know if this means I'm going to stay. I blush and admit I don't know. I introduce them to Caralys and they say it seems an easy choice to them. The women hit it off. Jerry suggests a local inn where we can hear a guitarist he knows, and before long we're there, claiming a corner table between dances, listening to his friend:

another old man, an ancient man really, with twinkling eyes and spotted scalp and a wispy comic-opera moustache that, dangling to his collarbone, looks like a boomerang covered with lint.

6.

”It's not that I hate my country,” Jerry says, when the women have left together, in the way that women have. His eyes shine and his voice slurs from the effects of too much drink. “I can't. I know my history. I know the things she's accomplished, the principles she's stood for, the challenges she's faced. I've even been around for more of it than I care to remember. But coming here was not abandoning her. It was abandoning what she'd become. It was abandoning the drive-throughs and the ATMs and the talking heads who pretend they have the answers but would be lucky to remember how to tie their shoes. It was remembering what life was supposed to be all about, and seizing it with both hands while we still had a few good years still left in us. It was victory, Robert; an act of sheer moral victory. Do you see, Robert? Do you see?”

I tell him I see.

“You think you do. But you still have a ticket out, day after tomorrow. Sundown, right? Ach. You're still a tourist. You're still too scared to take the leap. But stay here a few more weeks and then tell me that you see.”

I might just do that, I say. I might stay here the rest of my life.

He dismisses me with a wave of his hand. “Sure you say that. You say that now. You say that because you think it's so easy to say that. You haven't even begun to imagine the commitment it takes.”

But I love Caralys.

“Of course you do. But will you be fair to her, in the end? Will you? You're not her first tourist, you know.”

• • •

7.

Jerry has become too intense for me, in a way utterly at odds with the usual flavor of life in Enysbourg. If he presses on I might have to tell him to stop.

But I am rescued. The man with the wispy moustache returns from the bar with a fresh mug of beer, sets it beside him on a three-legged stool, picks up a stringed instrument a lot like a misshapen guitar, and begins to sing a ballad in a language I don't understand. It's one of Enysbourg's many dialects, a tongue distinguished by deep rolling consonants and rich sensual tones, so expressive in its the way it cavorts the length of an average sentence that I don't need a translation to know that he's singing a hymn to lost love long remembered. When he closes his eyes I can almost imagine him as the fresh-faced young boy staring with earnest panic at the eyes of the fresh-faced young woman whose beauty first made him want to sing such songs. He sings of pain, a sense of loss, a longing for something denied to him. But there is also wonder, a sense of amazement at all the dreams he's ever managed to fulfill.

Or maybe that's just my head, making the song mean what I want it to mean. In either event, the music is slow and heartfelt until some kind of mid-verse epiphany sends its tempo flying. And all of a sudden the drum beats and the hands clap and the darkened room bursts with men and women rising from the shadows to meet on the dance floor in an explosion of flailing hair and whirling bodies. There are children on shoulders and babies on backs and a hundred voices united in the chorus of the moustached man's song, which seems to fill our veins with fire. Jerry has already slid away, his rant of a few moments before forgotten in the urgency of the moment. I recognize nobody around me but nevertheless see no strangers. As I decide to stay in Enysbourg, to spend the rest of my life with Caralys, to raise a family with her, to keep turning pages in this book I've just begun to write, the natives seem to recognize the difference in me. I am handed a baby, which I kiss to the sound of cheers. I hand it back and am handed another. Then another. The music grows louder, more insistent. A wisp of smoke drifts by. Clove, tobacco, hashish, or something else; it is there and then it is gone.

I blink and catch a glimpse of Caralys, cut off by the crowd. She is trying to get to me, her eyes wide, her face shining, her need urgent. She knows I have decided. She can tell. She is as radiant as I have ever seen her, and though jostled by the mob she is determined to make her way to my side. She too has something to say, something that needs to be spoken, through shattered teeth and a mouth filled with blood.

During

8.

There is no sunlight. The skies are too sullied by the smoke of burning buildings to admit the existence of dawn. What arrives instead are gray and sickly shadows, over a moonscape so marked with craters and shattered rubble that in most places it's hard to tell where the buildings stood in the first place. Every few seconds, the soot above us brightens, becomes as blinding as a parody of the light it's usurped, and rocks the city with flame and thunder. Debris pelts everything below. A starving dog cowering in a hollow formed by two shattered walls bolts, seeking better haven in a honeycomb of fallen masonry fifty meters of sheer hell away. But even before it can round the first twisted corpse, a solid wall of shrapnel reduces the animal to a scarlet mist falling on torn flesh.

I witness its death from the site of my own. I am already dead. I still happen to be breathing, but that's a pure accident. Location is all. The little girl who'd been racing along two paces ahead of me, mad with fear, forced to rip off her flaming clothes to reveal the bubbling black scar the chemical burns have made of her back, is now a corpse. She's a pair of legs protruding from a mound of fallen brick. Her left foot still bears a shoe. Her right is pale, naked, moon-white perfect, unbloodied. I, who had been racing along right behind her, am not so fortunate. The same concussion wave that put her out of her misery sent me flying. Runaway stones have torn deep furrows in my legs, my belly, my face, my chest. I have one seeping gash across my abdomen and another across one cheek; both painful, but nothing next to the greater damage done by the cornice that landed on my right knee, splintering the bone and crushing my leg as close to flat as a leg can get without bursting free of its cradling flesh. The stone tumbled on as soon as it did its work, settling in a pile of similar rocks; it looks like any other, but I still think I can identify it out from over here, using the marks it left along the filthy ground.

I have landed in a carpet of broken glass a meter or so from what, for a standing person, would be a ragged waist-high remnant of wall. It is good fortune, I suppose; judging from the steady tattoo of shrapnel and rifle fire impacting against the other side, it's that wall which for the moment spares me the fate of the little girl and the dog. Chance has also favored me by letting me land within sight of an irregular gap in that wall, affording me a view of what used to be the street but which right now is just a narrow negotiable path between craters and mounds of smoking debris. My field of vision is not large, but it was enough to show me what happened to the dog. If I'm to survive this, it must also allow me to see rescue workers, refugees, even soldiers capable of dragging me to wherever the wounded are brought.

But so far there is no help to be seen. Most of the time even my fragmentary view is obscured by smoke of varying colors: white, which though steaming hot is also thin and endurable, passing over me without permanent damage; black, which sickens me with its mingled flavors of burning rubber and bubbling flesh; and the caustic yellow, which burns my eyes and leaves me gagging with the need to void a stomach already long empty. I lick my lips, which are dry and cracked and pitted, and recognize both hunger and thirst in the way the world pales before me. It is the last detail. Everything I consumed yesterday, when Enysbourg was paradise, is gone; it, and everything I had for several days before. Suddenly, I'm starving to death.

9.

There is another great burst of sound and light, so close parts of me shake apart. I try to scream, but my throat is dry, my voice a mere wisp, my mouth a sewer sickening from the mingled tastes of blood and ash and things turned rotten inside me. I see a dark shape, a man, Jerry Martel in fact, move fast past the gap in the wall. I hear automatic fire and I hear his brief cry as he hits the dirt in a crunch of flesh and gravel. He is not quite dead at first, and though he does not know I am here, just out of sight, a collaborator in his helplessness, he cries out to me anyway: a bubbling, childish cry, aware that it's about to be cut off but hoping in this instant that it reaches a listener willing to care. I can't offer the compassion Jerry craves, because I hate him too much for bringing fresh dangers so close to the place where I already lie broken. I want him gone.

A second later fate obliges me with another burst of automatic weapons fire. Brick chips fill the air like angry bees, digging more miniature craters; one big one strikes my ravaged knee and I spasm, grimacing as my bowels let loose, knowing it won't matter because I released everything I had inside me long ago. I feel relief. He was my friend, but I'm safer with him gone.

• • •

10.

I smell more smoke. I taste mud. I hear taunts in languages I don't recognize, cries and curses in the tongues spoken in Enysbourg. A wave of heat somewhere near me alerts me that a fire has broken out. I drag myself across ragged stones and broken glass closer to the gap in the wall, entertaining vainglorious ambitions of perhaps crawling through and making it untouched through the carnage to someplace where people can fix me. But the pain is too much, and I collapse, bleeding now from a dozen fresher wounds, having accomplished nothing but to provide myself a better view.

I see the elderly musician with the huge moustache stumble on by, his eyes closed, his face a sheen of blood, his arms dangling blistered and lifeless at his sides, each blackened and swollen to four times its natural size. I see a woman, half-mad, her mouth ajar in an unending silent scream, clutching a tightly wrapped but still ragged bundle in a flannel blanket, unwilling to notice that whatever it held is now just a glistening smear across her chest. I see a tall and robust and athletic man stumble on by, his eyes vacant, his expression insane, his jaw ripped free and dangling from his face by a braided ribbon of flesh. I see all that and I hear more explosions and I watch as some of the fleeing people fall either whole or in pieces and I listen as some are released by death and, more importantly, as others are not.

Something moving at insane speed whistles through the sky above, passing so near that its slipstream tugs at my skin. I almost imagine it pulling me off the ground, lifting me into the air, allowing me a brief moment of flight behind it before it strikes and obliterates its target. For a moment I wish it would; even that end would be better than a deathbed of shattered rock and slivered glass. Then comes the brightest burst of light and most deafening wave of thunder yet, and for a time I become blind and deaf, with everything around me reduced to a field of pure white.

• • •

11.

When the world comes back, not at all improved, it is easy to see the four young men in identical uniforms who huddle in a little alcove some twenty meters away. There is not much to them, these young men: they all carry rifles, they all wear heavy packs, they're all little more than boys, and their baggy uniforms testify to a long time gone without decent food. When one turns my way, facing me and perhaps even seeing me, but not registering me as a living inhabitant of the corpse-strewn landscape, his eyes look sunken, haunted, unimaginably ancient. He is, I realize, as mad as the most pitiful among the wounded—a reasonable response to his environment, and one I would share if I could divest the damnable sanity that forces me to keep reacting to the horror. He turns back to his comrades and says something; then he looks over them, at something beyond my own limited field of vision, and his smile is enough to make me crave death all over again. His comrades look where he's looking and smile the same way: all four of them showing their teeth.

The three additional soldiers picking their way through the rubble bear a woman between them. It is Caralys. Two stand to either side of her, holding her arms. A third stands behind her, holding a serrated knife to her throat with one hand and holding a tight grip on her hair with the other. That soldier keeps jabbing his knee into the small of her back to keep her going. He has to; she's struggling with every ounce of strength available to her, pulling from side to side, digging her feet into the ground, cursing them to a thousand hells every time they jerk her off her feet and force her onward.

She is magnificent, my Caralys. She is stronger, more vibrant, than any one of them. In any fair fight she would be the only one left standing. But she is held by three, and while she could find an opportunity to escape three, the soldiers from the alcove, who now rush to help their comrades, bring the total all the way up to seven. There is no hope with seven. I know this even as I drag myself toward her from the place where I lie broken. I know this even as she struggles to drive her tormentors away with furious kicks. But these boys are too experienced with such things. They take her by the ankles, lift her off the ground, and bear her squirming and struggling form across the ravaged pavement to a clear place in the rubble, where they pin her to the ground, each one taking a limb. They must struggle to keep her motionless. The soldier with the darkest eyes unslings his rifle, weighs it in his arms, and smashes its butt across her jaw. The bottom half of her face crumples like shattered pottery.

There is nothing I can do but continue to crawl toward her, toward them.

Caralys coughs out a bubble of fresh blood. Fragments of teeth, driven from her mouth, cling to what's left of her chin. She shrieks and convulses and tries to kick. Her legs remain held. The same soldier who just smashed her face now sees that his job is not yet done. He raises his rifle above his head and drives the stock, hard, into her belly. She wheezes and chokes. She tries to curl into a ball of helpless misery, seeking escape within herself. But the soldiers won't even permit that. Another blow, this one to her forehead, takes what little fight is left. Her eyes turn to blackened smears. Her nose blows pink bubbles which burst and dribble down her cheeks in rivulets. She murmurs an animal noise. The soldier responsible for making her manageable makes a joke in a language I don't know, which can't possibly be funny, but still makes the others laugh. They rip off her filthy dress and spread her legs farther apart. The leader steps away, props his rifle against a fragment of wall, and returns, dropping his pants. As he gives his swollen penis a lascivious little waggle,

I observe something wrong with it, something I can see from a distance; it looks green, diseased, half-rotted. But he descends, forcing himself into her, cursing her with every thrust, his cruel animal grunts matched by her own bubbling exhalations, less gasps of pain or protests at her violation than the involuntary noises made as her diaphragm is compressed again and again and again. It doesn't last long, but by the time he pulls out, shakes himself off, and pulls his pants back up, the glimpse I catch of her face is enough to confirm that she's no longer here.

Caralys is alive, all right. I can see her labored breath. I can feel the outrage almost as much as she does. But she's not in this place and time. Her mind has abandoned this particular battlefield for another, inside her head, which might not provide any comfort but nevertheless belongs only to her. What's left in this killing ground doesn't even seem to notice as one of the other soldiers releases his grip on her right arm, takes his position, and commences a fresh rape.

12.

There are no words sufficient for the hate I feel. I am a human being with a human being's dimensions, but the hate is bigger than my capacity to contain it. It doesn't just fill me. It replaces me. It becomes everything I am. I want to claw at them and snap at them and spew hatred at them and rip out their throats with my teeth. I want to leave them blackened corpses and I want to go back to wherever they came from and make rotting flesh of their own wives and mothers. I want to bathe in their blood. I want to die killing them. I want to scar the earth where they were born. I want to salt the farmland so nothing ever grows there again. If hatred alone lent strength, I would rend the world itself. But I cry out without a voice, and I crawl forward without quite managing to move, and I make some pathetic little sound or another, and it carries across the smoky distance between me and them and it accomplishes nothing but advise the enemy that I'm here.

In a single spasm of readiness, they all release Caralys, grab their weapons, scan the rubble-field for the source of the fresh sound. The one using her at the moment needs only an extra second to disengage, but he pulls free in such a panicked spasm that he tumbles backward, slamming his pantless buttocks into a puddle of something too colored by rainbows to qualify as water. The leader sees me. He rolls his eyes, pulls a serrated blade from its sheath at his hip, and covers the distance between us in three seconds.

The determined hatred I felt a heartbeat ago disappears. I know that he's the end of me and that I can't fight him and I pray that I can bargain with him instead, that I can barter Caralys for mercy or medical attention or even an easier death. I think all this, betraying her, and it makes me hate myself. That's the worst, this moment of seeing myself plain, this illustration of the foul bargains I'd be willing to make in exchange for a few added seconds of life. It doesn't matter that there aren't any bargains. I shouldn't have wanted any.

I grope for his knife as it descends but it just opens the palms of my hands and christens my face and chest with blood soon matched by that which flows when he guts me from crotch to ribcage. My colon spills out in thick ropes, steaming in the morning air. I feel cold. The agony tears at me. I can't even hope for death. I want more than death. I want more than oblivion. I want erasure. I want a retroactive ending. I want to wipe out my whole life, starting from my conception. Nothing, not even the happy moments, is worth even a few seconds of this. It would be better if I'd never lived.

But I don't die yet.

• • •

13.

I don't die when he walks away, or when he and his fellow soldiers return to their fun with Caralys. I don't die when they abandon her and leave in her place a broken thing that spends the next hours choking on its own blood. I don't even die when the explosions start again, and the dust salts my wounds with little burning embers. I don't die when the ground against my back shakes like a prehistoric beast about to tear itself apart with rage. I don't even die when the rats come to me, to enjoy a fresh meal. I want to die, but maybe that release is more than I deserve. So I lie on my back beneath a cloudscape of smoke and ash, and I listen to Caralys choke, and I listen to the gunfire and I curse that sociopathic monster God and I do nothing, nothing, when the flies come to lay their eggs.

After

14.

I wake on a bed of freshly-mowed grass. The air is cool and refreshing, the sky as blue as a dream, the breeze a delicious mixture of scents ranging from sea salt to the sweatier perfume of passing horses. From the light, I know it can't be too long after dawn, but I can tell I'm not the first one up. I can hear songbirds, the sounds of laughing children, barking dogs, music played at low volumes from little radios.

Unwilling to trust the sensations of peace, I resist getting up long enough to first grab a fistful of grass, luxuriating in the feel of the long thin blades as they bunch up between my fingers. They're miraculous. They're alive. I'm alive.

I turn my head and see where I am: one of the city's many small parks, a place lined with trees and decorated with orchid gardens.

The buildings visible past the treeline are uncratered and intact. I'm intact. The other bodies I see, scattered here and there across the lawn, are not corpses, but sleepers, still snoring away after a long lazy evening beneath the stars. There are many couples, even a few families with children, all peaceful, all unworried about predators either animal or human. Even the terror, the trauma, the soul-withering hate, the easy savagery that subsumes all powerless victims, all the emotional scars that had ripped me apart, have faded. And the only nearby smoke comes from a sandpit not far upwind, where a jolly bearded man in colorful suspenders has begun to cook himself an outdoor breakfast.

15.

I rise, unscarred and unbroken, clad in comfortable native clothing: baggy shorts, a vest, a jaunty feathered hat. I even have a wine bottle, three-quarters empty, and a pleasant taste in my mouth to go with it. I drink the rest and smile at the pleasant buzz. The thirst remains, but for something non-alcoholic. I need water. I itch from the stray blades of grass peppering my exposed calves and forearms. I contort my back, feeling the vertebrae pop. It feels good. I stretch to get my circulation going. I luxuriate in the tingle of the morning air. Across the meadow, a little girl points at me and smiles. She is the same little girl I saw crushed by masonry yesterday. It takes me a second to smile back and wave, a second spent wondering if she recognizes me, if she finds me an unpleasant reminder. If so, there is no way to tell from the way she bears herself. She betrays no trauma at all. Rather, she looks as blessed as any other creature of Enysbourg.

The inevitable comparison to Caralys assigns me my first mission for the day. I have to find her, hold her, confirm that she too has emerged unscathed from the madness of the day before.

She must have, given the rules here, but the protective instincts of the human male still need to be respected. So I wander from the park, into the streets of a capital city just starting to bustle with life; past the gondolas taking lovers down the canals; past the merchants hawking vegetables swollen with flavor; past a juggler in a coat of carnival color who has put down his flaming batons and begun to toss delighted children instead. I see a hundred faces I know, all of whom nod with the greatest possible warmth upon seeing me, perhaps recognizing in my distracted expression the look of a foreigner who has just experienced his first taste of Enysbourg's greatest miracle.

Nobody looks haunted. Nobody looks terrorized. Nobody looks like the survivors of madness. They have shaken off the firebombings that reduced them to screaming torches, the bayonets that jabbed through their hearts, the tiny rooms where they were tortured at inhuman length for information they did not have. They have shrugged away the hopelessness and the rampant disease and the mass graves where they were tossed beside their bullet-riddled neighbors while still breathing themselves. They remember it all, as I remember it all, but that was yesterday, not today, and this is Enysbourg, a land where it never happened, a land which will know nothing but joy until the end of everything comes again, ten days from now.

16.

On my way back to the hotel I pass the inn where Caralys and I went dancing the night before the end of everything. The scents that waft through the open door are enough to make me swoon. I almost pass by, determined to find Caralys before worrying about my base animal needs, but then I hear deep braying laughter from inside, laughter I recognize as Jerry Martel's. I should go inside. He has been in Enysbourg for years and may know the best ways to find loved ones after the end of everything. The hunger is a consideration, too. Stopping to eat now, before finding Caralys, might seem like a selfish act, but I won't do either one of us any good unless I do something to keep up my strength. Guilt wars with the needs of an empty stomach. My mouth waters. Caralys will understand. I go inside.

The place is dim and nearly empty. The old man with the enormous moustache is on stage, playing something inconsequential. Jerry, who seems to be the only patron, is in a corner table waiting for me. He waves me over, asks me if I'm all right, urges me to sit down, and waits for me to tell him how it was.

My words halting, I tell him it doesn't feel real anymore.

He claps me on the back. He says he's proud of me. He says he wasn't sure about me in the beginning. He says he had me figured for the kind of person who wouldn't be able to handle it, but look at me now, refreshed, invigorated, ready to handle everything. He says I remind him of himself. He beams and expects me to take that as a compliment. I give him a weak nod. He punches me in the shoulder and says that it's going to be fun having me around from now on: a new person, he says, to guide around the best of Enysbourg, who doesn't yet know all the sights, the sounds, the tastes, the joys and adventures. There are parts of Enysbourg, both in and outside the capital, that even most of those who live here don't know. He says it's enough to fill lifetimes. He says that the other stuff, the nasty stuff, the stuff we endure as the price of admission, is just a reason to cherish everything else. He says that the whole country is a treasure trove of experience for people willing to take the leap, and he says I look like one of those people.

And of course, he says, punching my arm again, there's Caralys: sweet, wanton Caralys, whom he has already seen taking her morning swim by the sea. Caralys, who will be so happy to see me again. He says I should remember what Caralys is like when she's delighted. He says that now that I know I can handle it I would have to be a fool to let her go. He chuckles, then says, tell you what, stay right here, I'll go find her, I'm sure the two of you have a lot to talk about. And then he disappears, all before I have said anything at all.

On stage, the man with the enormous moustache starts another song, playing this time not the misshapen guitar-thing from two nights ago, but something else, a U-shaped device with two rows of strings forming a criss-cross between ends and base. Its music is clear and resonant, with a wobbly quality that only adds to its emotional impact. The song is a slow one: a relief to me, since the raucous energy of Enysbourg's nights might be a bit much for me right now. I nod at the old man. He recognizes me. His grin broadens and his eyes slit with amusement. There's no telling whether he has some special affection for me as a person, or just appreciates the arrival of any audience at all. Either way, his warmth is genuine. He is grateful to me for being here. But he does not stop playing just to greet me. The song continues. The lyrics, once again in a language unknown to me, are once again still easy to comprehend. Whatever the particulars, this song is impossible to mistake as anything but a tribute to being alive. When the song ends, I toss him a coin, and he tosses it back, not insulted, just not interested. He is interested in the music for music's sake alone, in celebration, because celebration is the whole point.

17.

I think hard on the strange cycle of life in Enysbourg, dictated by law, respected as a philosophical principle, and rendered possible by all the technological genius the modern world can provide: this endless cycle which always follows nine days of sheer exuberance with one day of sheer Hell on Earth.

It would be so much easier if exposure to that Tenth Day were not the price of admission.

It would be so much better if we could be permitted to sail in on The Day After and sail out on The Night Before, enjoying those nine days of sweet abandon without any obligation to endure the unmitigated savagery of the tenth. The weekly exodus wouldn't be a tide of refugees; it would be a simple fact of life. If such a choice were possible, I would make it. Of course, I would also have to make Caralys come with me each time, for even if she was determined to remain behind and support her nation's principles, I could never feel at peace standing on the deck of some distant ship, watching Enysbourg's beautiful shoreline erupt in smoke and fire, aware that I was safe but knowing that she was somewhere in that no man's land being brutalized and killed. And there is no way she would ever come with me to such a weekly safe haven, when her land was a smoking ruin behind her. She would know the destruction temporary the same way I know it temporary, but she would regard her escape from the regular interval of terror an act of unforgivable treason against her home. It is as she said that time I almost lost her by proposing that she come back home with me, a suggestion I made not because home is such a great place, but because home would be easier. She said that leaving would be cowardice. She said that leaving would be betrayal. She said that leaving would be the end of her. And she said that the same went for any other attempt to circumvent the way things were here, including my own, which is why she'd despise me forever if I tried. The Tenth Day, she said, is the whole point of Enysbourg. It's the main reason the ships come and go only on the Day After. Nobody, not the natives like Caralys, and not the visitors like myself, is allowed their time in paradise unless we also pay the price. The question that faces everybody, on that day after, is the same question that faces me now: whether life in Enysbourg is worth it.

I think of all the countries, my own included, that never know the magic Enysbourg enjoys nine days out of ten, that have become not societies but efficient machines, where life is all about keeping that machine in motion. Those nations know peace, and they know prosperity, but do they know life the way Enysbourg knows life, nine days out of every ten? I come from such a place and I suffocated in such a place—maybe because I was too much a part of the machine to recognize the consolations available to me, maybe because they weren't available to be found. Either way I know that I've never been happy, not before I came here. Here I found my love of being alive—but only nine days out of ten.

And is that Tenth Day really too much to endure, anyway? I think about all the countries that know that Tenth Day, not at safe predictable intervals, but for long stretches lasting months or years or centuries. I think about all the countries that have never known anything else. I think about all the terrorized generations who have lived and died and turned to bones with nothing but that Tenth Day to color their days and nights. For all those people, millions of them, Enysbourg, with that Tenth Day always lurking in recent memory and always building in the near future, is still a paradise beyond comprehension. Bring all those people here and they'd find this choice easy, almost laughable. They'd leap at the chance, knowing that their lives would only be better, most of the time.

It's only the comfortable, the complacent, the spoiled, who would even find the question an issue for internal debate. The rest would despise me for showing such reluctance to stay, and they'd be right. I've seen enough, and experienced enough, to know that they'd be right. But I don't know if I have what it takes to be right with them. I might prefer to be wrong and afraid and suffering their disdain at a safe distance, in a place untouched by times like Enysbourg's Tenth Day.

• • •

18.

I remember a certain moment, when we had been together for three days. Caralys had led me to a gorge, a few hours from the capital, a place she called a secret, and which actually seemed to be, as there were no legions of camera-toting tourists climbing up and down the few safe routes to the sparkling river below. The way down was not a well-worn path, carved by the weight of human feet. It was a series of compromises with what otherwise would have been straight vertical drop-places where it became possible to slide down dirt grades, or descend from one rock ledge to another. Much of the way down was overgrown, with plants so thick that only her unerring sense of direction kept us descending on the correct route, and not via a sudden, fatal, bone-shattering plunge from a height. She moved through it all with a grace unlike I had ever seen, and also with an urgency I could not understand, but which was nevertheless intense enough to keep me from complaining through my hoarse breath and aching bones. Every once in a while she turned, to smile and call me her adventurer. And every time she did, the special flavor she gave the word was enough to keep me going, determined to rush anyplace she wanted me to follow.

The grade grew gentler the closer we came to the river at the gorge bottom. It became a mild grade, dim beneath thick forest canopy, surrounded on all sides by the rustling of a thousand leaves and the chittering of a thousand birds. Once the water itself grew audible, there was nothing but a wall of sound all around us. She picked up speed and began to run, tearing off her clothes as she went. I ran after her, gasping, almost breaking my neck a dozen times as I tripped over this root, that half-buried rock. By the time I emerged in daylight at a waterfront of multicolored polished stones, she was well ahead of me. I was hopping on one leg to remove my boots and pants and she was already naked and up to her waist in mid-river, her perfect skin shiny from wet and glowing from the sun.

She had led us directly to a spot just below one of the grandest waterfalls I had ever seen with my own eyes. It was an unbroken wall of rushing silver, descending from a flat rock ledge some fifty meters above us. The grotto at its base was bowl-shaped and just wide enough to collect the upriver rapids in a pool of relative calm. The water was so cold that I emitted an involuntary yelp, but Caralys just laughed at me, enjoying my reaction. I dove in, feeling the temperature shock in every pore, then stood up, dripping, exuberant, wanting nothing in this moment but to be with her.

She caught my wrist before I could touch her. "No."

I stopped, confused. No? Why no? Wasn't this what she wanted, in this perfect place she'd found for us?

She released my arm and headed toward the wall of water, splashing through the river as it grew deeper around her, swallowing first her hips and then her breasts and then her shoulders, finally requiring her to swim. Her urgency was almost frightening now. I thought of how easy it might be to drown here, for someone who allowed herself to get caught beneath that raging wall of water, and I said, "Hey," rushing after her, not enjoying the cold quite as much anymore. I don't know what fed that river, but it was numbing enough to be glacial runoff. Thoughts of hypothermia struck for the first time, and I felt the first stab of actual fear just as she disappeared beneath the wall.

The moment I passed through, with sheets of freezing water assaulting my head and shoulders, was one of the loudest I'd ever known. It was a roaring, rumbling, bubbling cacophony, so intense that it drowned out all the other sounds that filled this place. The birds, the wind, the softer bubbling of the water downstream, they were wiped out, eliminated by this one all-encompassing noise. I almost turned around. But I kept going, right through the wall.

On the other side I found air and a dark dank place. Caralys had pulled herself onto a mossy ledge just above the waterline, set against a great stone wall. There she sat with her back to the wall, hugging her legs, her knees tucked tight beneath her chin. Her eyes were white circles reflecting the light passing through the water now behind me. I waded toward her, found an empty spot on the ledge beside her, and pulled myself up too. The stone, I found without much surprise, was like ice, not a place I wanted to stay for long. But I joined her in contemplating the daylight as it prismed through a portal of plummeting water. It seemed brilliant out there: a lot like another world, seen through an enchanted gateway.

"It's beautiful," I said.

She said nothing, so I turned to see if she was all right. She was still staring at the water. She was in shadow, and a trick of the light had shrouded most of her profile in darkness, reducing her outline to a dimly lit crescent. The droplets balancing on the tip of her nose were like little glistening pearls. I saw, too, that she was trembling, though at the time I attributed that to the cold alone. She said, "Listen."

I listened. And heard only the sound of the waterfall, less deafening now that we'd passed some distance beyond it. And something else: her teeth, chattering.

She said, "The silence."

It took me a second to realize that this was the miracle she'd brought me here to witness: the way the waterfall, in all its harmless fury, now insulated us from all the sounds we had been hearing all morning. It was as if none of what we'd heard out there, all the time it had taken us to hike to this place she knew so well, now existed at all. None of it was there. None of it could touch us.

It seemed important to her.

At that moment, I could not understand why.

19.

I am in the little restaurant, thinking all this, when a soft voice calls my name. I look up, and of course it's Caralys: sweet, beautiful Caralys, who has found me in the place where we prefer to think we saw each other last. She is, of course, unmarked and unwounded, all the insults inflicted by the soldiers either healed or wiped away like bad rumors. She looks exactly like she did the night before last, complete with fringed blouse and patchy dress and two curling strands of hair that meet in the center of her forehead. If there is any difference in her, it lies in what I now recognize was there all along: the storm clouds of memory roiling behind her piercing black eyes. She's not insane, or hard, the way she should be after enduring what she's endured; Enysbourg always wipes away all scars, physical and psychological both. But it does not wipe away the knowledge. And her smile, always so guileless in its radiance, now seems to hold a dark challenge. I can see that she has always held me and my naïveté in the deepest possible contempt. She couldn't have felt any other way, in the presence of any man who had never known the Tenth Day. I was an infant by Enysbourg's standards, a man who could not understand her or the forces that shaped her. I must have seemed bland, dull, and in my own comfortable way, even retarded.

I find to my surprise that I feel contempt as well. Part of me is indignant at her effrontery at looking down at me. After all, she has had other tourists. She has undertaken other Projects with other men, from other places, trying time and time again to make outsiders into natives of her perverse little theme park to savagery. What does she expect from me, in the end? Who am I to her? If I leave, won't she just find another tourist to play with for ten days? And why should I stay, when I should just see her as the easy vacation tramp, always eager to go with the first man who comes off the boat?

It's hard not to be repulsed by her.

But that hate pales beside the awareness that in all my days only she has made me feel alive.

And her own contempt, great as it is, seems drowned by her love, shining at me with such intensity that for a moment I almost forget the fresh secrets now filling the space between us. I stand and fall into her arms. We close our eyes and taste each other's tears. She whispers, "It is all right, Robert. I understand. It is all right. I want you to stay, but won't hate you if you go."

She is lying, of course. She will despise me even more if I go. She will know for certain that Enysbourg has taught me nothing. But her love will be just as sincere if I stay.

It's the entire reason she seeks out tourists. She loathes our naïveté. But it's also the one thing she can't provide for herself.

20.

Jerry Martel stands nearby, beaming and self-congratulatory. Dee has joined him, approving, cooing, maternal. Maybe they hope we'll pay attention to them again. Or maybe we're just a new flavor for them, a novelty for the expatriates living in Enysbourg.

Either way, I ignore them and pull Caralys close, taking in the scent of her, the sheer absolute ideal of her, laughing and weeping and unable to figure out which is which. She makes sounds that could be either, murmuring words that could be balms for my pain or laments for her own. She tells me again that it's going to be all right, and I don't know whether she's telling the truth. I don't even know whether she's all that sure herself. I just know that, if I take that trip home, I will lose everything she gave me, and be left with nothing but the gray dullness of my everyday life. And if I stay, deciding to pay the price of that Tenth Day in exchange for the illusion of Eden, we'll never be able to acknowledge the Tenth Day on the other days when everything seems to be all right. We won't mention the times spent suffocating beneath rubble, or spurting blood from severed limbs, or choking out our lungs from poison gas. I will never know how many hells she's known, and how many times she's cried out for merciful death. I'll never be able to ask if what I witnessed yesterday was typical, worse than average, or even an unusually good day, considering. She'll never ask about any of the horrors that happen to me. These are not things discussed during peacetime in Enysbourg. We won't even talk about them if I stay, and if we remain in love, and if we marry and have children, and if they grow up bright and beautiful and filled with wonder; and if every ten days we find ourselves obliged to watch them ground beneath tank-treads, or worse. In Enysbourg such things are not the stuff of words. In Enysbourg a certain silence is just the price of being alive.

And a small price it is, in light of how blessed those who live here have always been.

Just about all Caralys can do, as the two of us begin to sway together in a sweet slow dance, is continue to murmur reassurances. Just about all I can do is rest my head against her chest, and close my eyes to the sound of her beating heart. Just about all we can do together is stay in this moment, putting off the next one as long as possible, and try not to remember the dogs, the hateful snarling dogs, caged for now but always thirsty for a fresh taste of blood.

"The mere absence of war is not peace."
—President John F. Kennedy

OUR HUMAN

At its onset, Barath's expedition to capture the beast Magrison consisted of one Human Being, one Riirgaan, one Tchi, and Barath himself, who was a Kurth. All were hated outcasts from their respective homeworlds, with nothing in common but their monstrousness in the eyes of their peoples, and their common greed for the bounty on the head of the even greater monster they sought.

Half the party died within their first few days in the rain forest. The Tchi, an effete disgraced academic of some kind, contracted a lung infection and was inconsiderate enough to confess his sins while writhing with fever. "I was a monster!" he cried. "I betrayed my oaths! I subordinated macrotext! I faked understanding of thematic unity!" It was almost a relief when the Tchi's spirit left him, midway through another anguished iteration of his transgressions.

The Human Being lasted only a few days longer. He had been a fugitive serial rapist, who before his sudden illness had enjoyed regaling his companions with detailed descriptions of his attacks on females of his species. Barath had endured these boasts but had trouble understanding why the human's deeds were crimes. After all, sex for the females of the Kurth was never voluntary the first time; it couldn't be, as they needed to be stalked and taken by force in order to enter heat. Rape was just part of the Kurthian biological imperative, accepted as necessary by both sexes. Human Beings seemed to have a different biological arrangement. Barath gathered that the species loathed those among their number who violated its spirit, but still couldn't see why a species as notoriously insane as Human Beings would make such a big deal over a simple breach of etiquette. Given time, and sufficient boredom, he might have pressed the human for further explanation. But then the human ate the wrong thing, or stepped in the wrong puddle, or did something else to encourage one of the many diseases that lurked in the jungle, and soon he, too, was gone.

This left Barath alone, save for his maddening final companion, Mukh'than. The Riirgaan had been sold to him as a learned guide who had been living in the Irkiirish jungle because that was the best way to study its fauna—not as a half-mad, unwashed exile squatting in the bush because no other place would have him. Either way, the lizard-face might have known the terrain and the natives as well as Barath's sources claimed, but he had all the personality of a pustule about to burst.

Barath almost killed this last companion the morning he discovered the parasite sucking at the soft meat between the armor plates on his right hind leg. It was a scaleworm, two claws long, glistening with the natural anesthetic the species uses to numb its hosts, and ready to burst after what must have been hours of feeding on him.

As Barath popped a claw and began to carve the beast from between his armor plates, Mukh'than watched with the unreadable fascination that had always so deeply annoyed Barath about Riirgaans. "You had better hope that's a female. In that species, the eggs are produced by the female but injected into hosts by the male. If that's a carrying male and he's had a chance to unload, you'll soon have hundreds of the creatures burrowing tunnels through your body. It isn't pleasant, nor is it quick. Just last year, I came across an infected Bursteeni who lingered an entire rainy season as he was eaten up from the inside."

Barath wanted to pop all twelve of his claws and give himself a pleasant little lesson in the finer points of Mukh'than's anatomy.

Instead he just lowered his head and proceeded with his impromptu surgery.

Mukh'than said, "You should clean that wound."

Barath grumbled. "You should mind your own business."

"You hired me for my guidance."

"And I'm beginning to regret my choice."

"If you want to find this village, I'm the only one who can help."

"That's what you say. And yet we seem to be lost."

"We are not lost," Mukh'than said. "We—" Then the skies rumbled, and he said, "Ah." Before the torrent could begin, he pulled Barath's sleepcube from his pack. The tent unfolded, expanded, and became a passable shelter for two, though the exterior canvas was already discolored from long exposure to the acidic Irkiirish rain.

"In terrain like this," he continued, once they were both inside the shelter, "it can be difficult to judge distances. Rivers change courses; tree cover changes shape. Even hillsides erode, reform, pick and choose their own topography. Too, we are using outdated intelligence, fifteen cycles old; for all we know, the entire village might have died out or migrated elsewhere. You were told this. You should show more patience."

The Kurth had a special treatment for people who urged patience at times of great urgency. It involved spikes and the careful placement of weighted stones. But Barath refrained. "I want the Beast. I want Magrison."

And Mukh'than nodded: one of several gestures his race shared with the race of the hated fugitive they sought. "So do billions of others."

Our Human remains huddled in the simple hut he built in the time of my firstfather's firstfather's firstfather, but we would know he was there even if the simple thatch walls were thick enough to muffle his hacking cough or his one-sided arguments with the many imagined ghosts of his past. We would know even if he wasn't too old and weak to wander far from his place. We would know even if his alien flesh didn't exude a rancid-fruit perfume subtle enough to tolerate but distinctive enough to serve as a constant reminder of his presence. We would know that our Human lurked inside the hut even without all these other reasons. We would know because the world around him ripples with the weight of the burden he carries.

Barath and Mukh'than were hours into the next day's travels, sloshing through a mulch of stagnant water and fallen vegetation, before Barath violated the oath he made to himself every morning and asked the loathsome Mukh'than, "How much further now?"

"Not far at all," said Mukh'than.

"That's beginning to sound like a fresh name for not knowing."

"Only if you have not paid attention," Mukh'than said. "Have you not seen the natives who have been tracking us for two days?"

Another trick of the Riirgaan's ego: withholding this basic intelligence until Barath's failure to notice emerged at its most humiliating. Barath rose to his full height, craning his neck to lift his armored head off the recess built between his broad, muscular shoulders. He saw nothing: just the stagnant water up to his lower set of knees and a dim hellish landscape littered with heaps of organic refuse. It was the kind of terrain a creature could hack through or burn through, but not see through. So he surrendered some more dignity: "What kind of natives?"

"The kind we're looking for," Mukh'than said. "Trivids."

There were three sentient species native to this world known only as Nameless: invertebrate jelly-things who drifted in its oceans, four-winged fliers who frequented the air above its poles, and the rarely-seen Trivids, who were native to this rain forest that dominated this region Irkiirish. None of the three had technological civilizations; nor did they have much contact with the illegal human mines that represented this sorld's only substantial link to interstellar commerce. Before this moment, Barath hadn't caught so much as a glimpse of any of them. But he'd been hoping for Trivids. "Where?"

"All around us. Throw a rock in any random direction and chances are you'll hit one. I count at least thirty."

Barath turned in a slow, deliberate circle, again seeing nothing but soggy deadfall. Or was he wrong? Over there, to his right: was that a telltale shifting in this place's damnable patterns of light? "Why are they hiding?"

"Since I've been communicating with them all day long, I would hesitate to call it 'hiding.' "

Barath's claws twitched. "Why don't they show themselves to *me*?"

"Perhaps they don't like your attitude."

"Mukh'than . . . "

"They're empaths. They sense these things."

"I can't turn my emotions on and off like a power switch!"

"Then look at it this way," Mukh'than said. "They're shy people. They've dealt with my kind before. They even know me personally. But your people are rarer, here. You're a mystery to them. And a formidable one: they don't like your size, or the look of your claws and tusks."

Barath sheathed his claws, sought a dry place to sit, and, finding none, lowered his armored rump into the mud. He could almost feel the parasites finding ways to get at the soft meat between his armor plates, but he was willing to put up with the discomfort as long as it tempered first impressions. "Tell them I don't bite."

Mukh'than produced some noises with his mouth and gestured with his fingertips.

Three Trivids appeared, passing from the unseen to the seen without any obvious transition. Thin, bony bipeds with sad, comical faces that reminded Barath of pie plates with beaks, they were taller than Barath had expected, towering a head and a half above Barath's height at full neck-extension. They each strode in the precarious manner of bipeds like Human Beings and Riirgaans, and wore body paint designed to blend with the splintered wood around them. But they were less intimidating than they intended—so lean and pale, so hollow-eyed and melancholy—that Barath almost laughed out loud at the fear he had begun to feel. They were worse than Tchi; so malnourished that the sharpened staffs they carried at their sides looked less like spears carried by warriors and more like walking sticks carried by the disabled.

The three creatures were clearly the same species, but there were gross physical differences between them: a ridge of jagged flesh across the shoulders of one, a gaping maw in the chest of another, an array of tentacles dangling from the jaw of the third. Sexual differentiation, Barath guessed, remembering something Mukh'than had said about the Trivids possessing three genders. If so, this could be a mated group, and the tentacled one, heavy in its lower abdomen, might have been heavy with child.

None of which interested Barath as much as the rag doll the ridged one wore on a knotted cord around its neck.

It depicted a biped, like them, and for that matter, like Mukh'than: a head atop four limbs. There was no detail. But the proportions didn't resemble theirs, or Mukh'than's. The head was too big, the arms too short.

As a representation of one of their own, it was pitiful. As a representation of a Riirgaan, it was complimentary. As a representative of one of Barath's people, it was insulting.

As a caricature of a human being, it was perfect.

Barath sat up a little straighter. “Mukh’than.”

“I see it.” The Riirgaan exchanged some pidgin sounds with the natives. “They say it’s a totem.”

“Where did they get it?”

More noises. “They say their human made it.”

Barath might have leaped to his feet at that, but his people, fierce as they could be in battle, had never been graceful risers. “They actually said human?”

“Clearly not. They don’t speak your tongue, my tongue, or the human tongue, Hom.Sap Mercantile. They said a word of their own invention, which I assume to mean Human. I’m not certain whether they see it as a category, a proper name, or a title. If you wish, I can come up with a subtler translation—”

“ ‘*Human*’s’ good enough. Introduce me. Tell them we’re happy to make their acquaintance and eager to see their human.”

Mukh’than obliged, listened to the jabber the natives offered in return, spoke some more, then turned his blank mask toward Barath and shook his head.

Barath’s hearts fell. The Human Being they sought was dead. They’d traveled all this way and the human was dead. The reward for his return would remain in the hands of the creature’s own people; Mukh’than would pocket his guide fee and return to his hovel in the jungle; and Barath would have to slog back up the river to the mine and continue working as beast of burden, trying to pay back the debt that had led him to such unpleasant labor in the first place. All because one human too old to care could not be bothered to keep his worthless heart beating long enough for somebody like Barath to come and claim him. “He’s dead?”

“He’s alive,” Mukh’than said. “And they say you can see him. But they also say they will not let us take him away.”

• • •

Our human has emotions and feelings that do not resonate to the same rhythm as our own. His feelings may not be outright painful to us—they do not prevent us from growing our food or raising our families; they do not make existence in his presence a torment—but they are, unmistakably, Other.

The Trivid village was a collection of mud and grass huts arrayed on an artificial island made of the same mud and dirt, supplemented with crisscrossed strips of cured frond. It was inhabited by maybe a hundred of the frail bipeds, including the thirty who had met Barath and Mukh'than in the jungle. At least a third of those who had stayed home were solemn-eyed young, who watched the off-worlders with a silence that could have indicated anything from awe to defiance. Few seemed to be doing work of any consequence. Several wore the human's rag-doll image on knotted cords around their necks. All stood by and watched as the party from the woods led Barath and Mukh'than to a straw hut at the heart of the tiny community.

The villager guiding them jabbered at Mukh'than until the Riirgaan translated: "He says their human lives here. He says that their human is very old and very frail and doesn't leave his hut very often. He hopes we will be kind to their human and understand his limitations."

"Tell the Trivid whatever he wants to hear."

After a few more moments of negotiation, the villager handed Mukh'than the handmade human totem from around his neck. The way was cleared, and both Barath and Mukh'than went inside.

The interior of the hut was dim and redolent with the stench of sickness and death. The dominant sound was the tortured wheezing of the emaciated figure lying on a wooden platform opposite the shrouded entranceway. The figure was indeed a human being, but not a human being of the sort Barath had encountered. Most of those had been young and robust, living on minimal sleep with maximum enthusiasm, enjoying exceptional health and vigor thanks to the treatments the mine owners leased from AIsource Medical. By contrast, this creature was even thinner than the natives outside and lacked even their vitality: he lay curled in a circle, one hand twitching, both eyes uncomprehending, his every breath a painful gasp, his skin disfigured by some kind of ugly skin-creases that seemed to have turned his face into a relief map of hilly terrain.

Barath felt repelled. "What are those?"

"Wrinkles. They happen to older humans. Their flesh starts to sag."

It was one of the most alien things Barath had ever been told about the Hom.Saps, who he'd considered pretty disagreeable already. "I've seen hundreds of humans and never encountered this before."

"Most of those who travel off-world get regular rejuvenation treatments. This human must have been deprived long enough for natural processes to come back into play."

"They're disgusting."

"I've seen worse. There is a small furry creature, native to a plateau on my world, which becomes a delicacy if it dies in sufficient pain. The natives of the region like to place a young one in a cage just large enough for its own body and feed it enough to make it swell to twice its natural size. As it fattens, the cage bars slice it in—"

Barath had endured more than his share of Mukh'than's enthusiasm for shocking details. "Enough. Let's confirm that he's the correct human."

The Human Being coughed twice, raised his head off the ancient pillow, and murmured a few words in Hom.Sap Mercantile. "I want Ravia."

"What is that?" Barath asked, as he removed the skin taster from his pack. "A refreshment?"

"A female of his kind," Mukh'than said. "A loved one, absent or long dead."

The skin taster was a flimsy thing, made for human hands, but Barath managed. He brushed the tip of the device across the old man's arm, withdrew, then projected a genetic analysis for Mukh'than's perusal. Mukh'than took longer than he needed to read the results, which was inconsiderate indeed, given that Barath couldn't read the only alphabet the reader could display, the over-complicated squiggles of Hom.Sap Mercantile.

The special tilt of Mukh'than's head more than compensated for the inadequate expressiveness of the Riirgaan face.

Barath didn't even need to ask the question. "It's him."

"Yes."

"Magrison? That's what it says?"

"Full positive," Mukh'than said. "It's the beast Magrison. There's no margin for error."

So shaken he didn't know whether to feel triumph or horror, Barath muttered a word he hadn't spoken since renouncing his faith. Magrison was *that* infamous. "All this time. All those people looking for him . . . "

"He had to be under a rock, to hide from the Humans. They have always raised so many monsters among their general population that they've grown very talented at finding those who choose to hide."

Barath grunted. "You probably consider yourself lucky your kind is less talented in that regard."

"Yes. And so must you. But what do you want to do with this one?"

Barath shuffled back and contemplated the figure. Sixty years, by the Hom.Sap Mercantile calendar, of hiding with people not his own, in squalor that must have reminded him of his fugitive status every day. Sixty years of knowing that the majority of his species fell into those who would have killed him right away and those who would have preferred to make his execution a neverending ordeal. Sixty years of evading the consequences of being a legendary monster . . . only to be revealed as a pathetic, senile invalid.

Barath, who didn't often feel sorry for anybody, would have felt pity for this man, were it not for the magnitude of his crimes against his own people . . . and the size of the bounty for his capture. "Do you know how many sentients would want to stand where we stand now? How many would kill to be here with a knife, a thresher, or even their own bare fists—just to do what this creature here deserves?"

"I hesitate to count," said Mukh'than. "But as for us?"

"We see whoever makes the decisions around here. We tell them who he is. We see if they're still so anxious to shelter him then."

"They will be," Mukh'than said. "If anything, more so."

The ancient Human Being spasmed, his coughs weak things barely audible beyond his pallet. "Where's Ravia?" he murmured. "I want Ravia."

Barath glowered at the emaciated figure sweating out his last days on the pallet. So many ways to retort to that. So few likely to get past the fog.

Our human is a creature who has had his life ripped from him, and who now leads a life he would not have chosen, among people who would not have chosen his company.

Alas, the Trivids had little sense of history and no sense of obligation to justice beyond their little swamp. Barath made Mukh'than translate at the start, but the constant repetitions of "You can't have him" grew so wearying he just left the Riirgaan to his work. The more Mukh'than wheedled with them the more obstinate they became, jabbering away in the pidgin that Barath could barely stand to consider a language, sweeping their arms in gestures he didn't need a translator to recognize as abject refusal.

The shadows cast by the forest canopy had grown considerably longer by the time the villagers dispersed, leaving Barath and Mukh'than alone in a village that seemed to have dismissed them.

Barath was so tired by then that he was almost happy for the chance to table the negotiations for the night. "No progress?"

Mukh'than touched a forefinger to his chin in the Riirgaan gesture of negation. "None."

"What's their problem? Do they worship him?"

"Venerate is probably more like it. They live only a quarter as long as untreated Human Beings, and therefore see him as a creature who has been part of their village life for generations. They consider any crimes Magrison committed before he came here ancient history."

"Do they even know what he did?"

"They know he did something bad, once upon a time. He has admitted this much to them. Sometime before he lost his faculties he even warned them that outsiders might try to take him into custody. But they don't know the specifics, and they don't care. He is too much a part of their lives for them to care."

"Maybe if you gave him the details," Barath said.

"Perhaps. I need to rest anyway. Maybe, in the morning, I will know the best way to make our case."

Barath could think of few things he desired less than sleep, as his people had minimal need for that condition. He desired another exposure to the prayers Mukh'than mumbled at night even less. But he knew the Riirgaan's needs were different from his own, so he assented.

They inflated the sleepcube and went inside for a few hours of protection from the insects and the muggy swamp-stench that saturated everything around the Trivid village. The air inside was not much better, given the olfactory consequences of a Riirgaan and a Kurth curled grubby and unwashed in close quarters.

It was a long night. Every few minutes in Barath's imagination, he leaped from the cube, batted the obstinate Trivids aside, seized the withered human from his bed, and collected the bounty. Then every few minutes he came back to himself, still curled beside his noisome guide, and still grimacing from his own dismay at not having done anything at all. It was intolerable for a sentient like Barath who had never seen the value of waiting.

Of course, impatience was a large part of the crime that had left Barath exiled from Kurth in the first place.

It hadn't been a serious offense, as such things were judged among his people. It wasn't killing without acceptable cause, or procreation without a cleansing fast. It had just been slovenly work: bored performance of a task contracted and paid for. Important people had been inconvenienced; a lucrative industrial concern had been shamed; a slave had been damaged beyond repair. It had all been tracked back to him. Barath would never be allowed back on Kurth unless he redeemed both his reputation and his finances—which was one reason he'd seized upon the claims of the dying Bursteeni he'd encountered at the mining camp infirmary.

The Bursteeni had claimed to have seen Magrison with his own eyes before illness felled him on his way to reporting this momentous discovery to human interests. To Barath, fallen so far that he might as well have been one of the slaves commanded by his people, the prospect of finding Magrison himself was a map offering a possible route out of hell. Even split between himself and his guide, the reward offered by the Hom.Saps could be enough to fund an outcast's way home. It could even be enough to fund a return with honor.

If the Trivids could be made to see reason.

If there were a way to take Magrison without their permission.

If.

In the midst of lighting a bowl of herbs—he claimed the intoxicating effect was essential for his nightly ceremony—Mukh'than said, "Do you know, we could satisfy ourselves with bringing back a scraping of Magrison's skin. After all, telling the human beings where to find him is almost as good as managing an actual capture."

Barath had thought of that. "They would have no reason to believe us. Samples were sent everywhere the Humans even thought of looking for him. Some have gone missing and later turned up in fraudulent claims."

"I know. But we could make a visual record. Bring back pictures."

"A child could fake those."

"But between the DNA and the pictures and their hunger to see this man caught—they would investigate, wouldn't they?"

Barath picked at the scab forming over his scaleworm sore. "The humans would still find a way to give full credit to whoever made the actual capture. We'd wind up with a small finder's fee, nothing more. No, it has to be all or nothing. We have to be the ones who bring him back. He has to be ours, if we want to earn the full reward."

Mukh'than lowered his face over the rising mists. "You sound like one of the Trivids. They consider him theirs, too."

"They're ignorant," Barath said. "They can't know the kind of monster he is."

Mukh'than was just a silhouette shrouded by a curtain of malodorous vapor. "And maybe it's just as ignorant for us to think that monstrousness on his scale can be reduced to a commodity for our profit. Maybe that's why we're not fit to have him."

The words hung heavy in the little sleepcube, with Barath remaining silent not because he concurred but because he saw no possible response to a statement so completely at odds with his own sensibility. Searching for signs of betrayal in the Riirgaan's sudden, unexpected burst of idealism, he wished he knew what the homeworld of the Riirgaans was like. It would be helpful to know if Mukh'than found the unrelenting mugginess of Irkiirish, or the forsaken wilderness of this world in general, an unbearable hell he would forsake principles to leave. After a long pause, he said: "You want him as much as I do."

"I have already said I do," Mukh'than said, as he lowered himself into the mists. "But perhaps not for all the same reasons."

Our Human once worked hard to earn his keep among us. When he was young, and the muscles still clung tightly to his oddly-proportioned bones, he made a point of helping us with the thousand and one small chores necessary to support our lives here. When a hut needed building, the Human lent his strength to the task; when food needed gathering, the Human grabbed a spear like the rest of us; when a child wandered off into the woods and needed finding, the Human searched as diligently as the Firstfather, Secondfather, and Firstmother. Even when we put down the work of our daily lives and sang hymns of praise to the spirits who built all things, our Human sat among us and raised his atonal voice with as much fervor as the most religious holies among us. It was a heroic effort, even if it was doomed to failure, for our Human knew as well as we did that he was not one of us and never could be, not even if the Spirits themselves came down from the sky to declare him an honorary member of the People. He trumpeted his alienness with every word that emerged, foul and unnatural, from his strangely-shaped lips; he came from a world where people walked on air and ate food that never touched the ground and mated in obscene couplings involving only Firstfathers and Firstmothers. Everything he said about his life among the people who had rejected him reinforced our awareness that he was different, that he was strange, and that he rendered us different and strange as well just by the act of living among us. He knew this, too, I think; and throughout the years of his life it made him as lonely as any creature had ever been.

When the next morning's negotiations began, the villagers all carried the human's crude totems around their necks. By the time their apparent spokesperson, a wizened member of the maw-chested sex, finished chanting an interminable string of gibberish that might have been anything from legal preamble to heartfelt prayer, Barath's head throbbed from sheer frustration. How nice it would have been to be able to resolve this by knocking their obstinate heads together!

Barath could only wonder how much Mukh'than was simplifying the story to accommodate the limited comprehension of the audience. These were people who had never been outside their swamp, who had never used weaponry more advanced than sharpened sticks, who had never seen more than a couple hundred of their own kind in one place. They were people who knew almost everybody in their world by sight, with the odd passing stranger a rare but tolerated anomaly. How could they comprehend a war fought worlds apart, over abstractions, between strangers who had never laid eyes on each other?

It was impossible.

But that's what Mukh'than needed to explain.

The hours crawled as the Riirgaan finished what he needed to say, but the time for words came to an end with daylight still remaining. Mukh'than returned to Barath's side, sweat glistening on the flat pads beneath his eyes. He grasped a water tube and sucked it dry, then wiped the moisture from his flat line of mouth.

Barath couldn't stand it. "What?"

Riirgaan feelings are impossible to read on their faces, but Mukh'than still managed to look haunted. "I think I may have made a mistake."

"What?"

"I told them that Magrison's victims outnumbered the leaves on the trees."

"And that's wrong?"

"Not if I'm trying to earn points for eloquence," said Mukh'than. "But very wrong if I'm trying to win their hearts. Images like that reduce a disaster to poetry, make it unreal, harder to comprehend—a joke compared to a familiar presence they've treasured all their lives."

"Tell them more, then."

"Saying more would only weaken what I've said so far."

Barath watched the Trivids confer among themselves. It was easy to tell that the villagers respected the gravity of their decision; they'd formed two dozen groups of three, lowered their heads and begun to mutter their soft liquid sibilants. Many fingered the Human totems around their necks, as if seeking comfort in a simulation of the man they had known. Another, a ridge-backed specimen who might have been moved by Mukh'than's case, gripped the doll so tightly that it punctured the doll's canvas skin, freeing the pebbles inside to spill onto the ground like parodies of blood droplets pouring from a wound. Several emitted a sour *blaat* that might have been their equivalent of weeping. Or laughter. It was impossible to tell whether they were devastated, or just rendered uncomfortable by the Riirgaan's evident belief that they should be.

Watching them, Mukh'than said, "Has it occurred to you, my friend, that this is all about monsters?"

"Eh?"

"Think about it. Our departed Tchi companion committed crimes that rendered him a monster in the eyes of his people. The Human Being we traveled with did the same. I know that you are no longer welcome among your own kind, for reasons you've neglected to share—and that the pathetic creature we wish to take into our custody is also notorious for reasons that make him a monster of the first rank. Did I ever tell you why I live in filth, rather than ever face another of my own kind? I promise you, you'll find it most instructive."

Barath said nothing.

But Mukh'than didn't wait for his approval. "I was a darr'pakh."

"I don't know that word."

"It's what we call a certain kind of teacher, one who is given total control over the life of a Riirgaan child, for one critical year in that child's development. During that year, before the child receives any other formal education, it's permitted no contact with friends, or family, or any adults other than the darr'pakh and the other students under the darr'pakh's care. Forbidden to speak, permitted only to listen, the child spends that year learning the one lesson most sacred to us, the one lesson we never share with outsiders, the one lesson we think every adult Riirgaan should know." Mukh'than dropped the empty water tube on the dirt and ground it beneath his foot, not stopping until it snapped. "I stopped teaching that lesson, Barath. After twenty seasons of pounding the same ideas into one student after another, I grew weary of my sacred task and simply abandoned it. I changed the lesson plan and spent one year teaching the students at my retreat another lesson, an irrelevant lesson. My crime was not discovered until after all my charges were returned to their families."

The Riirgaan's words had the bearing of broken stumbling things desperate to escape a place that had imprisoned them. But it did not seem to be pain that afflicted him. It didn't look like pain.

Barath would have asked what the false lesson was if not for the dread fear that the Mukh'than would have needed a full year to teach it. "Why?"

"Weakness. Boredom. The usual temptations. You know."

"And what happened when your people found out?"

The Riirgaan's shoulders shuddered again. "Among my kind, the sacred lesson must be learned that year, or not at all. The crime was thus irreversible. None of the children could go on to live useful lives. All were removed from their families. Most were committed to internal exile, or to institutions where they still rot today. Some of the unmanageable ones were euthanized." Mukh'than turned and cocked his head in a manner that could have been bitterness or amusement. "I was long gone. I knew the disgrace that awaited me otherwise. But given a chance, I would do the same thing all over again. The lesson changed me more than it changed them."

Barath, whose sense of morality had always been subject to his personal convenience, felt the special kind of revulsion that afflicts the merely flawed in the presence of genuine evil. He hadn't felt anything like this with Magrison. The human may have been something beyond all imagining once, but that which had burned in him before was all but extinguished by age and infirmity now. It still raged inside the Riirgaan. "Why would you tell me that story?"

"Because," Mukh'than said, with nauseating calm, "I don't want you to invest too much hope in my skills as a teacher."

Our human has been ancient, even by the longer-lived standards of his people, for longer than any of us have been alive. He was ancient even when I was a child still fresh from the litter, curious about anything and everything that walked the world around me, and fascinated most of all by the sad-eyed creature whose only purpose seemed to be storing unhappy memories. He is so old that holding on to breath could only be an act of open defiance against the spirit who brings release at the end of life.

The Trivids said no, of course. It was inevitable that they would: few peoples in their position would have surrendered something so familiar to charges they neither understood nor saw any reason to believe. They reported their verdict to Mukh'than, with all due solemnity; Mukh'than reported it to Barath, with the smugness of a being who has just had his brilliant predictions fulfilled; Barath muttered some of the fouler curses known to his people, with the resentment of a starving creature promised but repeatedly denied sustenance. Then the villagers dispersed, but for a single ridgeback who lingered long enough to leave the two off-worlders with one final message.

Mukh'than rubbed a finger across his cheek as the ridgeback scurried away. "It says they want us to leave. They say we make them uncomfortable: you with your anger, myself with . . . "—a pause, rare among the Riirgaan's usual smooth translations—"something they find just as disreputable."

"And yet they keep him. They don't consider mass murder disreputable?"

"They do," Mukh'than said. "But they still consider him theirs. They will let us stay another night, but we will not be safe here if we stay much beyond that."

Barath's claws emerged without his conscious consent. He clicked them together, feeling them scrape against each other, yearning for the warm bubbling reward of blood—though whether he most ached to slice the Trivids, the Riirgaan, or Magrison was something even he did not know. He did know it had less to do with the severity of the Human's crimes than with his own frustration at being denied. "We have weapons. Can we take Magrison by force?"

Mukh'than studied him for several seconds, his frozen features hiding a response that might have been anything from horror to enthusiasm. Transparent lids lowered halfway over the great empty blackness of his eyes. "Are you saying you're prepared to kill them?"

"If they get in our way . . . ."

"They'll get in our way," Mukh'than said, with absolute certainty. "If not before we take him, then afterward. Or do you think we can outrun the natives while carrying an invalid we'd need to keep alive?"

"We can keep them at bay. Threaten to kill him if they don't let us go."

"They'll still follow. And send runners to other villages. The further we run the more surrounded we'll be."

"Then we outfight them first."

"Kill one of them in such a fight and you'll have to kill all of them. Even assuming they don't manage to bring us down, a lone witness hiding somewhere beyond the tree line would be able to spread word of crimes committed against indigenes—and that's not all that popular a practice, even in this orifice of a world. Word of it will be up and down the river long before we reach the nearest outpost. We'd wind up retreating to the jungle and spending the rest of our lives dodging spears and living on bugs and worms."

It was pretty much how Mukh'than lived now, absent the spears, but Barath's short glimpse of the filthy lean-to the Riirgaan had constructed for himself had not recommended it as a lifestyle to be actively sought. But the need to suggest something, anything, kept Barath going: "The authorities might forgive us if we had the monster with us."

"The humans have a hateful history, but they're much more bound by the morality of interspecies protocol than you suppose. You can read the annals of their Diplomatic Corps if you doubt me.

But let us suppose we take your course. What if we kill them all, take our time getting back, and Magrison still doesn't survive our journey to the river? How will we be forgiven for filling a village with corpses just so we could produce the one the authorities want?"

Barath's claws now fairly throbbed with impotent anger. As much as it galled him to acknowledge that the twisted Riirgaan could be correct about anything, it was all true. Without the consent of the natives, they really did have no recourse grander than bringing the evidence back to what passed for civilization and hoping that the Hom.Saps who followed up played fair when it came to the reward. And yet, the prospect of a lengthy hike back to the river, enduring Mukh'than's company, without success to make up for it, seemed more nauseating still. "We'll think of something before we leave."

"Do you truly think so?" Mukh'than asked, then added a few sardonic words in his native language.

Suspecting an insult, Barath said: "What?"

"It is a couplet from an epic poem beloved of my people, words spoken by a despairing hero who has given up everything in a fruitless quest to find a villain who once committed a great crime against him. He wanders for years, goes hungry more often than not, suffers every indignity a traveler can suffer, becomes a ragged beggar and then an embittered ancient, only to find that all this time the object of his hatred has lived a rich and full life overflowing with bounty. Cheated of the justice he craves, he collapses in physical and moral exhaustion, shouting those words at the night sky. They mean, '*The Heavens always favor those who would reduce the heavens to ashes.*' It means that circumstances often conspire to free monsters of the consequences for their crimes . . . while those who hunt monsters destroy themselves by searching for justice. It's a charming fable that has provided no end of comfort to me through the years."

Furious, Barath said: "Because it means your hunters may never find you."

"Exactly. I take my victories where can I find them."

Once, there was still ample life in our human's aging bones—enough life, at least, that he still offered conversation to those few of us willing to oblige him. He cursed the bastards who were hunting him with a rage that made his eyes glow bright, and turned his voice into an open flame that would have seared any of them unlucky enough to stand exposed to its terrible heat. "Bastard" was of course a Human word, one of several harsh-sounding terms he used interchangeably with the far more reasonable vocabulary of our people. When I first heard him speak it, and the terrible hate he imbued it with, it conjured up a vague image of a terrible monster, like Our Human, only larger and blacker and better armed with claws and scales and teeth; a creature which could only inhabit the foulest of caves or the most monstrous of afterlives. As a child, the idea filled me with an infinite formless terror, and at night the spirits sent me terrible dreams about slavering Bastards come to get me. It did not make me afraid of Our Human, though. It made me feel sorry for a creature who had lost so much to such monsters. It was several seasons until Ctaas, who would become the Firstmother of my Grouping, but who was then a child as formless as I, heard him curse the bastards. In my presence Ctaas asked the Human the question I had been neither brave nor smart enough to voice: What Is A Bastard? Our Human had made that perverse coughing rasp that for his kind indicated vast amusement, and told us: A Bastard is a Human Being born without a Firstfather. It was even more alien than most of his answers, for we had never imagined that such an unnatural thing could happen, even among a species that only mated in Pairs. Our human brings so much wonder, so much terrible strangeness, into our lives.

• • •

Barath didn't want to sleep that night, but as he curled up for what should have been a few hours of alert rest, Mukh'than arranged and set fire to his bowl of precious herbs. The vapor was usually no more than an acrid tang, no fouler than the smell of the Riirgaan himself. But tonight it seemed stronger. Tonight the air around Barath turned as thick as the clouds in a blind thing's eyes, and something like unconsciousness came to claim him despite his intentions. His limbs grew heavy, his thoughts turned to crippled stumbling things, and his sense of time and place bubbled with contradictions. One part of him knew he was in a tent, among potential hostiles in a wretched village well beyond the few pockets of civilization that dotted this horrid world with no name. He felt the simmering fever at the base of his skull, the maddening itch where the scaleworm had gotten him, and the thousand and one smaller pains that came with any journey into places so inhospitable that the smallest steps exacted their price in blood. He even saw Mukh'than bending over him, murmuring words nothing like the prayers he had spoken every other night; and he experienced a moment of unease as the Riirgaan left him alone in a sleepcube filling up with intoxicating mist. He noticed, too, when Mukh'than returned with a rag over his face, carrying a knot of wriggling things at the end of a stick . . . and when Mukh'than left again. But another part of him was parsecs away, in the palace he would have built for himself upon returning home a success—a curtained place where a Kurth of distinction could luxuriate among his sycophants and slaves, inflating the victories of his youth into blessed lies.

It was such a joyous dream that he might have surrendered to it and died thinking it was his actual fate, but then the palace around him seemed to fill with smoke, and he found himself back in the sleepcube in Irkiirish, tasting his foul dinner of the night before as it burst from his mouth in an explosion of bile.

That was how he found out, before too late, that he couldn't breathe.

The air inside the sleepcube was now a gray mist that scoured his eyes—a lot like the Riirgaan's ceremonial intoxicants, only worse. Barath's lung was a burning ball of flame in his belly; his head a drum pounding out a song of imminent suffocation. He spat out the rest of the terrible taste in his mouth, rolled onto all fours, noted with distant rage that Mukh'than was nowhere to be seen, and for one queasy moment almost succumbed to the apathy that afflicts those so close to death that sinking all the way into that darkness seems less trouble than continuing to fight for life. Then anger took over and he drove himself forward, knocking over Mukh'than's stool and hammock, stumbling over his own pack, and ultimately finding himself trapped against the cube's flexible wall.

Once again he almost gave up, thinking gray thoughts of how little he had to live for anyway. He was a pauper. He was dead to his people. He was a friendless alien working subsistence wages for human beings on a world so forsaken that even its natives hadn't bothered to name it. There would never be any future for him, never any glory, never any redemption: just a wretched life and anonymous death.

Then the distant awareness that this wasn't just a stupid accident of some kind, but something else, ripped free a last defiant snarl. He popped his claws and punched holes in the soft canvas, carving stripes that his addled mind insisted on interpreting as wounds slashed in the flesh of an implacable enemy. Then he drove himself forward through the fresh exit, falling flat on his face in the mud created by a raging torrential rain. He vomited some more, tasted blood, and lay there hyperventilating as black fires burned at the edges of his consciousness.

It seemed a long time before his mind blazed with a single-word explanation.

Mukh'than.

He must have added something poisonous to his vapors.

Barath pushed himself off the ground, almost stumbling, but was able to rise to his hind legs, allowing the knuckles at his forelimbs to take the weight since his spine lacked the strength to support the far more awkward bipedal stance. His head lolled. He saw something white pulse between scales on his chest, and recognized it as a scaleworm, already growing fat on his blood. And there, further down, was another. And another.

Barath remembered the glimpse of squirming things at the end of Mukh'than's stick. Mukh'than had told him, just a few days earlier, to watch out for the males. Mukh'than would know what the males looked like. A Mukh'than turned malevolent—or, rather, revealing that he'd been malevolent since the beginning—would know just what to look for. How many had he found? Ten? Twenty? How many males in that many? And how long before they laid their eggs?

Barath's belly lurched. He spasmed, tried to expel whatever remained in his belly, and failed: there just wasn't anything left to bring up. For just a moment, thinking of the pain in store for him, he wished he could return to the apathy of near-death that he had just fought off at such cost and once again enjoy freedom from caring. But there was no reclaiming such a lost opportunity. As much as he might wish for death soon, right now he could breathe. He could think. He could hate.

He could see that the Trivids had been watching all along.

He sacrificed stability for height and rose on his hind legs, snarling like a beast as he did. The Trivids, gathered in the dark and the rain, reacted not at all. The anger burned in him again, and he stumbled forward, grabbing one of the ridgebacks by its neck. He wanted to shout, but the best he could manage was an explosive whisper. "Where is he?"

Either the Trivid had no fear, or his kind showed it in a manner Barath did not know how to read. It did nothing.

Barath wanted to tighten his grip and rip the creature's head from its shoulders. There was no reason not to. He had no future, and he had no cause to care for his reputation.

Then he saw the totem the Trivid held in its hand. They all held one: every single Trivid, holding before them all they had to show for Magrison's presence among them. Some held theirs higher than others, either stressing the object's power, or answering Barath in the only way they knew how.

Barath released the ridgeback, dropped to all fours, and moved toward the crowd—not because he wanted any of them, but because they stood between him and his murderer.

They moved aside.

And in the hut a few short steps away he found Mukh'than, an ardent lover curled beside the ancient human in his bed.

Our human described this Ravia as taller than himself, as thin as a reed, with a complexion the color of pebbled sand and sunny hair that descended to her shoulders in spiral ringlets. He said that since she was a Firstmother of his species and not a Firstfather like himself there were serious differences in the proportions of her body and his, but the descriptions themselves used terms that were unfamiliar to us. Once he said that every awful thing he had done, he did out of hate for those who had taken her. It is not a way of thinking we understand. But that is why we're Trivids. And why he's human.

• • •

Magrison was a knot of withered flesh with frayed cords for limbs. He gaped at the thatched roof above him, not seeing it, reacting not at all to the presence of the Riirgaan who lay naked beside him, stroking Magrison's pale white chest. Mukh'than seemed almost as insensate; he had closed both his transparent eyelids and the second layer of opaque ones that complemented them, and let his own mouth hang open, as if in parody of the human's slack-jawed senility.

The vague similarities between Human and Riirgaan anatomy that made some of the more unpleasant races grumble about not being able to tell those two species apart—similar heights and masses, bipedal posture, faces that arranged their features in approximately the same positions—seemed an obscenity in light of the differences that were visible when they lay side by side. Humans had limbs jointed at their midpoints; Riirgaan limbs had three segments. Humans had torsos a little like cylinders. Riirgaans were something like a prickly plant, with flat surfaces punctuated by spines. The proportions were off, too—especially the longer legs of the Riirgaan and the larger head of the Human. Nor did there seem, at first glance, to be any place where their respective parts could fit together. But that physical obstacle didn't seem to bother Mukh'than any more than the human's inability to respond did—and from the impassioned way Mukh'than stroked the collection of enflamed protrusions on his own belly, he didn't need the human's conscious involvement at all. Magrison's mere presence seemed to be enough.

When Barath charged them, Mukh'than was fast enough to grab his needle-gun and fire one shot, which dug a stinging furrow in the Kurth's side. But before he could fire a second, Barath's foreclaws were firmly imbedded in Mukh'than's wrist. The gun went flying into some dark corner.

The human clutched for his bed companion and murmured a single word in a voice filled with confusion and dust: "Ravia!"

Barath lifted Mukh'than off the bed by his impaled wrist. "Ravia? Is that who you are to him?"

Mukh'than threw a punch with his free hand. But it had no more effect than a single raindrop falling on stone. Without weapons, there was nothing any mere Riirgaan could do to get past a Kurth's armored hide.

Barath, feeling nothing but fury, drew Mukh'than closer.

Magrison reached for open air. "Don't hurt her! Please!"

Barath had never been good at reading Hom.Sap facial expressions, even after years of working for representatives of the species. The shifts from smile to frown to sneer and back again, so significant to them, had never struck him as anything more than random shifts of rubbery flesh. But it would have been impossible to miss the pain and desperation on the face of the slack-jawed old man, reaching with strength he no longer had to rescue the creature he thought he loved. Sickened, Barath faced Mukh'than again. "It isn't the first time he's begged for you in my hearing. He asked for you the other day too."

Mukh'than coughed. "He asked for Ravia . . . "

"Meaning *you*." Barath impaled Mukh'than's other wrist with another popped claw.

Magrison reacted to the Riirgaan's agony with a soft, weak cry of anguish.

"He loves you," Barath said.

"And I love him. He is the love of my life."

"You're Ravia?"

Mukh'than's voice was an agonized, breathless wheeze. "Ravia was . . . a female of his species. Mother . . . to his children. She died . . . as they died . . . in the war his enemies fought to avenge his crimes . . . "

"But he called you Ravia."

"When I am beside him, I am Ravia. I am a male of my own species . . . but I am honored to take the place of a female in his."

The arrogance in the Riirgaan's voice, dripping with satisfaction about his perverse liaison with a genocidal murderer of another species, was so infuriating that Barath couldn't resist retracting his claws and hurling the sordid little creature to the hut floor. Barath heard cracks indicating that Mukh'than broke bones when he hit but felt no diminution of his rage. He gave up on a clean kill right then and there, and instead decided to prolong his revenge by first shattering as many as the Riirgaan's remaining bones as he could manage. He lurched forward, ignoring Magrison's plaintive cries of "Ravia!", and falling on Mukh'than before the Riirgaan could crawl away into the dark.

"You killed the others in our party," Barath spat, grinding the Riirgaan's wrists for additional pain. "The Human. The Tchi. I don't know how you arranged it, but you made sure they died on the way here."

Mukh'than's response was a broken trill, distorted by agony, that nevertheless reflected real amusement. "That's right. You would be surprised how easy it was."

"You must have had trouble figuring out how to kill me."

"Not at all. I wanted you alive until now."

"Liar. I barely escaped the sleepcube."

More trills—but, as strained as they were, not frightened trills, but terrible triumphant ones. "If I had really wanted to suffocate you, you would already be dead. Remember the others. I know better jungle poisons than that!"

"I warned you not to lie to me!"

"It's no lie. If I wanted to smother you, why would I also infest you with scaleworms? What would be the point of that? If you suffocated in the cube they would die as fast as you did. I wanted only to incapacitate you for a while . . . to keep you from noticing the scaleworms I planted until after they laid their eggs and began what's going to be a much slower death. You will not make it back to the river no matter how quickly you travel. You will grow weak. You will collapse. You will linger. You will be in pain, an invalid, mad with delirium for an entire season, maybe two—something these Trivids can care for and consider theirs, so I can have more time to spend with the precious dying thing I consider mine. I have done it before, with other wanderers in this jungle. My only mistake with you, you vulgar brain-dead animal, was misjudging your metabolism . . . thinking the fumes would hold you longer, and give me time to get away. But that doesn't matter, not to you. You're still a corpse too stupid to realize it's started to rot."

It was far too early for Barath to feel the scaleworm larva digging burrows inside him, but for a moment he imagined the sensation anyway: a pounding, burning agony, multiplied a thousandfold for every second he was riddled with holes. He shook away the image, lowered himself closer to the traitor who had done this to him, and demanded: "Why?"

"Because I love him. For the same reason they love him."

Barath pressed the tip of a claw against the soft underside of Mukh'than's throat. "And that is?"

The Riirgaan's black, inexpressive eyes were pools filled with the knowledge of his own oncoming death. Perhaps that is what permitted him to speak without exhaustion, without fear. "Because in a place like this, where we live without hope, where we live among creatures with no hope . . . all we really own is the magnitude of our own sins." He closed the opaque lids over his eyes. "Don't you see that that's what makes him such a treasure to them? How much it must comfort such a people, to claim ownership of such a demon?

How much it comforts me, to care for one whose own crimes were so much worse than mine? Or how much it should gall you, in the presence of such fallen greatness, to remember that your own life was destroyed by a crime so petty?"

The crushing silence that followed was thick enough to bury any hope of answer.

"What I did," the Riirgaan said, "I would do again. It was a sin that made me proud. Can you say the same of your sin, Barath? Was it as grand?"

Barath gutted him. Thanks to the temperature differential between Kurth biology and the Riirgaan equivalent, the blood that geysered against Barath's chest plates was a thin cold soup, as unsatisfying a vengeance-trophy as any enraged Kurth had ever known. His rage unspent, Barath raised his forelimbs above his head and brought them down hard, shattering the Riirgaan's skull, driving the brains and bone fragments into the dirt. It should have helped. But the traitor's blood hadn't warmed any; nor had Barath's rage cooled. It could never cool. Not when he was still dying, and there was no one left to avenge him.

Part of him thought he still heard trilling.

Magrison didn't seem aware that anything unpleasant had happened; he just stared at the ceiling above him, his mouth agape, his slug of a tongue licking his dry withered lips.

"Ravia," the human said. "Ravia."

Barath didn't bother to get up off the floor. He just crawled over to the bed and loomed over the ancient figure, wanting Magrison to see something monstrous in his own tusked, blood-spattered face. He needed that; to achieve monstrousness in the eyes of a monster would have been victory of a sort.

But the old man didn't see him, really: was no more aware of Barath's presence than he was of his beloved Ravia's absence. If he saw anything, it was just the darkness and the fog comprising an exile far crueler than that which he'd chosen for himself so long ago. Perhaps he still experienced memory-flashes of the people he'd hated, the plans he'd made, the atrocities he'd carried out; perhaps they gave him moments of satisfaction, or raw crushing guilt. Perhaps he could live long enough to be taken from here and condemned to whatever execution his fellow humans wanted for him. But time and decrepitude had already provided a darker sentence.

"I should kill you," Barath said. "Do what everybody wants done. Get that much satisfaction out of this, at least."

Magrison's lips curled in an expression that might have been a smile. He whispered something in a language Barath didn't know, coughed, fought for breath, then whispered the same words again; though whether he spoke to Barath or to some phantom resident of the lost world where he lived was something the Kurth would never know.

Then the human closed his eyes, and did not move again.

Barath regarded the empty thing for a long time, thinking of a world filled with familiar shapes and abandoned opportunities. He thought of all the things the human had done and all the other human beings who would have danced if they'd known he was dead. He thought of his own crimes, wondered if anybody would have searched entire worlds to bring him to justice, concluded that in the end nobody would have cared, and wondered if that made him more or less pathetic than a monster fading in twilight. He didn't wonder whether the monster he contemplated was Magrison or Mukh'than, because in the end it didn't matter.

When he left the hut some time later, he wasn't surprised to find the entire population of the village gathered at a respectful distance. Every Trivid was there: every mated adult, every child.

They all carried the human's totems, and they all faced Barath with the incurious calm of creatures who already knew everything that had happened inside. A few made sounds Barath took to be questions, or possibly invitations. He stared back, expecting them to attack en masse, not caring much whether they did or not. Then one—a ridgeback, who Barath supposed to be the same individual who'd represented them before—stepped away from the crowd, approached Barath, and placed a single gentle hand atop Barath's head.

It took Barath a heartbeat to understand that the Trivid was offering welcome.

Of course.

As a people, they were so bereft that their greatest dream was the chance to replace one dying monster with another.

The Trivid approached again, and once again placed its hand on Barath's head.

Barath growled the last coherent words he'd ever speak to another sentient being. "I won't be your next bloody human."

The Trivids cocked their heads, trying to understand.

But by then Barath was leaving the village, on the first step of a journey that he knew he'd never live to complete.

Maybe if he pushed himself to the limits of his strength he'd at least be able to travel beyond their ability to carry him back.

The bones of our most recent human sit in an honored place. They are massive things, sculpted in proportions nothing like our own, sitting in a mound of scales we peeled from his form after he breathed his last. He died four days from our village, falling apart as he lumbered away from our offers of hospitality, cursing us, snarling at us, and throwing stones every time we tried to draw near. He was not like our other humans: neither the ancient one who lived with us for so many generations, or the black-eyed lover who so often shared his bed. This human was a giant thing with tusks and scales and claws, who walked on all four limbs instead of the two our previous humans preferred. This human looked so little like the other two, who in turn looked so little like each other, that it's difficult to see how they could all be creatures born of the same world. And unlike the other two, this human never told us of his crime—though the crimes committed by the other two, which they described to us often, were so beyond imagining to us that the offenses committed by the giant tusked thing must have been just as terrible, just as great.

It is a powerful thing, indeed, to have the bones of three such humans among us, in this place which has known no such wonders . . . so powerful a thing that skeptics among us sometimes wonder if all three of these creatures were indeed of the same species. After all, they looked nothing alike. How could all three be human?

But we see no point in such doubts. We have heard what humans are.

And we know a human when we see one.

CHERUB

Childbirth always means pain, and not just for the mother who must strain to expel both the squalling infant and its parasitic demon rider from her womb. It also torments those of us who must stand around the outer wall of the birthing shed and watch, both eager for our first look at the baby and dreading our first glimpse of the hateful attached thing bearing the face of the corruption in that child's heart.

It is midday. A peremptory daylight enters the shed in stripes, illuminating the dust in the air, but not the bleakness of these last moments before we discern the nature of the monster who will accompany the child into the land of the living. My beloved wife Faith squats in the center of the room, slick with sweat and tears. Her straw hair clings to her cheeks, and her toes sink into the diarrheic puddle she expelled as the ordeal entered its final stage. She has uttered curses since dawn that prove the common wisdom that women turn savage during birth: oaths of terrible hatred directed against the child inside her and I the man who planted the seed. I believe she would kill me, and it, right now, just to be rid of the pain.

I know I'm right about the rage because of her own personal rider, a hideous idiot monkey-thing riding piggy-back on her soft shoulders, whose spindly leprous arms lead to scaled claws buried knuckle-deep in her temples, leers at me over the top of her head. It is the embodiment of everything that is bad about this mostly good woman I married, and it mocks me with the deep pleasure it takes in her suffering. Its tiny piggish eyes and moron leer, all sharp teeth and pointed tongue, manifest the vindictive cruelty my darling wife is prone to whenever the world requires more of her than she can freely give. Despite the genuine affection she has always shown for me, Faith has also always been capable in heated moments of flinging words that flay all my self-respect away in a single lashing sentence. Even as she strains with the effort of expelling our son, her rider's face betrays the few secrets Faith bothers to keep, her unspoken resentment of every passing disappointment I've ever caused her rippling across its noxious features like pus flowing from a septic wound.

Nor am I any better. My own demon rider, whose petty features betray my cowardice, my pettiness, and my secret selfishness, tightens its grip on my skull and tickles the part of me that cares not for Faith's pain and wants only for this long, stinking, noisome day to end. I'm certain that Faith can see that and I can only hope that she sees the best of me, the part of me not embodied by my rider, as easily as she can see the worst.

The men of the village form a circle around the wall of the shed, their arms linked in the traditional last gesture of defiance against whatever evil thing comes to join us atop the child about to burst from Faith's slit. They are silent. Their riders keep up an animated conversation between themselves: not one we can hear, thank the Lord, for if riders spoke aloud their voices would drown out our own. It is not a nice conversation. The riders make faces, they make obscene gestures, they laugh long and hard, they pull their talons from the bore holes in our skulls and nail them in again, in cruel emphasis of their dominion over us. I think they are arguing between themselves. I think they are wagering on the new arrival. I think they are as tired of the wait as we are.

On either side of me, my brothers Noah and Eben hold my arms, counseling strength. They have always been good men, but Noah's gibbering imp of arrogance and Eben's stone-faced golem of coldness peer over their respective faces. I am entitled to hate my brothers a little for this, and no doubt my own rider—(that loathsome many-eyed insectile thing, that whispers obscene things to me in the night, that assures my wife of the vile rape fantasies I must sometimes employ to keep me hard during the act of love)—now shares that secret with them, over whatever pretense of a grateful look I can place on my own merely human features.

Then Faith screams, her voice hoarse and breathless. "They're coming!" The word becomes a bellow as she puts all she has into the final push, expelling a gout of blood and the head of a baby, which for a moment dangles between her spread legs, glistening scarlet. She gasps, takes a sideways crab-step to relieve the horrendous cramps in her knees, and squeezes again. My newborn son lands in the dirt we're all heir to, the dirt that greets us as we enter the world and embraces us again as we leave. There is of course something on the back on his neck, something as soft and as rounded and as new to the world as he is: the passenger that will define much of what he is, even now grasping him by the neck, cementing its grip on who he will be.

This is the most terrifying moment, for any parent. In my life I have attended births where the first sight of the rider was enough to prove that no joy would ever come from the child, where the rider's distinct features branded its human mount as thief or rapist or murderer, and the babe for all its apparent innocence was revealed as naught but a seed from which nothing but evil would ever grow. True, even those were usually permitted to live, for even a future murderer might be able to live a worthy life blessed to his kin until the moment he commits his terrible sin, and remains possible to value such a person, even if it will always be impossible to look at them without some inner voice raising that dread question, *when*? But that is still a shattering thing to see for the first time, on what should be a day of celebration.

And even that would not be the worst. I still have nightmares about that foul morning some five years gone when my neighbor Jeremiah's son was born and the thing on his back bore the face of something so savage that we could scarcely bare to look at it: an awfulness that we could only compare to riders of legend whose human hosts had not just killed once or twice out of greed or rage, but slaughtered freely, sometimes entire families and sometimes entire populations, in sprees driven only by their sheer love of killing. When Jeremiah took the child from his shrieking wife and headed for the village well, we all knew what he intended to do, and none saw the point in stirring a muscle to stop him. After all, he'd borne his own murderer imp since birth, and the time had now come for him to live up to it.

Now I have to behold my own child, and see whether the sins on his back bring more heartbreak than joy. My brothers release me, and I join my darling Faith, who still strains with the afterbirth. I tell her I love her and I take a deep breath and lifetimes later raise my son from the filthy puddle that is his first introduction to a debased and sinful world.

He is a tiny thing, bearing the correct number of arms and legs and a scrunched-up face indignant about the ordeal just forced on him. He coughs out a mouthful of liquid and then starts to cry, a high-pitched, angry wail that assails me his fury at me for inviting him into a place this filled with pain and fear. I sense that he is strong, and before I allow myself to feel the first stirrings of love for him turn my attention to the creature on his back, which is of course even smaller than him, and so covered with slime and blood that it is at first impossible to determine its true nature. Somebody hands me a wet cloth, so I can clean it enough to see; and as I wipe away the blood and the piss and all the other shiny effluvia of life, I first feel fear, and then puzzlement, and then relief, and then the dawning amazement of a man faced with the kind of miracle no man dares hope for.

From the shadows, Eben asks me what it is.

The tiny creature clinging to the back of my son's neck is beautiful. It is pure and it is innocent. Its face is as smooth and as unmarked by any of the possible cruelties or follies as the mirrored surface of a lake can be when undisturbed by wind or current. Its eyes are closed, its expression sweet. Its hands are not the sharp, raking claws we all know from our own riders, but hands that could belong to any other baby's, and they cling to my son's neck without breaking the skin, their touch more gentle caress than possessive grasp. It is absolute innocence personified: something that exists only in legend, something that no man I know has ever worn, something no parent I've ever heard of has ever dared hope for.

"It's a cherub," I say.

Fifteen years later, I am at home tending to my infant daughter, when Eben rushes in with the bad news. My son Job has been beaten and robbed again.

I wish I could say this was a shock. It is not the first time, or the tenth, that others have seen my son's innocence as weakness, and done whatever they wanted to him, whether robbery, bullying, or—on one terrible occasion—rape. His back is a relief map of scars, his face a history of all the brutal things other boys have done to the one perfect boy who will not defend himself for any reason. Many of these are also visible on the back of his rider; not just because our riders tend to take on the same ravages time inflicts on us, but because more than one boy ridden by something foul and angry has attempted to peel my son's harmless rider away, with fingernails and sticks and even knives, in the apparent belief that the boy envied and despised by all should not even be left that which marks him as what he is.

I know it is my duty to go with Eben, to tend to the son cursed by a birth that failed to sufficiently damn him. I should, but I feel a great weariness, the kind that only comes after years and years of watching someone you care for live through one torment after another. I am tired of hearing that the other boys have beaten him. I am tired of hearing that strangers have robbed him. I am tired of hearing him lashed with the kind of horrible words that leave barbs in the skin and continue to fester even after the surface wounds have healed.

It is not that I don't know of other children who have been almost as brutally treated; there is a man in my village, Jared, ridden by a thing of perverted carnality, whose fifteen-year-old daughter Ruth avoids all eyes as she carries his latest rape-spawn to term. Everyone knows what Jared does to her at night. But she at least bears the imp of a future patricide on her back. She deserves what she gets and he deserves what she will do. A case can be made that Jared is only doing what he has to do, to punish her in advance for the inevitable moment when she will destroy him. But what of Job, who has never sinned, and never will sin? Who, it seems, may even be incapable of sin? How does he deserve what they do to him? How will his scales ever be righted?

I glance down at my new infant daughter Miriam, who is round-faced and beautiful and (I know from the hateful second face grinning at me over the smooth curve of her head) a brat, a user, a castrating bitch who will someday brandish her sex like a weapon to manipulate men who will give up their dignity and their principles for a mere moment of her favor. When she is old enough to know what her eldest brother is, she will doubtless manipulate him as well, showing him moments of kindness in between vivid demonstrations that she feels nothing for him but contempt. I feel no fear about her ability to make her way in the world. If anything,

I take comfort in fearing for the world's capacity to survive her attentions.

Faith enters from the other room leading our other son, the dull-eyed seven-year-old Paul, who is not feeble-minded as he would like us to believe but (we know from the features of the creature on his back) has an utter contempt for anyone but himself and a low and animal cunning that leads him to pretend dependence on others in order to get them to do things for him. It was difficult to remain patient with him when he resisted toilet training as a means of remaining a coddled, indulged infant; it will be even more difficult to endure the selfish, spoiled, half-formed being he will be as an adult. I know that my rider's face clarifies the depth of my growing disgust for him, so I turn to Faith, who has aged thirty years in the past fifteen, and tell her that I need to go to Job.

Even as she takes Miriam to me and coos to her, the rider on her back flashes the mien of any mother who sometimes hates her own children, for making her worry about them, for making her spend time on them, for making her subsume everything she is to them. Paul, jealous of any attention spent on any human being other than himself, starts to tug at her sleeve. Faith reassures him, her sweetness never wavering even as her rider underlines how much she'd like to kill him.

I tell Eben to take me to my eldest son.

The two of us trudge through the streets of our village, which are cold and ankle-deep in slush from recent snowfalls. I do not look at the familiar faces of my neighbors, or at the faces of those who ride them. I do not look at the liars or the thieves or the bullies or the connivers or the bigots or the hypocrites or the self-satisfied stupid. I do not look at the adulterous or the violent or the ones who show compassion but exult when others feel pain. I do not look at the boy who kicks dogs or the girl who twists her little sister's hair when their parents aren't looking. I do not look at the other boy, the surprisingly gentle one who everybody knows will kill somebody someday, and who once tearfully confessed in my hearing that he wishes he didn't know, because the knowledge leaves him unable to look at any other person, even the girl he likes, without wondering if that's his future victim. And when I pass the glass window of Judah's bakery I do not look at my reflection in the glass. I never look at my reflection in glass.

It is not that long a walk, overall. It is only an eternity.

In less than ten minutes we arrive at the crossroads on the edge of the village, where a small crowd has gathered around my bleeding son. There are wagons, some drawn by oxen and some by horses, left untethered in the grass, as their owners hopped down to bear witness. Two local girls who have always been kind and even loving to Job, despite what I know about their true natures from the savage crones clinging to their respective backs, tend to his wounds, cleaning the gash in his forehead and staunching the copious flow of blood from his nose. He whispers something to one of them, and she blushes. Then he sees me and his wounded but still beautiful features brighten at the sight.

As always, it takes my breath away, to see nothing hiding behind that love but more love; it is not something I'm used to.

This is the beautiful and the terrible thing about my boy Job. He is always as he seems. When he smiles, there is nothing behind that smile but warmth. When he offers to lend a hand, there is nothing behind that generosity but an eagerness to help. When he is hurt by others and later professes forgiveness, it is true forgiveness and not the kind of grumbling, suppressed resentment that amounts to vengeance, biding its time, but the absolute inability to pollute himself with grudges of any kind, even when he has been wronged so grievously that he could be forgiven for seething with hatred. He puts me, puts all of us, to shame. Maybe that's why he's so hated. People may think they despise those not as virtuous as themselves, but there's no end to the reservoirs of wrath we bear for those we know to be better.

He tells me what happened. There was a gang of them. They came upon him as he returned from the next town with the goods I sent him to get, and swarmed him like rats, ripping his clothes, kicking his ribs, stealing his money and taking his goods. In the end, they took turns pissing on him.

I am livid. "Who?"

"You know I can't tell you. I won't subject them to your anger."

"If you won't give names, it'll only happen again. You'll never know a moment's peace."

I know it's the wrong argument as soon as the words leave my mouth.

He says, "I already know peace." And there is no denying that, in the same way that there is no denying that the sun rises, or that rain falls from the sky.

There is no denying that because, even now, even after its mount was savaged by savages, his cherub sleeps. Riders never sleep, not even when they ride those marked by indolence and sloth. A man's sins always cling to him, even when he slumbers. Like all married men, I sometimes spend time on sleepless nights studying the features of the woman who shares my life, and even when her own face is a peaceful mask buried by the false death of sleep, her rider is always peering over the tousled curve of her hair, miming its endless caricatures of all the waking woman's sins. But in all these years Job's cherub has never once opened its eyes. It has always hugged his back in gentle acceptance of all that befell him, its dozing features testifying to a soul as placid, and yet as possessed of great depths, as a vast becalmed sea.

This is not a state of being I understand, as I would track down those responsible for this outrage and carve their punishment from their own flesh, with even less mercy than they showed my son . . . but then my passenger has always borne the features that mark me as vengeful at heart, and Job's has always borne features marking him as a boy who refuses to hate.

"Tell me their names. I won't hurt them. I'll just make sure they never hurt you again."

He tells me, "I'm sorry, father. I forgive them."

From deep in the surrounding crowd there's a rumble of derisive laughter, the kind a bully makes when he dismisses a weaker soul's right to conduct his life without fear. I recognize the laugh before I turn, and find myself cursed by the awareness that it comes from a man who either knows who beat my son, or happily participated. He is a man known to me, whose own boys bore bruises and furtive looks before they grew old enough and large enough to become, like their father, blights on the lives of any with the misfortune to know them. He says, "It is like they all say. Your son is useless."

The man's name is Kenneth. He owns a pig farm outside of town, but lives better than his income from that enterprise could explain were it not supplemented by extortion and theft. He has burly arms and a weather-beaten face marked by too many scowls and not enough smiles; his shoulder-length red hair and beard frame his harsh features, always unruly, always catching the wind in a manner like a corona of fire.

These are the things I know of Kenneth. I know that he is stupid, in the way that the worst cruel and bullying men are stupid: that he is incapable of considering any concerns but his own, and sees any objections to his conduct as a personal affront, demanding of punishment. I also know that he is crafty, in the way that the worst cruel and bullying men are crafty; that he knows how to hurt people, and when, and has an infinite imagination when it comes to breaking them. I know that his wife is little more than a despised slave, who rarely opens her mouth for fear that he'll shut it for her. I know that he lives with four other women, each of whom joined his extended family while barely more than children, at least two of whom he simply took from their families and rendered utterly devoted to him by the simple method of alternating brutality with unexpected kindness until they were willing to do anything he asked of them if it guaranteed the latter. I know that he has punished their prior families for trying to interfere, that homes have been burned, and livestock killed. And I know that, even without his rider's terrible visage, a mask of cruel self-satisfaction not all that much more offensive than Kenneth's own, it would be just as easy to see it in the set of his tiny black eyes.

A couple of his younger sons, who are still not coarsened to the degree he wants, refuse to meet my eyes. The three eldest meet them with defiance, enjoying my hatred. All five of their riders grin at me, their demented faces as exultant in their evil as Kenneth has always been in his.

Whether they witnessed the beating or not, everyone in the crowd knows at once that Kenneth directed his sons to beat and rob mine: and that he doesn't care that we know.

The old man sneers. "Your son's a woman. If you took his trousers off you would find a hole where a boy should have a good strong rope. A true man would have dirtied his knuckles with the blood of at least one of the scoundrels who attacked him, or at least now had the stones to name them. This one's less a boy and more a mushroom, planted in shit, born without backbone and doomed to wither as soon as the sun strikes him."

Even as I stand, my hands curl into fists. But I know it's no good. I cannot stand against Kenneth alone, let alone his sons. Nor will any of my neighbors stand with me; certainly not Job, whose gentle right hand even now reaches up to touch my wrist, to assure me as always that this is nothing, that he can bear it, that no wound can be inflicted on him that his infinite soul will not heal.

I have never wanted to kill a man so much, and I have never been as shackled to the cowardice that is the least of my sins. I burn from the awareness that my rider shows Kenneth both.

His look of answering recognition is the worst thing I've ever seen.

"Leave him alone," I say, "or I'll kill you."

He chuckles and gathers his sons for the journey back home. I have no doubt that were I to wade into them with angry fists, and by some miracle reduce them to as battered a state as they left Job, I would find in their pockets the money they took from him, and in their cart the goods they stole; and I know that were I to raise my voice and demand that the other onlookers aid me in finding justice for my boy, there would be no takers. Even those who hate Kenneth agree with him on this: innocence has made Job worthless, as far as defending himself is concerned.

Even so, the moment would not pain me quite so much if one of the two pretty girls tending Job did not stand up and leave him behind, to hop aboard Kenneth's wagon and sit pressed up against one of his sons.

Three years later, Leah enters our life for the first time.

She has been brought to us by her father, a man whose rider marks him as a cheat and occasional petty thief, but there is nothing in its manner or in his that marks him as anything but a parent who loves and cares for his daughter. I might keep an eye on my coin purse, but I believe him when he says that his only concern is for her.

Leah is a fragile wisp of a thing, with skin so pale it is almost translucent and hair so blonde that it is almost white. I would mistake her for albino if not for the tracing of freckles that form a constellation across both cheeks and the tip of her nose. She has weak eyes, by which I mean that she refuses to meet mine, not even when I speak kindly to her, and not when I tell her, in all honesty, that she is a pretty girl and that I am charmed by her face. In truth I am even charmed by her rider—it is no cherub, like my son's, but it is so unmarked by anything terrible that it might as well be, resembling an innocent babe in all ways but for a powerful stormy affront about its eyes. It is not a happy thing, but neither is she. I have seen riders like hers on the shoulders of other souls too sensitive for this world, souls so helpless at fending off the cruelty of others that they don't even grow inured to the sharp and cutting places inside themselves. It is the look of self-hatred, which can be as great a sin as any other, a look that anyone would recognize as the mark of a possible future suicide.

Leah and her father, who are strangers to us, come from a village further down the coast and have spent weeks on the road, traveling here. The reason is of course obvious. It is often said that a marriage can only be happy if the rider of the man and the rider of the woman betray sins of equal weight. A man whose rider marks him as an epic monster will bring nothing but misery to the life of a woman whose rider marks her as one whose sins amount to little more than weakness. And certainly a woman of cutting tongue and demeaning temperament will always drain the life from a man whose rider embodies nothing worse that a shiftless soul. No man or woman seeking some semblance of happiness should ever join with anyone much worse than themselves, else they risk bearing the weight of their partner's rider as well as their own.

Leah's father has always despaired of finding her a man capable of treating her with the kindness she will need to survive. And our greatest fear for Job's future has always been the impossibility of finding him a wife who would not take advantage of his unassuming nature and enslave him in ways beyond the chains that should be forged by love. It is indeed part of why we have ordered him to remain close to home, these past few years; not just because of the danger he faces from rapacious people like Kenneth's family, but because too many of the local girls have divined at a glance just how much power they would have over him if ever they ensnared him into marriage. I have seen what rides the shoulders of those with the kindest eyes and sweetest faces and shuddered at the thought of my poor son, subjected to their version of love without any rider of his own to provide him the strength he would need to have any will of his own.

So, yes, I understand why Leah's father thinks his daughter and my son might be the greatest hope for one another. But as we all sit together in our home's largest room, the unshuttered windows admitting a hot dry wind from the west, the conversation erupts only in fits and starts. Three-year-old Miriam cries nonstop and tugs at her mother's leg, upset beyond reason that the gathering isn't about her. Ten-year-old Paul, who always resents the attention she gets, tugs at her ear and makes her cry. Leah averts her eyes to avoid meeting Job's, he struggles to find words that won't be embarrassing or shameful, and the air itself thickens like amber, trapping us all in an afternoon that seems to have stopped like time.

A few minutes after Faith goes into the other room to stir the stewpot—Paul following so closely behind her that he might as well be a second rider, clinging to her with the insistent intimacy of a mistake—I mutter that I better go check on her and find my beloved wife weeping in utter despair that anything will ever turn out all right. Nothing I say to her, no reminder of how shy I was the day we met, will staunch the tears. I ask her what's wrong. She draws close and beats at my chest with her fists, while Paul continues to tug at her apron. She asks me, "What did God think he was doing, when he gave us one son too good for this world?"

This prompts a tantrum from Paul, who hates the special regard his mother has for Job. The screeching begins.

Dinner is grim.

It is not until much later, when the smaller children have been banished to bed and the adults have wandered to a different part of the house to talk about something, anything, but the fiasco we believe we're experiencing, that I look out the window and spot something in the gathering twilight that takes my breath away.

Unnoticed by any of us, Job and Leah have stolen off together, to the edge of the meadow, well within the distance we have declared safe for him but farther than he has ventured since the last time he was rendered bloody from a neighbor child's hurled stones. It is late in the year, and the sun is just starting to set. They stand facing one another, but not eye-to-eye the way they would be if about to kiss. She's looking down at his feet, her long hair hanging like a curtain over any emotions that might be betrayed by her features. He's doing something that most people would consider obscene even in marriage, and downright scandalous when seen in two young people who have only met a few hours ago: reaching past her face to stroke her unhappy, self-loathing rider on the back of its head.

From the window, I can see the face of Leah's rider far more clearly than I can see her own. I can see that stormy scowl so redolent of misery resist his touch, and even grimace from resenting it. And then I see that scowl falter, come back as angry as ever as the rider realizes it's losing, and then disappear completely. The rider's features smooth over, becoming placid. Its eyes close. It adopts the expression of a baby lost in sleep. It becomes a cherub, as unpolluted by darkness as his own.

As Leah looks up to face my son, the curtain of blonde hair falls away from her delicate profile, revealing cheeks slick with tears that are just beginning to curl into an unaccustomed smile.

Job and Leah don't kiss, yet, but instead just stand there looking at one another, their lips moving in words I would almost kill to hear. She looks down again, but this is just a flicker, a moment of vestigial reflex no longer relevant after a lifetime. Her rider continues to doze. His never stirs. The setting sun makes the meadow glow red, cradling boy, girl, and riders in what might as well be a wreath of flame.

The news that a boy and girl ridden by cherubim—his that way from birth, hers created by a moment of kindness from him—have betrothed spreads from village to village, bringing not just curiosity-seekers but monsters, seeking to spread the hurt as a matter of principle. Our neighbors close ranks. Many of those who abused Job in the past take to watching the roads in and out for strangers whose riders signal their intent to do harm.

Even that human viper Kenneth takes part, driving his boys against a caravan of ragged and unshaven men whose riders all bear faces marking them as the worst kind of vindictive destroyers, the kind of men who spread misery not out of greed or hatred but for the sheer joy of shattering the lives of those more fortunate than themselves. Kenneth and his sons confront this wolf pack, determine that they have come from many miles away to entertain themselves by committing malicious mischief against this couple they have heard about, this man and woman who consider themselves so special, and with remarkable efficiency sent them on their way, missing coin-purses, wagon, clothing, a number of teeth, and in one case a right eye. I do not forgive Kenneth and his family for what they have done to mine in the past, but I now give him a nod when we make eye contact encountering one another in public. Maybe he's decided that his family has tormented Job enough.

My brothers, alas, are less sanguine about our newfound hope for a better future. They buy me ales at the inn and congratulate me on the upcoming new addition to the family but turn dark as the brew poisons their blood and hint at bad times to come.

Noah says, "I fear for the children of such sinless people. Whether ridden by cherubim or demons themselves they'll have the misfortune of growing up with parents unable to summon enough anger or hatred to protect them from anyone not quite so pure."

Eben has other worries. "They will have trouble if they become parents. A mother and father without so much as a dark thought in their heads will never be able to tend to children prone to lies, cruelty, or worse." He goes on to tell us the story of a mother and father he knew during the five years he lived further down the coast, whose riders were, though not quite cherubim, also not quite formidable enough to arm them against their son, who was a little monster. By the time that boy reached adolescence, he ruled their home like a despot, reducing mother and father to beasts of burden too terrified to do anything but indulge his slightest whim. Nor did it ever end for them, for why would such a little monster ever seek a life away from his parents, when his parents were so incapable of denying him?

Eben tosses back another drink and tells me that I should take special care that Paul does not end up like that. "You need to take him in hand now or know the nightmare he will become later."

It is all true, every word of it, but from the way my other brother Noah peers with sudden alarm over my shoulder I know that my rider reflects the extent of my growing anger. He mutters some words about how I should take all this as well-meaning advice and not as mockery.

I allow myself to be mollified, and return to my drink. But when I walk home, later that night, more than one of my neighbors, passing me on the way, walks a little faster when they see me, or the terrible aspect of my rider. For I know that my brothers are right.

I sleep that night in a downstairs bed to avoid frightening Faith with the rage of my rider. She will never miss me, not when Paul still insists on sleeping between us, a living barrier erected to exclude his invasive father from the territory on his mother's side of the bed. My dreams are terrible, though when I wake I don't remember how. With dawn still hours away I trudge to the outhouse and return, taking a protective detour past Job's door, which is always ajar, an invitation to a world that he insists on treating with trust. He is sleeping. I stand there for long minutes and listen to him breathing, marveling as any father would at the miracle of a boy now on the threshold of becoming a man, and reeling from the terrible vertigo that can only be known by a parent of a child in danger.

Job and Leah become husband and wife seven months later, in the tradition of our village. We stand them in the public square, carve a tight circle in the dirt around both, and bid spend four hours back-to-back, their riders pressed together in mutual acceptance of the respective sins borne by both man and woman. This has always been, by our teachings, the most intimate covenant by which the betrothed can demonstrate not just their love for one another, but their acceptance of the very worst to come.

Tradition among us holds that if either the bride or groom can be driven from the circle before the time is up, their sins will always stand between them and that they must therefore not be wed. Friends, family, and strangers are encouraged to surround them shouting whatever they can, to drive the pair apart . . . sometimes bribes, sometimes declarations of love, sometimes just mocking recitations of all the reasons why they're bound to make one another miserable. In my day I have seen many a wedding end with the bride breaking down in tears and fleeing, face in hands, minutes before the end of that four hours, and have never doubted the ceremony's efficiency at preventing marriages doomed to misery.

Other villages do it differently, I hear. Eben says that some far from here, which he visited during the years he spent as a wanderer, have a specific series of prayers recited by a designated holy man. This makes no sense to me at all, as I have never seen a man anywhere who could be called holy. Even Job isn't holy, the more appropriate word for him being *innocent.* All I know is that if I ever did meet a self-professed holy man who claimed the power to preside over the most intimate moments of my life I wouldn't let him speak prayers about anything having to do with my family unless I first spent long minutes examining whatever rode on his back. I personally suspect that the riders of these holy men may be even worse than those carried by those of us who don't claim freedom from sin.

For hours Job and Leah stand back to back inside the small circle, the spine of his sleeping rider pressed tight against the spine of hers, both demonstrating a level of divine peace well beyond the reach of those of us whose riders snarled and spat and brandished our worst secrets on this special day. Both Job and Leah are calm, smiling, confident of their ability to outlast the ordeal.

Outside the circle, the required ritual abuse by our neighbors is mostly restrained, limited to little more than good-natured teasing. The unmarried girls cavort and waggle their tongues at Job, promising him endless nights of wanton abandon should he abandon his foolish devotion to this girl with no idea how to set a fire in a wedding bed. The unmarried men advise Leah that they understand her ignorance in these matters, but feel obligated to tell her that Job has a root doomed to remain soft for life and that she'd be better off spreading her legs for a man who can make his stand at attention. There is a bad moment when Kenneth strides from the crowd and circles the pair, looking over both of them as if appraising pigs that have come to market, but after two orbits he nods his head and ambles away, with a nod at me that I can almost consider friendly. It is never possible to tell for certain, but there is nothing in his eyes or in the eyes of his rider that betrays simmering malice against my son and his bride. He doesn't seem to be letting the day pass without incident only so that he can indulge his cruel appetites later. There is reason for hope.

The afternoon is of course not completely without trouble. Paul, who we gave the honor of drawing the circle, grows upset that his contribution is over with and that he is no longer the focus of all eyes. He starts whining that he's bored and then wailing that he wants to go home, and is unstirred by appeals that this is his brother's day and that he should be as happy for him as we all are. Miriam gets sick from something she's eaten and is soon as cranky and as inconsolable as her middle brother. The tension Faith has felt up until this day combined with the poor behavior of our younger children makes her blame me for being so useless a father.

But all of this falls far behind next to something else I see, something that I have never heard tell of happening before, and that as far as I can tell only I can see, because I will afterward question my wife and friends and neighbors and find not a one who confesses to beholding what my eyes are blessed to behold now. As I watch, amazed, Job's sleeping rider turns its little head and, without ever opening its eyes, brushes its lips against the cheeks of Leah's rider. Her rider, without opening its eyes, turns its head and kisses his on the lips. Both riders then turn their attentions back to those they ride. I look up at the faces of my son and his bride and see from both blinding smiles that both are fully aware of what just happened, and both know what it means. This is not just the only possible union for a boy born without sin and a girl who lived too long without hope; nor is it just the loving union we all hoped for. It is the kind of union they write about in the stories, the kind that is not supposed to happen in the real world. Maybe it is why even Kenneth would not wield his evil against them. I can only dare to hope, my knees turning weak at the thought.

As the ceremony ends a great weight lifts from me as a cheer erupts from my friends and family and neighbors and the couple is mobbed by well-wishers who hoist them aloft and carry them about like trophies for long minutes before once again allowing their feet to touch the ground. Another cheer splits the sky as the couple kiss a second time. Job embraces his mother and then me and tells me that it does his heart well to know that I was watching on this glorious day. Leah kisses me on the cheeks and tells me that she will take joy, from this day forward, in being able to call me father. Even Paul senses the tug of family and congratulates his older brother. The songs and dancing begin, and then the feasts. It should be the happiest day of my life.

I can only wish I knew why I remain afraid.

Another two years later, something big happens. I do not know how to classify it in my heart. There must be a special word for an event of staggering undiluted evil that can only stun you with its depravity, that you are bound by all standards of human decency to regard with and that you cannot help face with any emotion darker than relief. But I do not know it. I can only report what's happened and try to measure my feelings later.

Kenneth has been murdered.

It should be no surprise. His family has if anything gotten worse over the past few years, robbing homes and stealing livestock and growing their little colony of corruption by taking girls by force and making them too frightened to leave. In the last three years, three men who decided to stand against him had their homes burned, and one disappeared on his way home from an errand, leaving no signs of the nature of the misfortune that befell him. Kenneth was always in a public place, making himself visible, whenever these things happened, though he never showed any surprise whenever somebody came running from a distance to report the news. Nor were his sons anywhere to be seen. There was always a terrible, mocking knowledge in his eyes, showing us how much he relished our awareness that the responsibility remained his even when his hands were empty and displayed in plain sight. He loved our impotence.

I have always known that it was just a matter of time before somebody did what so many have wanted to do.

Noah, who witnessed the event, brings the news while I am at Job's house helping adding a room for the baby now only two months away. We have been working all afternoon, enjoying the heat of the day and the slick sheen of sweat our labor summons to our skin, and when Noah rides up, his horse shining from a hard gallop, we wave at him, thinking at first that he's only come to help us. But then he gasps out the news and we put down our hammers and we step away from the skeletal frame of the nursery under construction and join my brother on the front porch so he can tell us what happened while we were here preparing for the miracle of new life. After a few seconds Leah comes out preceded by her belly to hand him a cup of water, then stays to listen.

This is what he tells us.

It happened a little more than an hour ago.

Kenneth rode his open wagon into the village to pick up some supplies he's sent for, accompanied by his eldest son and the youngest of the young girls to join his extended family. She is Amelia and she is fourteen and she has been with him with three years, a relationship that began when she reported being raped by him at eleven, changed when she recanted two days later, and became whatever it is now when she left her parents and two younger sisters and moved in with Kenneth, calling him her "husband." Following the usual pattern, her parents expressed outrage and appealed to her neighbors to help them rescue their darling girl, receiving little help before inevitably showing up bearing cuts and bruises and frightened expressions to go along with their insistence that it was all a misunderstanding and that Amelia's new marriage had their blessing. The girl has rarely been seen in public, since then. Today, the first time in months, her little belly was as swollen with new life as Leah's.

Kenneth pulled his wagon up to the community store, tied up the horses, then took his boy and went inside to get and carry out his goods. It took several trips. Amelia remained silent where she sat, not answering anybody who tried to speak to her. A crowd started to form. By the time Kenneth and his son finished the loading, half the village was there, many surrounding the wagon in a crowd five bodies thick.

Shaking his head, Noah tells us that Kenneth was not afraid, even then. He had always been untouchable and he thought he was untouchable still. When he took the reins and told the crowd that they better move, because they were hemming him in, he had the eyes of a man who was memorizing faces. His rider's burning visage declared a dozen separate vendettas. Then somebody, it could have been anybody, shouted a call to action. Somebody, it could have been anybody, dragged Kenneth's son from his seat. Somebody, it could have been anybody, grabbed Kenneth as well and forced him to the ground, where he was engulfed by a wave of shouting people.

He would have survived the beating.

But somebody, it could have been anybody, stabbed him in the heart.

So far, nobody had confessed to seeing who drove the blade between his ribs, though a number of the people there had long borne riders bearing the face of murder and a number bore riders bearing the face of complicity. No one will testify against a killer. In a sense, they may all be killers.

I do not know how to feel about this. Kenneth's family hurt someone I loved as much as anyone I loved has ever been hurt. There was once a time when I might have snuffed out his life myself, had I believed there was a chance that I might get away with it. But either I've grown soft with the years or the long time he's left my loved ones alone have diluted any hatred I feel. No weight has been lifted from my heart.

Leah, looking sad, asks, "Is his son all right?"

Noah tells her, "As all right as any boy can be when his father is murdered mere steps away from him."

"And the girl?" Job asks.

Noah tells him, "She is unharmed as well. She has been brought to the home of her mother and father, neither of whom she has seen in more than a year. There is no telling whether she will stay there, rather than return to Kenneth's family, but for the moment she is where she should be."

Job says, "Good."

It is his only immediate reaction.

After a little while Noah takes his leave of us and gets back on his horse, to bring the news to some of our more distant neighbors. We return to working on the new room. More than a hour passes, by my estimation, before I ask Job to stop.

He puts his hammer down and waits.

"If you were not the man I know you to be, and if I were not with you all day today, I would have wondered all my life whether you'd been the one to put that knife through that bastard's ribs."

Unhurt and unsurprised, he says, "But I am, and you were."

"True. But with the man dead, there's no reason to not tell me the truth. Was Kenneth the one who beat and robbed you, that last time?"

"Yes. Him and one of his sons. I won't say which son, but it was one of them."

"God. Are you all right?"

He considers his answer a long time before answering. "If you're asking me whether I feel any pleasure at Kenneth's death, the answer is no. It solves nothing. The world is still awash with brutality, and becoming part of it, even taking distant pleasure in it, interests me not at all. All I feel is sadness for a man whose rider so bubbled with hatred and pain that he could only achieve release by sharing it."

"But don't you feel safer?"

"Of course not." He takes up his hammer again and strikes a protruding nail just once before looking ill and putting the tool down. "One day I was born. Someday I will die. What takes place between the beginning and the end is too short to fill with fear. The bad days happen from time to time, and more must be coming, but I've had far too many good ones in between to give the bad more weight than they're worth."

My vision blurs. "You're a far better man than I'll ever be."

"No, I'm not. I will not lie to you, father. I fear that I'm not the man you and so many others believe me to be. I'm capable of hating people who hurt me, and wishing for bad things to happen to them. But I don't want to hurt anyone back. While I'm alive I just want to live the best life I can, and this is the only way I know how."

I know him well enough to recognize the closest he ever comes to annoyance. It hurts him, hurts everything he is, to be pressed for some form of celebration at his old tormentor's death. It is the chief disadvantage of having a paragon for a son. Sometimes, many times, I cannot live up to him.

It is only late that night, as I lie beside Faith, that I wake and realize that it must not have been Kenneth I've feared all these years . . . for in asking Job whether he felt any safer, I neglected to notice that I do not.

The wheel of time continues to turn. Life in the village becomes much more peaceful without Kenneth around to prey on us. His sons heed the warning that there is only so much their neighbors will take from them, and scale back their criminality, without ever ceasing it. Leah strains a day in the birthing shed and presents Job with a son they name Isaac whose gentle rider betrays no sin worse than mischief. I put the baby in twelve-year-old Paul's hands and he looks down at his new nephew with harmless bafflement, almost dropping him when the baby's lips burble over with cheese. Miriam toddles about, stealing hearts with sideways glances. Leah brings me a jacket she has made for me and kisses me sweetly on the forehead, telling me that I am her second father, blessed for raising a man who could tame her rider and teach her that life can be an occasion filled with joy.

While playing with my grandchild I catch a glimpse of my face in a mirror and am stunned to see that my own rider has been tamed as well. All my adult life I have tried to be a good husband to Faith and loving father to the children, but I have also always been aware, as much from the way it felt in my heart as from the terrible aspect of the second face peering over my own, that it has always been more the act of a man pretending to be good than a man who could just be. I have always told myself that this is true for everybody, because we all feel the weight of our riders and we all know the evils we bear. It does not mean that the good among us are frauds. But I have always felt that way anyway . . . until this moment when I see the reflection in the glass and realize for the first time that happiness, years of fighting the worst in myself, and the example of a man better than any I ever hoped to be, can calm the greatest beast. My rider's gnarled features have smoothed, its aspect turned more human than ever before. It is not the peace Job and Leah know. But it is still more than any man could ever hope for. I turn to Faith, beaming, and see her beaming back, her own rider as soft and innocent as it has ever been. This may be the most loving moment of all our years together.

We make love that night: the kind of love that only long-marrieds can make, when they are reminded of how hot their flames burned in youth.

I don't know why, but I remain awake long after Faith has surrendered to sleep, all the strangeness of the world large in my thoughts. After a long time I kiss the back of my dozing wife's hand and go to the common-room, lighting a candle so I can look at myself in the mirror again. My face is lined with the kind of furrows that come with years, and hard work, and broad smiles, and—it stuns me to see—wisdom.

My rider, wide-awake and curious, blinks at me, wondering what I'm up to. I find myself, wondering, idly, if its current strange purity would be at all affected by deliberate and conscious evil on my part. It is the kind of game played at least once by every child who ever picked up a mirror, tired of making silly faces at themselves and wondered if their rider could be induced to do the same.

It could be done. The philosophers say that our riders don't define us. We would not be perfect people, if we were lucky enough to be born without them. We would instead be people whose sins were hidden, who could conceal their most vile natures behind the most angelic countenances. We would never know if a man was fated to become a rapist, or a woman a murderess; we would not find out until the sins were committed, and the evidence of their crimes lay bleeding on cold earth. There would even be those of monstrous aspect but innocent hearts condemned for deeds committed by others: a terrible thought that speaks to alien possibilities, and worlds even worse off than our own. What would the world be like, if the prisons could fill with innocent men?

I have not indulged in this kind of experiment since I was young. But a strange whim drives me to make the attempt now. I concentrate on the very worst atrocities I can think of, trying to mean them as more than ridiculous abstractions. *I will go back to our bed and take Faith by force. I will go to Miriam's bed, take her by the ankles, and smash her skull open against the wall. I will do what some monstrous parents do and take Paul as a man takes a woman. I will go out in the night and knock on Job's door, pretending an emergency just so I can strangle him with my bare hands once we are alone. I will hold Isaac below water and*

I cannot go on. I am too sickened by even thinking these things, and feel shamed for allowing them to take root, for even a moment, in the imperfect soil of my mind. Maybe I am an evil man, after all. But my rider just blinks at me, its expression as placid as before, marked only by the confusion of a child who has just seen his father spouting inane gibberish.

Our riders are part of us. They know our pretenses. They know what we are and what we only pretend to be. I cannot summon enough pretend evil to fool my own, any more than I could have summoned enough pretend good.

Maybe that's what prevents true evil from overrunning the earth.

I put down the mirror, blow out the candle, and return to my wife's side, imagining myself at peace.

And then one day two years afterward Job shows up at my front door carrying Isaac's shattered body.

If a man's life is like a ribbon of time, stretched out upon the earth and extending from the moment his parents conceive him to the moment some bedridden old man releases his last breath into a world that has long since robbed all of his reasons for living, then there are during those years moments that cut like daggers, that can plunge from the sky and snap that ribbon in two. They can even be poisoned, these moments, carrying toxins so foul they shrivel everything to come and everything that came before. Any happiness that ever existed becomes a lie, any hope that ever beckoned a fraud.

I don't refer to my grandson's death. It has only been one day since he toddled away from his mother and some damned drunken wagon-master crushed him in the road. It has only been one day since I saw his chest staved in, his little body opened by a scarlet groove where his ribs should have been. It is only one day since I heard Faith scream when she saw him, one day since I had to look into the eyes that had been laughing, just earlier that morning, now burst cherries in a darling face.

All of that was terrible and all of that was like having all the joy torn from the world, but that is not what tears the ribbon of my life in twain and poisons everything that came after and came before. It cannot be. I have lived a long time. I have had people I love die before; parents, friends, and once before all that the baby sister I had to go along with my brothers, who drowned at seven and left a hole I still feel after a life of never mentioning her name. I know that life is what you live in between watching the people you care about die, and though it breaks my heart it is not the dagger that cuts my life in half and makes all our lives a lie.

That happens later in the evening, when we are all gathered at Job's home, offering what shallow comfort we can. Leah sits on the floor, her eyes staring, her hands shaking, her rider once again assuming the self-hating aspect it possessed when first we met. Faith sits by her side, whispering one empty reassurance after another. Miriam stays close to me, stunned by her first encounter with death in all its fullness. Noah and Eben stand silently by the wall, their hands folded before them, their shaggy heads turned toward a floor that fails to offer any clues as to what they can do to make the tragedy bearable, if not better. Job answers the many knocks at the door and accepts the condolences of neighbors who have heard about the tragedy and want us to know how sorry they are, kindly ushering away those who want to come in long after a lesser bereaved father might have gone mad.

At one point I recognize the visitor at the door as one of Kenneth's sons, a brute who I've always believed to have participated in Job's beating, and though he comes hat in hand and delivers his condolences in the tone of a man who dearly wishes he could be anywhere else, I feel the fury rise in me and almost race to the door to lash him with all the hatred of a father and grandfather irate that this pig still breathes while Isaac waits at the gravedigger's house for his new home beneath dirt. But Job takes his old tormentor by the hand and thanks him, with a sincerity that shames me, as so many of the examples he's set have shamed me.

The worst begins not long after that, as Leah starts talking about her fallen baby boy, the way he ran and played, the golden way he laughed. The memories wound her so much she starts to sob again. Job rushes to embrace her, to tell her that Isaac is not truly gone and all that nonsense. Faith holds her hand and murmurs sweet lies of her own, and all this might help, but I cannot tell, because we're entering the worst of it, that horrid point in the shattering grief of the bereaved mother that only comes after the immediate shock of the tragedy passes and she finds herself seeing for the very first that this is now her world, the only world she'll have.

And there's no way to get past this moment except by living it, and in another few seconds we might be able to, but my other son Paul, who at twelve is more than old enough to know better but who has been simmering throughout all of this with the impatience known only to those who need every moment to be about themselves, incredibly chooses *this* of all possible moments, *this* one, to start tugging Faith's sleeve and start whining that he's bored, that he's hungry, that he wants to go home . . .

Job curses him and shoves him away.

It's a light shove, even if it does leave Paul sitting on his rear end with a comical look on his face. It would be forgiven from any bereaved father, seeking a moment's respite from a brother half his age who has never been anything but entitled brat. But from Job, who has never in his entire life lost his patience, it hits with the impact of a thunderclap.

All sound in the room ceases.

Job's lips move without making sound. He peers down at Paul and then at Faith and then at me, and each time he bears the look of any man caught in a monstrous lie. For the very first time I am able to see beyond his placid and compassionate eyes to an infinite and stormy place beneath. His face contorts with what might be shame and might be rage, though it's impossible to tell because he has never betrayed either.

The shock is so great that it cuts through even Leah's bottomless grief. She blinks up at him and says, *Job?*

He flees past my gaping brothers and barrels out into the night. Noah and Eben make to go after him, but their hesitation allows me to beat them to the door, where I assert my responsibility as father. Eben relents, muttering about this being the first time he could be sure the boy was even human. I glare at him and he looks away, before I depart.

It is not long before I find my son, kneeling in the meadow with his forehead pressed against a bare patch of dirt. He shakes and sobs as he pounds his fists against the ground. I can only approach and kneel beside him, allowing him to wail, thinking of how I might have acted if a catastrophe just as stupid had taken him, or Faith, or Paul, or Miriam. After a few seconds I say, "Come on, son. You need to be better than this."

Without looking up at me he murmurs, "Why?"

"Because this isn't you. Because your wife and your mother expect you to be strong . . . and when you're not, it scares them." I hesitate. "And me."

The sound that bubbles up from the ground strikes me first as chuckle and then as sob, and then as some terrible mixture of the two, celebrating and mourning all at the same time. He claws furrows in the ground with his fingers and mutters something I cannot hear, something followed by the long seconds of weeping and then by the same words, repeated in a voice as empty as the shell he must feel he's become. "This is me, father. This has always been me. You just never really knew who I was."

I pull him upright and face him. "Yes, I did."

This, again, seems to strike him as hilarious. He giggles and weeps, the tears pouring from him in waves. "I thought I could be a good man. I thought I could live the life of a good son, a good husband, a good father. I thought I could do it and that nobody I loved would ever be hurt."

"It's not your fault. These things happen."

"You think so?"

"I know it, Job. You're the best man I've ever known."

"Oh, Father." He bows his head and lays his fists against my chest, pounding me with a frustration that, even now, he keeps in check. "I keep telling you. I'm no man at all."

"Don't be ridiculous, son. That's just the likes of Kenneth talking—"

He chokes on his snot and tears. "No, it's true. I'm no man. I've sinned more than any true man could, every second of every day you've known me. I sinned by being liar and murderer and thief all at the same time, taking everything that belonged and ever would belong to another. Isaac's death is just one of my punishments . . . and I'm afraid, so afraid, that the way you'll look at me from now on is another."

I have no idea what he's going on about, not right away, but my incomprehension shatters him further, and he falls back to hands and knees, clawing at the ground as if hoping to dig himself a home there. Knowing only that whatever's bothering him, however foolish, is as real to him as Isaac's death, I draw closer and wrap my arms around his back, lending him the strength that is all I have to offer.

It is while I am doing this that the little creature on his back turns its little infant head to face me. Though it has made its own soul known once or twice in its many years among us, it has up until now always been the placid embodiment of innocence, the one quality we all remember from childhood that we all lose as we make the foul compromises required by life.

But now, in the instant before it opens its eyes, it occurs to me that innocence is not always a measurement of virtue. It can also be the domain of fetuses or infants, those who have not yet known life, or ever been permitted it.

The thing clinging to Job's back opens its eyes and looks at me. I see through those eyes into a soul that should not be rider, but man: a soul trapped there by another, that now wakens after a lifetime of sleep.

For the very first time, I know the true face of my eldest son . . . and understand what that makes Job.

THE SHALLOW END OF THE POOL

I don't know which one of us woke up first. I do know that when the light changed, illuminating a sky that the wire above us sectioned into little diamonds, I was curled like a wounded ball by the concrete steps, my skull pounding from the beating I'd taken, my arms numb from lack of circulation and my jaw aching like a dead thing attached to my skull with six-inch nails.

You would have expected us to have collapsed in opposite corners, in the traditional manner of the gladiators we were, but when I opened my eyes I saw that we'd slept only a few feet apart. His eyes were already open, and though it was hard to tell, he seemed to be smiling.

My Mom the Bitch lived in a desert fortress.

At least that's what my father had always told me, sometimes whispering the words, sometimes slurring them, sometimes growing so tired with the same old stories that he spoke in a monotone, making the words sound like a prayer from a faith he could no longer believe.

She'd nursed me when I was born. But things had already gotten bad between my parents by then, so bad that after less than another full year of trying they split the kids between them. She took my twin brother Ethan, and Daddy took me, raising me to remember her as the Psycho Bitch she was.

I didn't lay eyes on her again until the summer of the year I turned sixteen.

On that sweltering day in August my father and I flew to Vegas, rented a car, and drove four hours into the desert to a place where the local roads almost disappeared under the windswept sands. There we took an almost invisible turnoff, and navigated another forty minutes along an abandoned road to the skeleton of a sign that had, once upon a time, decades ago, advertised roadside cabins.

The resort had never been prosperous. It was just a place for travelers on a budget to rest their heads for the night. Now, it was a wreck, hidden behind a natural outcropping of stacked boulders that God had arranged to look like praying hands. Once, the rocks had protected the guests from road noise. These days the barrier hid the blackened skeleton of the main office, the three cabins still standing out of the original eight, a swimming pool that hadn't seen water in years, and the mobile home where the Bitch lived with Ethan. I don't know if the cabins were still officially owned by anybody, nor do I have any idea how the Bitch had ever managed to find such an isolated place to live.

We pulled up in a cloud of dust to find the Bitch on the mobile home steps, smoking a cigarette, dressed in faded jeans with torn knees, and a sleeveless white t-shirt. She'd aged since the last photograph I'd seen, which dated back to some months after my birth. She'd been young and pretty in that one. But her skin had leathered and her hair, once a shiny brown, had gone gray and stringy, with a long white lock that crossed her face in the shape of a question mark. When she grimaced at our arrival, she revealed a front tooth missing among others yellowed from tobacco and time.

Leaving the rental's A/C was a shock. The outside temperature had been edging into the high nineties in Vegas, but here it was more like a hundred, in air that seemed more dust than oxygen.

Daddy said, "Hug your mother."

I crossed the seventeen steps between myself and the stranger on the mobile home steps. She put her arms around me and called me honey, even as her fingers probed my back, testing the bunched muscles there for any signs of flab. "My God, Jen. I remember when you were just a baby."

I cut the hug short. "I'm not a baby any more, Mom."

"No. You're not." She squeezed my upper arm, testing its solidity with strength I would not have expected from her. "She's an Amazon, Joe. Better than her pictures."

And that was just hateful mockery, because I knew what an Amazon was, and what one wasn't. An Amazon is tall: I was still three inches shorter than Daddy. An Amazon hacks off her right breast: I still had both of mine, and I daily cursed the hormones that had built them into a pair of fleshy curves softer by far than my bulging arms, my corded shoulders, and my granite abs. I was strong, and I was compact, I'd used diet and exercise to reduce those unwanted tits to the smallest size the genetic roll of the dice would allow, but I was still only a girl, the Amazon status we'd strived for a goal that would forever remain beyond my reach.

Daddy must have been thinking the same thing. "Where's the boy?"

The Bitch raised the cigarette to her lips and took a drag so deep the paper sizzled. "Inside."

"Call him out."

The Bitch took another long, slow drag of her cigarette, just to demonstrate that she wouldn't be hurried by the likes of us. "Ethan! Your father's here!"

Ethan emerged from the mobile home, screen door slamming.

In all my life I'd seen less than thirty photographs of my brother. They were what Daddy gave me instead of birthday or Christmas presents. As per the agreement that had governed the relationship between parents since the day of their dissolution, the two of them provided each other with such updates twice a year, just to keep each side apprised of just how the other was developing. Our basement dojo has a wall, tracking Ethan's metamorphosis from the chubby-cheeked toddler he was when last we saw each other, to the thick-jawed, iron-necked bruiser he was now. Watching that chest fill out, those arms swell, those muscles layer upon muscles, and those eyes grow dark as coals, in what amounted to time-lapse photography of a monster sprouting from a seed, had spurred me on more than any number of Daddy's lectures or rewards or punishments. Nothing communicated the urgency of hard training more than those pictures. Nothing made my own situation look more and more hopeless, for while Ethan and I were twins, the nasty combination of gender and genetics had provided him with a body much more hospitable to muscular development than mine. His last measurements, sent with glee six months ago, had already declared him a foot taller and some fifty pounds heavier than myself, with less than one percent body fat.

He was even bigger now. The last six months had provided him with another growth spurt. He was stripped to the shorts, by design I think, his hairless pectorals gleaming with the sheen left by his latest workout. His face, tanned to near blackness by the brutal desert sun, was so dark that the unpleasant white glow of his teeth stood out like a searchlight at the bottom of a deep well. His greasy shoulder-length black hair completed any resemblance he might have had to Tarzan. Next to him, the Bitch was a wisp in danger of being blown away by the next strong wind. He dwarfed her, and dwarfed me.

If my father had raised an Amazon (a label I rejected), then the Bitch, with her exacting cruelty, had raised a Greek God.

There were flaws. The enlarged jaw and forehead testified to the hormonal imbalance inflicted by steroid abuse. I had a touch of that myself, and had endured taunts about my face in most of the schools I'd briefly attended. Like mine, his chest was lined with hairline scars from training accidents and, I think, punishments. Unlike me, he was so very muscle-bound that his flexibility had suffered. He moved with the clumsy deliberation of a stop-motion dinosaur in a fifties monster flick. I moved better than that. And, like the Bitch, he couldn't really smile, at least not at us: the closest he could manage was an uneasy grimace.

"Hello," I said.

His voice was thick, his consonants guttural. "Hello."

Once upon a time, we had drifted together in the same womb, knowing nothing of the venom being passed between those who had brought us into this life.

The Bitch said, "Hug your father."

My behemoth of a brother turned the head on his massive tree-trunk neck, and narrowed his eyes as he took in the figure of the man whose seed had provided half of him. Hatred burned in those eyes. He took two steps and enveloped Daddy in an embrace so tight that I half-expected to hear the crunch of shattering vertebrae. Unlike the Bitch, who had made a big show of hugging me back, Daddy just let his arms hang motionless at his sides. It was a brief hug. After a second or two my brother stepped back, his social obligations fulfilled.

Daddy said nothing.

The Bitch's eyes glittered. "Aren't you going to say I've done well?"

"I don't have to say it. I can see it."

"Then aren't you going to say I should be proud?"

"I wouldn't give you the satisfaction."

"Bastard." Her eyes turned to me: "I'm sure the two of you have a lot to talk about, after all these years. You can spend some time together this afternoon, if you'd like. Your father and I will need the rest of the day to finish work on the pool."

Daddy could not have been happy about this development, as

private time between my brother and me had never been part of the family agenda. But the state of war between my parents had not gotten to where it was by either showing fear in the face of a challenge. "I have no problem with that. She'll need a few minutes to get ready, but after that, they can have the rest of the day if they want."

I coughed. "No."

Her head swiveled. "What?"

"This is just stupid. What are we fucking supposed to do, become friends now? That's just psychological warfare. I want to get this bullshit over with."

Ethan's eyes glittered, but not with the anger I might have expected. "You sure? There's plenty of time for that."

Daddy said, "I suppose we could use your help setting up."

I said, "There's that, too."

My mother and father let out a shared sigh.

"I'm sorry you feel that way," said Ethan.

Damned if our parents didn't look a little regretful too.

"All right," Daddy said. "Give us about half an hour to get settled and take stock, and we'll meet on the patio."

"You can use Cabin Three," the Bitch said.

I backed away from her and Ethan, staying between them and my father until I could get behind him and concentrate on retrieving our trunk from the back seat.

Ethan and the Bitch just stayed by sat the mobile home steps, watching us.

Measuring me.

Cabin Three turned out to be surprisingly well-preserved, given that so many of the others had either burned down or collapsed. I'd expected cobwebs, scorpions, and an inch and a half of dust.

We got a freshly swept wooden floor with a pair of bare box-spring mattresses with fitted white sheets. There was no air conditioning, which meant that the temperature was stifling, but the walls seemed solid enough, and the fresh screening on all the windows promised some protection from the local flies. There was no toilet, but there was a note to the effect that Ethan had dug a fresh outhouse for us, a short walk into the desert. For a sink we had a porcelain basin and a gallon jug of warm bottled water.

Daddy and I had lived in worse during my endurance training in the Sierra Nevadas, one long summer about three years earlier. That place had been so rickety that my last task, on the last day, had been to demolish it with my bare hands. By the time I was halfway done my knuckles bled and my fingers were studded with splinters. He had called me his best girl.

Without a washroom, settling in amounted to little more than dumping the bags on the unmade beds, so I took care of that, changed into a fresh white t-shirt bearing the name of a dojo I'd attended in Seattle, and then went around back to inspect the empty swimming pool. A leftover from the roadside cabin days, it and the cracked, weed-ridden patio surrounding it were the only paved things in the Bitch's entire homestead. It was kidney-shaped, three feet deep at the kiddie steps and thirteen feet below the rusted brackets that had once anchored the diving board. The bottom was pitted and streaked with years of windswept sand; there was also the corpse of a little black bird in the deep end, buzzing with flies. The air shimmered. Without any water to cut the sunlight, the walls had nothing to do but reflect the glare at one another, turning the entire bowl into a natural reservoir for heat.

Lifeguard chairs sat on both the concave and convex sides of the pool. They looked new, or at least recently wiped clean. So did the long and narrow tarpaulin, a few yards into the desert, there to keep the sun off a cylindrical shape three feet high and thirty feet across.

I asked, "That the chain-link?"

"That's the chain-link." Daddy licked his lips as he surveyed the deep end. "Check out that grate."

I dropped to my knees, grabbed the lip of the pool and hopped in, landing on my feet. The grate Dad had seen was a rusty square a half-meter on each side, covering the ancient water filtration system. The metal was so hot from the sun that I recoiled from my first touch, but I swallowed my pain, slipped my fingers through the holes in the mesh, and pulled it loose. It weighed maybe thirty pounds. The drain beneath it narrowed and curved out of sight, marked only by more sand and the skeletal remains of a mouse.

"Nothing hidden there?" Daddy asked.

"Nothing," I said.

It had been worth checking out. There could have been anything in that little well. A knife. A gun. Even a big rock. Any number of possible hidden weapons.

"Better get up here, then."

"All right." I didn't replace the grate, but instead used it to scrape the dead bird from the bottom of the pool, and hurl it over the side and into the desert. Not that I'm all that squeamish about having dead things around, but I prefer not to smell them when I don't have to. After a moment's further thought, I tossed the grate itself onto the patio, a safe distance from my father. "It's pretty solid. It probably qualifies as a weapon."

"It shouldn't be an issue," Daddy said. "Neither one of you will have arms free."

"You know. In case."

"Not saying it's a bad idea, hon. Besides, it's done."

I grabbed the edge of the pool with my fingers and climbed

back up. The temperature was well over a hundred on the patio, but even that was a relief after the sizzling conditions in the oven down below; my t-shirt was already so saturated with sweat that the cloth had gone transparent over my breasts. I peeled the material off my belly and fanned myself with it, once or twice, just to get some cooler air in there, but it didn't help.

Daddy kneaded my shoulders. "Are you ready for this, Jen?"

"I guess I have to be."

Wrong answer. "Are you ready for this, Jen?"

"Yes. Yes, Daddy, I'm ready."

"You're not scared?"

"Maybe a little."

"Good. It helps to be scared. Fear is a survival trait. I wouldn't let this go any further if you weren't scared. But you're also ready?"

"Yes."

"Are you sure? There's no room for any doubt here."

"I'm sure. I know why this is important."

He really was proud of me. That was the main thing, which had carried us through all the years of hard work. He had invested everything he had in me, and I had invested everything in living up to what he wanted. I was still feeling a glow when his hand moved to the side of my head, and tugged at a braid. "What about this? Now or later."

"Later's fine," I said. "We can do it last thing."

"Okey-Dokey," he said.

A few minutes later Ethan and the Bitch came around, and we set to work on the arena.

The chain-link was a high-quality, thick mesh, lighter than it looked but still a bitch to work with at the quantities we needed. It took all four of us, working in grim concert, more than an hour to unroll it from its resting place over the desert sand, past a section of patio, and over the pool itself, until it covered the basin entirely. Pronouncing the effects good, Ethan then went away and came back with the aluminum braces and steel bolts necessary to secure it against the patio. By the time we were had finished lashing it down, our shared mother and father had exhausted themselves and had retreated to their opposing lifeguard stations, eyeing each other over the construction with the resigned air of nations that had always been, and would always be, at war.

By then, of course, I knew that turning down the day of truce had been a good idea, not only because our parents wouldn't have ever gotten this job finished, but because all this time working with Ethan had provided me an excellent opportunity to gauge his strength, his speed, his endurance, his dexterity, and most of all, his eagerness to begin.

Like me, he was hungry for this.

He might have dreaded it once, but his years of training had like my own worn away any of his own dreams and ambitions, and left him eager for nothing but the moment that we'd enter the pool together.

At about four o'clock, the sweat pouring down our bodies in waves, my brother and I used a pair of wire cutters to peel a three-sided flap away from a section over the steps leading to the shallow end. Descending, we explored the territory in the wader's area on hands and knees, testing the feel of the concrete against our bare skin, determining just how close we could come to standing before chain-link scraped against our backs or the tops of our heads. My smaller size and greater flexibility gave me an advantage here. I could run about in a doubled-over crouch that still gave me several inches of clearance, in places where Ethan could only struggle along in a hunchbacked, half-crippled lurch confined by the low ceiling. That advantage vanished as we both moved on to the Deep End. In the Deep End, where we could both stand fully upright, unimpeded by any low ceiling, the advantage of weight and strength was entirely his own. The gaping hole left by the removal of the grating presented the only equalizer. Either one of us could stumble into that one without warning, if not breaking bones, then at least crippling us long enough to cede advantage to the other.

We circled that hole together, thinking the same thoughts, then parted.

After several minutes of contemplative silence, we addressed each other with our backs against opposite walls.

Ethan ran a hand through his hair. "You do good work."

"Thanks. You too."

"I'm sorry you didn't want to come with me today. There's some great rock formations about twenty miles from here. I figured we could do some climbing and have ourselves a little picnic on the summit."

"That might have been fun," I allowed.

"Yeah." He kicked at the dust with the toe of one boot. "Would have been nice to have some fun. I don't even remember what it's like anymore."

"Boo fucking hoo."

"Yeah. I guess you know what it's like."

"And then some."

He seemed to hoard his next question before letting it go, all in a rush. "I'm sorry, but I have to ask this. Did he ever fuck you?"

"Who?"

"The Bastard."

Even then, it took me a second to figure out who he meant. "You mean, *Daddy*? Christ, no!"

"Did he ever make you blow him?"

If he didn't stop this, I was going to break his neck right here and now. "Is that what she told you?"

He relaxed. "Don't take it the wrong way or anything. I'm just saying, you never know. Not considering the kind of shit he used to do to her."

"He never did anything to her but take what she dished out."

"According to him."

If he was trying to anger me, he was doing an awfully good job. "I don't know what fucked-up stories she told you, but she's lying. She was the bad one."

"How do you know?" he countered. "Were you there?"

I thought of all the things Daddy had told me about her, from all the dreams she'd denied him, and all the petty betrayals she'd used to wound him, to all the words she'd used to castrate him. "What about you? Did you ever fuck the Bitch?"

He didn't object to me calling her that. "She offered once. About four years ago. I was thirteen, and half out of my head from jerking off fourteen times a day. She was already working five nights a week at the Horny Jackal, putting away enough cash for my training, so helping me out too wouldn't have meant all that much more. When I said I'd rather not, she didn't push it. Instead she got one of her co-workers to pay me a visit every couple of weeks."

"Ewww," I said.

"It wasn't too bad. But then she finally saved enough money to support us out here, and all that stopped."

"What do you do now?"

"Nothing, I think those shots have done something to my balls. I don't even think about it anymore." He drew another line in the dirt. "You could just give up, you know. That's what the rules say. Say you can't beat me and we won't have to do this. We can just go rock-climbing tomorrow instead of today."

I shook my head. "I can't do that to Daddy. Unless you want to give up instead?"

"Can't do that," he said. "Not all by myself. Not and miss the whole point of being born in the first place."

"Yeah, well." I shook my head, pushed myself away from the wall, and met him at the pool's deepest point.

We clasped hands.

He said, "Nice meeting you, Jen."

I said, "I'm gonna kill you, Ethan."

Would you believe he looked hurt?

Why did he have to go ahead and make me feel shitty like that?

Daddy and I went back to the cabin so he could shave my head.

I can't say I wasn't bothered. I owed my hair a lot. For all too long, sitting in school among soft boys with flabby necks and skinny girls with toothpick wrists, all of whom indulged their pretend adolescent cruelties without assets enabling them to last thirty seconds against a genuine real-world enemy, I'd had to pretend that I didn't hear the whispers. I heard them pointing out the crewcut and the enlarged jaw and my tree-trunk biceps and the nose flattened by a punch in the years before I'd learned to see an attack coming. Before Daddy relented and let me grow my hair long—always with the understanding that I'd have to cut it again for my match with Ethan—I'd heard them wonder just what the hell was I was supposed to be anyway. The long blonde hair helped, as if I wore it right it placed me within shouting distance of pretty. There'd even been a boy once, and sweaty gropings on the couch in his parent's basement. It had been fun enough, though that had ended, painfully, the one time he put a hand on me without warning. Unfortunately, that incident happened on school property. Daddy had apologized and paid for the Emergency Room visit. I took the one-week suspension knowing that the lesson would not need to be taught again.

The hair was a loss. But I had always known I wouldn't be wearing it long, around my brother. Long hair was dangerous. It could get in my eyes and blind me at a crucial moment. Maybe I'd have a chance to grow it back and maybe not.

Daddy sat me down on the bed, used a pair of scissors to cut my hair short, the electric shears to reduce what was left to stubble, and a straight razor with medicated shaving cream to make my scalp baby-smooth. By the time he was done the mattress was itchy from liberated blonde. Then, surprising me, he opened up the suitcase and showed me a big floppy white hat.

"For afterward," he explained. "I think you'll look pretty in it."

My eyes welled. I hid it well, batting my eyes at him, in the manner of any southern belle.

By six we were still so far from sunset that the sky hadn't even faded to a darker shade of blue. But more than half of the pool bottom was already in long shadow, the other half a surreal fresco of diamond-shapes cast by the fencing. Ethan and I had both consumed our last food and water and both taken our final opportunities for a civilized bathroom break. Daddy had given me my final instructions, which mostly consisted of strategies I already knew: to exhaust Ethan's wind by keeping him on the move, to retreat to the shallow end whenever I needed a breather myself, to be careful around that gaping hole in the deep end and to lure him into it, if I could. I was kind enough to react to all of these suggestions as if they were new and exciting ideas.

When he was done he gave me yet another hug, told me that I was his special girl, and promised me that things would be different once this was over. He said I could have anything I wanted. He made the mistake of asking me to name the first thing I'd want for myself when we were done, and for the life of me I couldn't think of anything. My life had never been about anything other than today and the idea of wanting something afterward was so ridiculous that it might have been spoken in another language entirely. When he pressed the point I couldn't speak the first answer that came to mind, which was that chance to go rock-climbing with Ethan. That was just stupid. By definition, there'd be no Ethan. So I just said, "Maybe we'll go shopping."

He kissed me on the forehead and said, "Sure."

By half past six, Ethan and I were stripped, greased, and in the process of being fitted with our respective hobbles.

Our parents had recognized, while Ethan and I were both still toddlers, that even with equal training he would probably still emerge with a substantial edge in brute strength. That appraisal had turned out to be an accurate one, but Daddy had pointed out that even Ethan wouldn't be able to end the fight with a single punch, or crushing bear hug, if unable to use his arms. Mom had agreed to taking corrective measures on the single condition that I was prevented from fighting dirty, by which she meant the use of teeth or nails.

Our gags, which buckled tightly around the backs of our shaved heads, were steel bits sheathed in a layer of rubber thick enough for us to sink our teeth into. Our arms were cuffed behind our backs and held in place with canvas sheaths laced to the shoulders and fastened around our necks to prevent either one of us from curling into a ball to pass the cuffs under bent legs. The getup was confining, but I'd practiced in it for hours and could still high-kick without losing balance or strangling myself. Nor would it affect my stamina. Just six months ago I'd run the equivalent of a marathon with both arms tightly strapped behind my back.

I hadn't ever worn the getup against a similarly-hobbled opponent tasked to kill me, but that was all right. By now, this felt far more natural to me than that sun bonnet. Ethan, standing at attention while the Bitch tugged at the laces binding the sheath to his arms, looked like he felt the same way. He even managed to wink at me, though I don't know just what the hell he thought he was communicating.

Daddy announced that it was a quarter to seven. The sky was definitely a darker shade of blue now. The sunlight was just a thin slice of brighter concrete, beveled with distorted diamond-shapes, on the eastern edge of the pool. The Bitch led Ethan in through the cutaway flap above the Shallow End steps, escorted him all the way to the pool's deepest point, kissed him on the top of the head, then withdrew. Daddy helped me down the same steps, sat me down in the Shallow End, told me that whatever happened I would always be his daughter and that he would always believe in me no matter what, then abandoned me as Ethan had been abandoned.

Neither one of us could see the other. It was, after all, a kidney-shaped pool, which meant that as long as we stayed at opposite ends we were hidden from one another by the curvature of the walls. Apart, neither one of us would be able to tell how the other was doing. The only way to tell was to risk meeting in the middle.

Above us, Daddy and the Bitch got to work repairing the flap so that neither of us would be able to use it to escape. It wasn't a fancy patch. They just looped wire through the links, sewing the loose edges together. The two of them worked side by side, not speaking, not deigning to look at each other, but working as a unit just the same. Both their faces seemed shadowed, given the fading brightness of the sky. I wished I could see if Daddy was looking at me, but I couldn't tell for sure. I didn't think he was. Sweat stung my eyes and I had to look away.

Not long after that, our parents stood together and tugged at the flap. The fresh seal held. They turned their backs on each other and disappeared from my sky. A few seconds later, Daddy appeared again, this time sitting high on the lifeguard chair on the convex side of the pool. The Bitch took her own position on the lifeguard chair opposite him. I shifted position, got my feet under me, rose to a half-crouch, and waited.

Daddy said, "All right, kids. Make us proud."

Ethan did not disappoint me.

He was too smart to come at a run. He came around the bend at a fast walk, his eyes dark as he searched for me, half-hoping I'd meet him halfway.

I remained where Daddy had left me, waiting.

Ethan was neither disappointed at my lack or initiative nor contemptuous of my cautious start. He slowed and stopped at the midway point separating the Shallow and Deep ends of the pool. He paced that invisible line between us, his muscles tensing, his shoulders cording from what must have been a hideous effort to wrest himself free of the sheath binding his arms. The sheath held, as he'd probably known that it would. He grimaced through his gag, mumbled a word his mouth was not able to properly form, then advanced another step uphill. Another two. His eyes rolled toward the sky, as he felt the space between the top of his head and the wire link narrow to inches. He bent his knees and advanced still further, still testing our battlefield, painfully aware that I would not just allow him to march up and put me out of my misery.

I still didn't move.

Ethan advanced further. Now he had to crouch—not all the way, not so much he couldn't keep both eyes firmly focused on me, but enough to unbalance him, enough that he could feel his advantage of height and weight diminishing with every step he took. I could see sweat cutting through the sheen at what would have been his hairline. He paused again, braced himself for the inevitable moment when I charged, and tried to persuade me with a look that hanging back was no good, because he was ready for any attack I could muster.

I didn't move.

He advanced some more.

I saw his balls. I knew what balls looked like; I'd seen them close up, on that boy whose name I couldn't even remember. These looked tiny and purple. The steroids had shrunken them to a fraction of their natural size.

Had I been able to talk, I would have mocked him for being a dickless wonder. It might have upset him, made him sloppy.

He took another step, reminding me that it was a waste of time to contemplate strategies I couldn't use.

Another step.

I faked to the right.

He recognized my move as a feint, and anticipated a move in the other direction.

Another fake and I actually went right. A heartbeat before we collided I saw him brace for impact, but he expected me to hit him mid-body, at his center of gravity, where his superior weight allowed him to compensate. So instead I hurled myself at the ground and swept his legs with my own.

He went down.

Everybody's fallen down. But few people appreciate just how much we rely on our arms to protect our heads from damage during a fall. Falling forward, we throw out our hands and take the damage there, turning a potential cracked skull into a mere pair of sprained wrists. Neither one of us had the option now. Ethan managed to compensate enough to take the bulk of the impact on his knees, but even that did not stop his fall, and when he landed flat on his chest, his head whipped forward, smashing nose and forehead against the hard concrete ground.

Without the knees, that fall might have been enough to finish him all by itself.

Daddy cried, "Good one, Jen!"

I managed a weak kick to Ethan's calf as he rolled away, but didn't waste time waiting to see where he went after that, not with life or death riding on who rose first. It was early, still. I got my feet under me and backed off, giving Ethan the space he needed to back against the wall and take stock of himself. His nose was broken and bubbling blood from both nostrils: good news, as that would obstruct breathing. There was more blood in the seams between the teeth clamped against his bit-gag. He couldn't have bitten his tongue or cheeks, but maybe I'd loosened an incisor or two. Another advantage, in that he'd have that sickening taste to deal with.

But his eyes were still smiling.

Daddy yelled, "Don't overestimate him, baby!"

Ethan came for me again.

I faked another dodge to the right, but he changed course without even trying hard, and I tried to duck and roll, but that was going for the same trick twice in a row, and he was ready for that, lowering his head and reaching me before I could move away.

He drove his head into the softer flesh below my ribs and drove me off my feet, the force of his charge carrying me all the way to the concrete wall of the pool. The impact drove the air from my lungs. I gasped as my head whipped back against the wall with a force that I experienced as a burst of blinding white light. Before I could recover he smashed the top of his head against my jaw, driving my skull against the concrete a second time. And then a third.

"Finish her!" yelled the Bitch.

He might have.

I only stayed up because Ethan's body kept me from falling.

He rammed me again. My legs thrashed and my feet left the floor.

He was bearing all my weight now, driving me into the concrete so hard that I didn't have time to fall.

"Put him down, honey!" yelled Daddy.

If I'd had the use of my hands I could have taken out Ethan's eyes. If I'd had the use of my teeth I could have ripped out his throat. I only had my legs, which didn't have the proper angle for a worthwhile kick.

But I didn't need to kick him to put him down, not when the wall was right behind me.

Not when he was keeping me from falling.

I braced the bare soles of my feet against the concrete, took another skull-rattling impact with the wall just to gather my fading strength, and at the moment when he pulled back for another power-driving charge pushed off with everything I had.

It wasn't enough to send him flying backward, as I'd hoped. But it did throw him off balance. His greased skin lost traction against mine. He tried to shift, but then he fell left and I fell right and we both hit the bottom of the pool in a tangle.

I landed on top, driving my knee into his shriveled balls with a force that made him double in two.

"That's a girl!" Daddy yelled. "Now finish him!"

But I was in no shape to risk more close contact, not with my vision going gray from the beating I'd taken. I rolled away, got my feet under me again, and managed to get to the opposite wall just as Ethan was also getting back to his feet.

He looked like hell, sweaty, out of breath and the entire lower half of his face gleaming with blood. I don't know what I looked like, but as he went in and out of focus I knew that I had to look worse.

He shouted something through his gag, something that emerged as a series of bubbly roars. He could have been telling me to fuck myself. Or he could have been saying that I was his sister and he was sorry he couldn't love me. Or he could have been describing all the ways he wanted to make me suffer before I died.

It didn't matter what he wanted to say. Or what I wanted to say. Our vocabulary was limited. This fight was the only conversation we had left.

Fortunately, he'd had enough for now.

He looked away and staggered toward the Deep End.

I went for the Shallow.

Dad shouted encouragement from above. "That's good, honey! Pick your opportunities! Don't waste yourself going after him until you're ready!"

The Bitch cried, "I love you, honey!"

And so came the night.

The stars surprised me.

It wasn't the first time I'd spent the night outdoors. I'd had that summer in the Sierra Nevadas, and the endurance treks in the Mojave, and long nights shivering in tents on Alaskan glaciers. I'd been so far from cities that if anything had happened to me it would have taken days or weeks to make my way to the first emergency room capable of giving me so much as a single stitch. I'd learned just what the sky could look like in the rarefied places untouched by smog or the glare of neon lights. I'd seen those distant suns glowing by the thousands, each so bright that they might have been tiny campfires just beyond my reach. I had grown bored by them.

I had never seen stars as bright as the stars looked tonight. They were so brilliant that the sharpest stung my eyes and made my vision blur. Whenever I moved, some twinkled out of sight, eclipsed by chain-link. I had never seen them so close, so mysterious. I had never seen other eyes looking down, from those distant places, wondering about us the way I wondered about them. I had never known that some of them had to be fighting for their lives, to settle conflicts begun long before they were even born.

There was no moon. Daddy and the Bitch had decided that we shouldn't schedule this for a night with a moon. But the stars still provided enough glow to reveal the shape of the cracked white concrete walls. I could see the way the concave side curved off into the distance. The shadows were deep enough and large enough to provide any number of possible hiding places for my brother, but I could hear his bubbling snorks—representing a constant effort to keep his nostrils clear—and as far as I could tell it came from all the way around the bend. We were still at opposite corners.

I was thirsty. When I leaned the back of my head against the wall, my skin stuck, revealing a dried clotted mass back there. My teeth ached from biting into rubber for so long. My arms were in agony. I was nauseated, but didn't dare throw up, not when the gag would have forced me to swallow it or choke. I hadn't heard Daddy or the Bitch shout their little encouragements for quite a while, and couldn't tell from the shapes of lifeguard chairs silhouetted against the night sky if they were still up there watching.

It must have been about midnight that I squirmed away from the steps, which had been the closest thing I had to a refuge, got my feet underneath me, and padded over to the gentle curve to my immediate right. I crouched there, hesitated to make sure I was alone, and peed. Drizzle ricocheting off the puddle peppered my right ankle. A rivulet flowing downstream puddled against my heel. I wondered not for the first time how female dogs managed to keep their paws dry. After a few seconds, feeling better, I straightened out and put some distance between myself and the only toilet I'd have for as long as this battle lasted.

A million miles away, Ethan snorked again.

With his nose obstructed by the break, just breathing had to be exhausting him. It would deny him sleep, deny him rest, deny him even enough air to stay strong. He could get some around the gag, but it wouldn't be enough to keep him going forever. Even if I did nothing at all, and stayed out of his way, his probable life expectancy in the pool must have already been cut in half. I only wished I could be sure that what was left was still shorter than mine. After all, I'd suffered a head injury. The nausea and dizziness was a sure symptom of a concussion capable of deepening into coma as soon as I drifted off.

I had to make another go for him.

Padding along the warm concrete floor of the pool, which had not yet given up all the heat of the day, I made my way toward him, stopping every step or so to keep him from triangulating my position from the sound of my breath. Not that stealth mattered all that much. The thin layer of grit at the bottom of the pool made every step crunch like an old-fashioned soft-shoe.

I tried not to think about how big he was and how badly he'd hurt me the last time we'd faced each other.

In my head, he'd grown to twice his actual size.

In my head, he was an ogre, towering over me like any other creature of old fantasies, with arms the size of tree trunks and a head that blotted out the sky. In my head, I only came up to his waist.

An image from an old stop-motion movie intruded, painting Ethan as a roaring Cyclops, scooping up badly-imposed sailors to bite in half with one chomp of his oversized jaws.

I cursed my imagination. This was stupid. He was nothing but a big, stupid, overdeveloped boy too clumsy for his own good.

He was just my brother.

Daddy had said, "You're better than him, honey."

He had said, "You'll win as long as you have heart."

He had said, "I have faith in you, Jen."

The Bitch might have said any number of things like that to Ethan, but then, she was the Bitch, and she was used to lies and deceit. Just look at all the things she had done to Daddy.

When Daddy said things like that, he told the truth.

I made it to the line that separated the Deep and Shallow ends. The bowl ahead of me was inkier and, it seemed, deeper than it had any right to be. I couldn't see the far wall. There was too much shadow there even to admit the distant light of the stars. It was too black to see Ethan, but I could still hear his breathing, somewhere ahead of me. It was ragged, wet, and labored. It didn't sound like he was lying down. I got the clear impression that he was standing against the far wall, beneath what would have been the diving board, confident in his own ability to meet my advance with a strength that trumped my own.

He was accurate enough there. If he was waiting for me, I should turn back.

I took another step to be sure.

Something nearby smelled like a sewer.

I still couldn't see him. I listened for him and all of a sudden couldn't hear him either.

I couldn't bring myself to hope that he'd died in the last few seconds. More likely, he'd realized I was close and was holding his breath and long as he was able, to keep me from being able to track him.

That trick worked for two as well as one. I couldn't close my mouth or pinch my nostrils shut, but I held my diaphragm tight and held my next breath as long as I could, counting off the seconds.

Ten. Thirty.

One minute.

I could hold my breath for two.

More, since my life depended on it.

Ninety Seconds. Still no sound from him.

He couldn't be dead. I could feel him.

Was he moving toward me?

Coming up on two minutes. My heart was pounding.

Two minutes. Still silence.

Would I even be able to hear him over the roar of the blood in my ears?

Two minutes ten.

It was not breath that alerted me. It may have been a soft, padding thump or a rush of air or the instinctive connection between siblings, but I knew I was being charged.

I spun, not knowing which way to dodge. Something massive struck a glancing blow against my right side, and kept going, the impact enough to make me lurch to the left in a clumsy dance that barely kept me on my feet.

I heard a metallic clang.

Rushing past me, he'd scraped the top of his head against chain link.

That had to hurt.

It didn't knock him down, but it did make him grunt.

I gasped as best I could, and whirled to face him in case he made another charge. I saw a gleaming wetness at just about eye-level and identified it as his gag, slick from hours of blood and drool. I had just enough time to register him racing toward me at terminal velocity. I went to my knees, looked up, caught another glimpse of an Ethan-shape occluding the sectioned starscape, and for just a heartbeat knew what it must have been like, in Jurassic times, to be a tiny animal cowering at the tyrannosaur shadow standing between me and the primordial sky.

He went over me hard.

I heard a thud, a crack, and a subsequent moan.

That had to have killed him. He had rushed me too hard and gone over me in what felt like a somersault. He would have had to smash his head again, maybe broken his neck, at the very least dislocated his shoulders or fractured a leg. He must have sustained some kind of injury, maybe even something internal that would seep his life away.

I peered into the shadows and saw a huge form, glistening from wounds and other liquids, dragging itself toward the farthest wall. The snorking breath started again. He wasn't dead, then, only hurt. And there was no way of telling how hurt. It would be just like him to fake something worse if that meant drawing me close.

I thought of how large he'd seemed in the darkness, and more than just gathering thirst filled my throat with sand.

I'd peed all I had just a few minutes ago, but I lost another couple of drops now.

I couldn't go after him again. Not while it was still dark. There'd be more light in the morning.

I retreated, refusing to turn my back on the giant in the darkness, not feeling safe again until I was on my knees again, curling up beside the steps that represented my only refuge. The stars above still twinkled in and out of existence when eclipsed by the overhead wire.

All at once, they blurred.

I didn't want to kill him anymore.

I wanted to kill the Bitch. I wanted to grab her by her stupid witchy hair and smash her face into the concrete again and again until her head staved in and the pavement turned red from blood and brains. I wanted to scream at her, call her names worse than the obvious cunt and whore and demand to know where the fuck she got off doing this to her son and her daughter when we'd both be so much better off if she'd just close her withered lips around a double-gauge.

I wanted Daddy. He had done the same thing. But he was Daddy.

"You can't cry," he'd told me. I'd been flat on my back pressing weights and he'd been spotting me. "You're strong and you're brave and you have more heart than anybody I've ever known, but if you don't get him right away and it goes into hours or days, then at some point it'll all be too much for you and you're going to want to cry. You'll know what it means because it'll be the first sign that you're losing heart. You can't let it happen. You'll have to shut it down, wall it off, put it away before it takes over and it's all you have left. You have to make yourself too hard to break." I'd told him I would and he'd said, "That's a good girl."

When he called me a good girl, I felt capable of anything.

But I hadn't heard his voice in hours.

Had the Bitch done something to him?

Or were things even worse than that?

Was all this just a joke to them? Or, worse, foreplay? Were they together in that shithole of a mobile home sharing six-packs and nuzzling each other's necks while they laughed over the big hilarious joke they'd played on the kids?

Were they in the car together, lighting out for parts unknown while wondering which of their two science experiments fell first?

"You'll even lose faith in me," he'd said. "But you'll know I love you, honey."

Unless that was just another part of the trick.

I couldn't cry. But there were too many hours between now and morning, and my eyes were burning.

I don't think I fell asleep. I think I passed out.

I saw myself running, the summer Daddy and I spent in the

Cascades. I rose before dawn, performed three hundred pushups, then donned my wrist and ankle weights and hit the woods for a twenty mile run. It was the time of day when the chill left over from the night before turned the dew into frost, and the grass into stiff needles. The air ripped at my lungs like fire and my breath trailed behind me in a necklace of little clouds. Daddy had pointed out one ravine that could be leaped as long as I used a fallen tree propped up against a living one as an acceleration ramp. It was a tricky stunt even in perfect light and an almost suicidal one in woods still marked by the failing shadows of the previous night, but I'd mastered it, always landing in a duck-and-roll that plastered dirt and leaves to my back in a mortar of warm sweat. Even a perfect landing was hard enough to knock the breath out of me, but I always got up and kept going, As a younger girl, running other courses in other environments, I'd cracked ribs and once or twice broken fingers, once even run headlong into a low-hanging branch that ripped a gash in my forehead and freed hot burning blood to seep down into my eyes. It hadn't slowed me down. I'd been blinded but I'd returned home without slowing down. I couldn't depend on vision when so many possible attacks depended on targeting the eyes.

When I woke the sun had arrived, illuminating a sky that the wire above us sectioned into little diamonds. I was curled by the concrete steps, my skull pounding, my throat burning, my arms numb from lack of circulation and my jaw aching like a dead thing attached to my skull with six-inch nails. I would have expected Ethan and I to collapse in opposite corners, but instead we'd fallen only a few feet apart, in a togetherness unexpected for two people who wanted each other dead. His eyes were already open, and though it was hard to tell through all the gear on his face, he seemed to be smiling.

His nostrils weren't bubbling. I wondered if he was dead.

I shifted position and prodded him with a toe.

He blinked. The gagged smile broadened. He murmured a series of vowels that should have been indistinguishable as words, but which his sunny tone communicated perfectly.

"*Unnnh Aww Innh.*"

And *good morning* to you, too.

I couldn't make myself believe that he'd been too injured to chance attacking me as I slept. Or that he'd been too afraid. More likely he'd experienced a spell as lost and as despairing as mine, and had wanted nothing more than to spend the remaining hours of darkness close to another living being. Even if that person happened to be me. Maybe especially if that person happened to be me.

I wasn't ready, either physically or emotionally, to take advantage just yet. I just nodded hello, squirmed and crawled my way to a safe distance, and then got to my feet. Dizziness, thirst, and whatever damage the concussion had inflicted made me wobble, but I managed to stay upright.

I took a deep breath and almost gagged on it. Even with half the pool still in shadow the air was still so warm it felt more like soup.

We could stay in the narrowing shadows on the eastern side of the pool for most of the morning, moving west when they were replaced by the lengthening shadows of the late afternoon. It wouldn't protect us from the heat, but it might save us from being burned to a crisp by the sun.

That was funny. Us. Like we were a team or something.

And either way, there'd be no shadows at noon.

We were going to cook.

The two lifeguard chairs were still unoccupied.

They'd left. Daddy and the Bitch had patched together their differences and were now sipping champagne in their jacuzzi in some swank resort in Reno. Daddy must be saying, *too bad about the kids. Yes, what a shame. They were both so respectful. Do you know,*

May, I once asked her to go fifteen days without food, as a survival exercise, and she just did it, without even arguing? That's right. She sat in her room, growing paler and paler, her cheeks growing gaunt and her skin going pale, and in all that time, May, all that time, she never one said, Daddy, I can't do this anymore, I need something, just a little soup, just a little bread, just something to stop my stomach from cramping? It was enough to make me wonder, May, just what the hell else I could ask her to do. Would she have put out her eyes? Cut off her own hand? Press the right side of her face against a hot frying pan and not move even as she felt her skin scar and sizzle from the heat? We should be proud of ourselves, May. The way we raised them, and all.

Daddy wouldn't talk that way. The Bitch would, but Daddy wouldn't.

Daddy was better than that.

Daddy loved me.

The world grayed. I shook the spots away and stumbled forward, walking the perimeter. I noted the drying blood stains on the floor and on the walls, I found a crack emitting a battalion of ants and, at the moment I entered the Deep End, a dead rattlesnake, its head and midsection crushed almost flat. It puzzled me for a while until I figured out the story. The concrete of the patio above, with its talent for sucking up heat during the day and radiating it slowly at night, rendered it a natural beacon for snakes. They must have loved the place, and with the empty pool considerably warmer, it must have been just as natural for them to crawl in, from time to time, their idiot reptilian brains too shortsighted to realize that once they made the drop they would not be up to the task of finding a way out. Ethan and the Bitch must have had their hands full, clearing the place of pissed-off rattlers without getting bitten themselves. And of course, they hadn't bothered to warn us of the danger: not when a fortuitously-stranded snake could spell defeat for a girl who hadn't been told.

This one must have taken Ethan by surprise.

Had it bitten him?

I couldn't be that lucky.

I looked over my shoulder and confirmed that he was still curled by the Shallow End steps. The sweat and the grease had plastered the sand to his body, giving him a white, powdery appearance. But he didn't seem sick. He'd rolled over and was watching me with a calm, unbothered curiosity.

My eyes burned.

I went deeper, not knowing what I was looking for. The deep end was just a filthy oval, covered with dust and bird shit and brilliant in the morning glare. When I reached its lowest point I caught a whiff of something foul, and followed the odor to the drain hole, where I found pretty much what I should have expected to find. Removing the grate had been doing Ethan a favor. It had given him a place to do his daily business without having to worry about stepping in it. Looking closer, wrinkling my nose as I was hit by the awful rising stink, I further noted that he'd suffered diarrhea. This was disgusting, but good news for me, as the single greatest factor in living through this was probably surviving dehydration, and he'd have no chance to replenish what he'd lost.

As if on cue, my own stomach gurgled.

Christ.

The heat and the conditions were doing the same thing to me that they were doing to him.

I considered making use of the drain, decided not, and went back to the Shallow End.

The sun was higher in the sky now. The shadows cast by the pool's eastern curve now covered less than a third of the pool bottom. I made the mistake of glancing at the sun and recoiled, my vision a purple blob. That sun wasn't golden. It was white. It was pure, malevolent heat, pounding down on us like a thousand hammers. How high was the temperature going to rise today, before the shadows came back? A hundred ten? More?

Ethan had settled in under the shadows, his bound arms against the convex wall, his knees curled up against his chest. He looked at me, then at the empty space beside him, and then at me again. He repeated himself, and when I failed to get it, repeated himself a third time.

I got it.

It was stupid to fight now. Not with shelter a more immediate need.

Might as well wait out the day, survive if we could, and make another go at each other tonight. We'd both be weaker then, but that only meant that we'd both be that much closer to finishing this.

If there was a finish. If Daddy and the Bitch came back.

I selected a spot two body-lengths from Ethan, put my back to the wall, and lowered myself into a bent-kneed squat. It was as relaxed a position as I was willing to attempt, around him, one that would allow me to jump away in a heartbeat if he went for me.

I didn't think he would.

If we couldn't outlive the day, what was the point?

The hours crawled. The sun rose in the cloudless sky. The air grew hot, then sweltering, then brutal, then hellish. Our refuge of shadow narrowed, the razor-thin line between mere unbearable heat and deadly sunlight drawing closer to our curled legs. The sweat pouring down my face collected against my lips, investing the rubber bit with a foul, salty taste. My tongue swelled. I tried not to look at the opposite wall, already so bright from reflected glare that my eyes compensated by conjuring gray spots at the edges.

The shadow wasn't protecting us enough.

Sunburns don't only happen to those who expose themselves to direct sunlight. Sometimes it's possible to hide in the shade, all day long, and still suffer painful burns. It all depends on the reflectivity of the surrounding surfaces.

Ethan and I were in a big white bowl, facing one of its big white walls. Spared the worst of the sunlight, we were still absorbing enough reflected radiation to cook us more slowly. Ethan, who was darker than me and had the base tan one would expect from a boy who had spent years training under this sun, would tolerate it better than I would, with my much fairer skin. But we were both burning. By the time the zone of shadow came within a finger's-length of his knees, his face had turned lobster-red, and sprouted the first of what would soon be many sun-blisters on his forehead.

He didn't move, though. He didn't shift position, to protect the parts already burned with the parts that had spent these hours protected by canvas and shadow. He didn't even lower his head. He just faced forward, his eyes closed, his expression serene and confident even as his lips cracked and the sweat pooled in the furrows between his muscles began to shine like tiny sun lamps. Not once did he let me see that it was bothering him.

By then I already knew that I was losing.

My skin was on fire. My tongue was a dry, swollen worm scraping the roof of my mouth like sandpaper. Something had gripped my bowels and twisted, turning everything inside me to acid. I'd fouled myself and not even realized it. When I moved, I could feel the stored heat rising from me in waves.

I felt snakes crawling over me. They were burning snakes, with razors instead of scales, and when they slithered over my breasts they left gaping wounds behind. They went away and were replaced by flies, each as hot as embers snatched from a fire, each with little buzzsaw wings that, twitching, shredded whatever remained. Then came the worms and the maggots. I threw up, choked on it, managed to get it down again, decided that the long day had to be over after all these hours of hell and looked down to see that the cutting edge of that line of direct sunlight hadn't moved any closer to me in the year or so I'd been hallucinating.

I cried. I don't know how many tears came out, but I cried. I didn't care if Ethan heard me. He knew how much this was hurting.

I couldn't fool him about that.

Even if I'd lied to him about Daddy.

"You have to be a rock," Daddy said. He had come to me early in the morning of my twelfth birthday, his eyes dark and his thing dangling from his thatch like a blind, rooted worm. "You have to take whatever happens to you. A broken nose is nothing. A broken leg is nothing. A broken rib is nothing. A lost eye is nothing. Days without sleep or rest, more pain than you can imagine, it's all nothing. He will hurt you any way he can, everywhere that you're soft enough to be hurt. He can even try to rape you, if he wants—after all, he's a boy, and that's always been one of the best ways for boys to hurt girls. It'll be even worse for you if it happens, because you'll know all along that it's your own brother doing it. Of course, if you're strong enough, he won't be able to. You can make it more work than it's worth. You might even make it the last dirty thing he ever tries. But even if he does manage to pin you down, and hurt you in that special way, you'll have a chance as long as you know that you can get past it. And the only way to know that is to know that you've been past it before."

He'd only done it that one time.

And I knew almost immediately that it hurt him as much as much as it hurt me, because when I tiptoed to his room the next morning, clutching the carving knife I'd plucked from its rack in our kitchen, thinking only of not letting him do that to me again, planning to separate him from the thing he'd jammed up inside me, I'd found him sitting on the edge of his bed, his head in his hands, his shoulders wracked by convulsive sobs. He hadn't seen me as I'd padded up behind him, not so fired by certainty now, my right arm trembling as the knife grip grew heavier and heavier and the sobs coming from the broken figure before me resolved into self-recriminations about what kind of monster he was. And I'd thought about burying that knife between his shoulder blades and watching his life blood seep into the sheets as he fell over dying but not dying so fast that he couldn't turn his head and gaze at me and see that I was the one who had done this to him, his stunned expression betraying a hurt a thousand times worse than the pain of the wound or the violation I'd suffered for a few short minutes in the middle of the night. He really did love me. He was my Daddy. And so I dropped the knife and threw my arms around his shoulders and wept, "I'm sorry, Daddy, I'm sorry, I didn't know," and he grabbed me back and buried his head in my shoulders and cried, "I'm sorry, I'm sorry, I had to, I didn't want to but I had to, you had to experience it once," and I said, "I know, I know, I know," and then it was all about him feeling bad and me trying to make him feel better, because I loved him, as he loved me, which meant that I would have to let him do it to me again if he thought it would help. He just wanted to make me strong, that's all.

I was a rock. Nothing could hurt me.

I looked down through the haze and thought I saw little plumes of steam rising from skin that now seemed scarlet enough to have been dipped in blood. I recoiled, gasped as the burns I already had chafed against the concrete and the sodden canvas of my arm restraints, and shifted position to pull my knees a few inches further away. It wasn't much of a reprieve, I knew. It would give me, at most, a few extra minutes of relative protection.

The line advanced, and touched skin again.

I hadn't seen Ethan move, but he was lying down now, pressed against the curve of the wall with the paler skin of his back, partially obscured by the canvas restraints binding his arms, presented to the sun that would soon be attacking both of us with all its considerable force. The skin on the top of his head was also fire-engine red, and popping with blisters. He was so still that he could have been dead. But I could tell from the corded tension in his shoulders that he was still alert, still strong, still aware of the toll this was taking on me. I should have been mad at him for not grunting or something, just to make sure I followed his example, but I couldn't blame him. He was my brother.

I lay down and rolled against the wall, pressing my face against the gentle curve that marked the junction between pool wall and pool floor. The seam, seen up close, turned out to be littered with the curled, blackened forms of ants, similar to the living ones I'd seen before, these baked to a crisp by previous mornings or afternoons. Their thoraxes pressed against their abdomens in pretend fetus positions, their little legs outhrust as if in protest. If they all came from the same colony, which was likely, then they all had the same mother, and they'd all died here, as we were dying here, as the siblings they were.

Ethan and I had more in common with them than with anybody else on the planet.

My throat thickened.

When the line of fire touched my skin again, there was no longer any safe place to retreat.

I don't know how long I was unconscious, but as I came to there was a dead weight, several times my size, pressing down on me.

I didn't care. If I was buried alive at least I'd soon be dead. If I was being attacked at least I'd soon be dead. If I was being raped at least I'd soon be dead. I was beyond feeling or wanting anything at all.

After a long time I registered the slippery feel of bare flesh, slick with sweat. It took me a while to identify it, because my nerve endings were all on fire, but eventually I registered as a naked human being, taller and broader than myself, covering me, shielding my head, my torso, my bound arms, and most of my legs, from the direct rays of the sun. I was still burning alive, and still dying of thirst, but the sun itself was no longer touching me, not even in reflection.

The weight made me protest. "*Unnnh!*"

The heavy body bore down, pinning me, but not making any further move as long as I refrained from struggling.

I passed out again.

My mind wasn't working very well, because it wasn't until much later that I realized it was Ethan protecting me.

It didn't make any sense to me. He had tried to kill me last night. If we survived the day he would no doubt try to kill me again. The sooner I fell, the better off he was—at least, as long as Daddy and the Bitch intended on ever coming back for us, which was far from certain.

Had I been able to talk, I would have asked him just what the hell he thought he was doing. Had he been able to talk, he might have told me.

I might have thanked him. I might have called him stupid.

But we weren't able to talk. And I was in so much pain by then that I might not have made any sense anyway.

The sun climbed as high as the sun ever goes, and began to climb back down.

As soon as there were shadows worth inhabiting he stood and nudged me with his toe until I managed to rise. We swayed together, in an inferno, the air rising in waves between us. He was seared black, his face an unhappy landscape of dried blood, blisters, and peeling skin. He had puffy half-moons under both eyes, and a dry scab sealing one nostril: the reason I hadn't heard any snorking for a while, and the chief reason why, with his mouth gagged the way it was, his ability to breathe at all qualified as a miracle. I didn't like what his expression had to say about the way I looked, but at least he didn't try to keep me from seeing it.

I didn't have to see what I looked like, though. I could already tell. I could see the baked red of my breasts and the big fat sun blister forming on the tip of my nose. I'd been sick and I'd been feverish and at some point in the last hour or so my bowels had erupted with more liquid waste that hadn't had anywhere to go but except down my legs. All of it was peppered with grit and sand and packed together with congealing grease. I don't know how much body weight I'd lost from sweat, stress, and illness, just over the past few hours, but if it didn't show on my frame it must have shown in my face, and in my eyes, the same way it showed in his. We were both the walking dead, and we both looked it.

And it was as the walking dead that we shuffled together, across an infinite wasteland of burning concrete, the few short steps to the narrow strip of blessed shade that had begun to swell against the opposite wall of the pool.

We put our backs to that wall and slid downward, this time sitting side by side, secure in a truce that would last until the sun was no longer a common threat.

I forgot who said it. Maybe Daddy did. But whoever put the words together knew what he was talking about, when he said that sometimes Paradise can be nothing more than a Hell not quite as bad as a Hell you've already known.

It must have still been well over a hundred degrees in the shade, but I could already feel the temperature start to drop, and that made it Paradise.

At least until our insides felt the change, and the chills began to wrack us.

I asked him, all of once, why we couldn't just hide from her.

I must have been six at the time. I couldn't have been much older. I know that I'd been hearing the horror stories of my mother for as long as I could remember, and that it hadn't been all that long since I'd been able to place her in a category removed from Rumpelstiltskin and the Wicked Witch and the Evil Stepmother and the other imaginary monsters of the fairy tales that I'd somehow managed to pick up without my father's notice.

I'd had bad dreams since the night I realized the Bitch was real.

So I asked him. Did I really have to visit her someday? Couldn't we just go somewhere far, far away? Wouldn't she just get tired of looking for us, and go away?

He'd gotten very serious and very sad.

"Just how many years do you think you'd have to hide?"

I felt them burning me before I had any idea what they were.

I'd spent the last few hours with my back against the pool wall, my legs curled against my chest in what would have been a fetal position had my arms been free to link fingers around my knees. My internal thermostat had been veering from one extreme to the other for some time now, alternating the wonderful sensations of being burned alive with those of everything inside me being turned to ice. I'd popped sweat after sweat, feeling steam rise from my skin as the rivulets of perspiration poured down my sides in waves; and then, reacting, I'd shivered with a fever that turned the world around me arctic. For hours on end my teeth would have chattered if they could have touched at all. My throat continued to ache for water, and the shadows, lurching toward the opposite wall to reclaim our battlefield for night, gained ground in a herky-jerky rhythm that served to emphasize just how much of the day I was spending too far gone to notice the passage of time.

Sometime after the shadows advanced to within a foot of the opposite wall, I was attacked by balls of fire.

There were dozens of them, each as hot as molten iron, each as solid as ball bearings, each impacting against my skin at the same instant: most striking my face and legs, but some hitting the top of my head and others burrowing down my back to burn my spine like acidic flame. The agony was so profound that I convulsed, shrieking through my gag, hurling myself against the pool floor with a desperation to escape that superseded any worries over how much the impact was going to hurt. I smashed my head again and didn't care. I heard Ethan roaring in equal pain, somewhere to my immediate left, his deeper cries as inarticulate and just as uncomprehending as mine.

More acid fell. It didn't stop falling. I felt my skin shriveling, turning black, peeling away from the bone, becoming flakes of ash which blew away like little embers.

Then a little made its way past my lips, somehow making its way past the gag and past my still-clamped teeth, and I found myself sucking at it with something like awe.

It was water.

It didn't feel like water, not against my skin, but against my tongue and dribbling down my throat it was just warm, refreshing water, tinny to the taste but better than wine.

A dribble went down the wrong pipe and I started to gag. I raged at myself for choking on this wonderful gift I had begun to think I'd never know again, forced the coughs to silence after only a minute or two of nonstop hacking, and stood, raising my face to the wonderful shower. Drops seemed to sizzle as they struck my ravaged cheeks and forehead. They still felt like acid against my burned flesh, but I didn't care. Thirst trumped Pain. I could feel my strength coming back with every drop I sucked down.

Somewhere above me, Daddy said, "Don't swallow too much, little girl. You'll get sick. Just turn around and I'll clean you off!"

I couldn't see him, as the water had washed the salt caked on my forehead into my eyes, but I staggered about in a circle, as he'd commanded. All at once the flow concentrated, no longer a diffuse spray but a tight, burning stream, battering my buttocks and my inner thighs to force away all of the day's collected filth. The agony of the moment was enough to make my guts clench. I staggered a step or two away, driven by the instinctive urge to escape the source of the suffering, but Daddy kept the stream focused and on target until every bit of the foulness was gone.

Then he turned off the water, leaving me wracked and trembling. There was vapor rising from the concrete.

"There," Daddy said.

I could still hear water patter against concrete. Looking up, I saw Ethan, still being hosed off. The current stream targeted his face, in order to wash away all the dried blood. The force of it rippled his cheeks, maybe making it easier for him to drink some. As he turned, the pool dust, washing off his muscled skin in waves, revealed shoulders turned so scarlet from the sun that he might as well have been dipped in blood. The top of his head, and the arc of his shoulders, had become a mass of popped blisters. His nose had swollen to almost twice its original size, and had a distinct blue tinge that worried me.

I don't know why it worried me. I should have wanted him to die.

Daddy said, "Come over to the steps. I want to take a look at you."

I pulled my eyes away from Ethan and staggered back to the shallow end, forgetting to duck as the chain-link grew low enough to scrape the top of my head. The contact with it felt like being branded. I groaned, went to my knees, and scrambled as best I could to the Shallow End steps.

Daddy was kneeling just above the wire. He wore a red-and-yellow Hawaiian shirt, mirrored sunglasses, khakis, and a big straw hat. He looked tanned and rested and proud. When he saw me close up his mouth made a little O of sympathy. "Looks like you had a rough day, honey. I'm sorry to see it."

I tried to speak through my gag. "*Wheeehhh wuhh oo*?"

He understood me. "This dump has no running water and no well. The Bitch has to drive to town every couple of days, to fill up gallon jugs, and she was already almost out."

"*Unnh! Wheehhhh wuhhh OO?*"

"Calm down, kiddo. You have every right to be a little annoyed. But it's about a ninety minute drive, each way, and she wasn't about to go all by herself when she was afraid I'd take advantage of her absence to help you out when her back was turned. We had to be fair about this. So I had to go along to help. And then while we were there we decided to surprise you by renting a tanker and hose, and the place made us wait almost four hours before one was available." His mouth went grim. "Try to spend four hours with the Bitch trying to be civil in public. Just try. We even had to make nice over lunch in some diner with a one-eyed waitress. That was an ordeal you should be happy you missed."

Something hiccupped in the back of my throat. My vision blurred. I didn't know whether I was going to throw up or scream until the sound came out and it turned out to be laughter. It was the one-eyed waitress that did it, I think. I couldn't help picturing a fat woman in pirate gear, complete with patch, parrot, and peg-leg, slinging hash while Daddy and the Bitch exchanged small talk over the menu. I even wondered if they'd tipped well. Probably. I didn't know my Mom's custom in that regard, but Daddy knew how to charm the ladies. He just didn't know how to pick a good one.

Daddy perked up. "Anyhow, we're both back for the duration now, and now that we're here it looks like you've given as good as you got. You have a bit of an owie on the back of your head, but it looks worse than it is, and he's got to be suffering from that mess you made of his face. Plus his burn seems to be shaping up even worse than yours. Pick your moment tonight, or at the very worst sometime late tomorrow, and I'm sure you'll have no trouble putting him down for good."

His eyes softened, turning moist in the way they only did in training, whenever I'd broken some new boundary with sweat and blood and back-breaking effort. He pressed his hand against the chain-link, and extended his fingers through the diagonal windows between the wires; I raised my head to feel the touch of his hand and almost moaned at the way even that soft contact tortured the taut skin of my scalp. He couldn't tell that I wasn't craving his love. I was just hoping that if I was nice enough he'd remove my gag and give me a nice, cold cup of water. The few drops I'd sucked down hadn't come close to satisfying me, and the mere thought of enduring any more time without another taste was almost more than I could stand.

I argued my case through the gag, but my voice trailed off in a mouthful of dust.

"I'm so proud of you," he whispered, turning away all at once so I wouldn't see him cry.

The real suffering didn't manifest until after the air cooled. But as the sky turned purple and then black, every part of me caught on fire, raging at the slightest physical contact. I could avoid most of the pain by simply not moving, but the straps that held the canvas bindings around my arms and the bit gag firmly planted in my mouth both felt like razors heated over an open flame. I couldn't focus past it. It was like a landscape larger than myself, so vast in every direction that I couldn't even see its furthest horizons. It only ceased to overwhelm when I moved an arm or leg and in that way distracted myself with some other pain just as large, just as unbearable. Daddy and the Bitch, who had returned to watching the show from their respective lifeguard chairs, must have been bored beyond reason for much of the early evening, as both Ethan and I spent those hours at opposite ends of the pool, unconscious more often than we were awake, trembling with chills even as we panted from the heat.

We must have resisted the inevitable for hours.

I don't know what time it was when I crawled from the Shallow End steps, found the strength to get to my feet again and stagger, in a precarious lurch with only distant relation to the upright, to the invisible line separating the Shallow and Deep Ends.

Daddy called down from above. "Thattagirl. Show him what you're made of."

The Bitch summoned her own champion. "Don't give up, Ethan! I'm proud of you!"

After a long, snuffling pause, my brother shuffled out of the darkness.

The darkness spared me actual eye contact, or even a clear look at his face. All I saw was a vague, threatening presence, still larger than myself, still more formidable than myself. All I heard was ragged breath and a weak, liquid bubbling that may have been heralded the return of the blockage in his nostrils. The stench was the worst, all sour sweat and festering waste, the perfume of a creature all but dead who had yet to lie down.

"Come on, honey!" the Bitch cried. "You can do it!"

Ethan shuffled forward another step, and then stopped, swaying.

I couldn't see his eyes.

But the last day and a half had been a silent conversation between us, punctuated by moments of equally incomprehensible brutality and mercy. I didn't need to see his eyes to know something I hadn't really appreciated before.

He hadn't ever really wanted to do this.

He'd offered me a way out, at the start, but I'd imagined it the kind of formality one warrior exchanges with another, in the last few minutes before any duel to the death. I'd believed him when he'd said that he had no other reasons for being born. But now that I'd spent twenty-four hours with him, in the shared hell we'd been training for all our lives, I found I knew differently. He'd meant what he said. He'd taken his last opportunity for escape, and I'd thrown it back in his face.

Had I accepted his offer of a quiet afternoon together, on our last day before our descent into the pit, he wouldn't have stopped the jeep at those rock formations twenty miles away. He would have kept going, picking up a main road and staying on it until long after we'd left the State and the swimming pool behind. Daddy and the Bitch would have set up the chain-link barriers together, waited in vain for our return, and then come to the shared conclusion that we weren't coming back. They might have been upset and they might have been disappointed and they might have been relieved that the contract between them had finally been broken by somebody other than themselves. They might have flayed each other with recriminations, each blaming the other for raising a child disloyal enough to break free. They might have parted as bitter enemies who no longer possessed the weapons they had honed to hurt each other. Or they might have descended into the pool themselves, with or without the hobbles they'd chosen for us, to finally face each other without proxies, on a battlefield that would have put a period to everything that had turned the air toxic between them. Whatever happened to them, I realized, would not have mattered. Not with Ethan and I already miles away, and adding more distance between our lives and theirs with every moment we breathed free.

He had tried to shock me awake, asking questions he'd already known the answers to.

I just hadn't been ready to hear him.

We shuffled the last few steps toward each other. I rested my forehead against his shoulder and murmured something useless. He made a noise no more articulate.

"What the hell is this?" the Bitch demanded.

"Come on, kids!" Daddy urged. "Mix it up already!"

We were both sorry.

But we both knew this couldn't end until it ended the only way it was allowed to.

I reared back and slammed my forehead into Ethan's broken nose, feeling it collapse again under the impact, hearing the crunch of cartilage and the gasp of pain.

"Good one!" Daddy yelled.

Ethan staggered back a step, but recovered quickly, advancing with a speed I could not have expected, to drive his knee into my gut. It hurt even more than most belly-shots because my gag cut off most of my air's natural escape route, making my cheeks balloon from a mouthful of exhaled breath unable to leave as fast as its force demanded. I doubled over, spun, and fell over on my side, hitting the pool bottom with a thud that rattled my entire spine. My spine exploded again as he spun and slammed his right heel against my lower ribs. I felt something crack, as my eyes tried to well with tears but couldn't come up with the moisture they needed to cry.

The Bitch yelled, "Finish her!"

Daddy screamed. "Get up, get up, get up!"

I arched my back, whipped my legs up and around, and delivered a pile-driver kick to Ethan's crotch. I would have recognized the impact as solid even if the pain of impact hadn't rebounded all the way to my waist. I would have heard it in his liquid gurgle and in the blind thud of his next clumsy steps.

From the way he staggered, those stunted balls of his were just as sensitive to pain as the normal kind. It'd only take him another second or two to shrug it off, and come after me again, but I had no intention of giving him that much time.

I pinwheeled my legs, flipped to my feet, lowered my head, and charged him, striking his midsection with my right shoulder. He was already off balance and struggling to remain upright. The tackle drove him off his feet, his legs flailing against the pool bottom, his arms straining at their canvas binding as his body obeyed the urge to regain balance.

We both screamed through our respective gags: Ethan because he knew what was happening and myself because a tidal wave of white agony had flared down my back at the moment of impact. Daddy and the Bitch were screaming too, but at the moment I no longer gave a shit about them. I no longer gave a shit about anything.

The only thing that mattered, in this last second before the ground gave way, was driving Ethan back, further into the Deep End.

Then his left foot sought solid ground where there was none.

He didn't fall backward right away, which might have been better for him. He had just enough balance left to compensate as the pool bottom disappeared beneath him. His left leg sank into the drain hole, and his right slipped out from under him.

He took the bulk of the initial impact just under his left knee.

Even as I heard the wet splat of the first blood freed by the break, he was still off-balance, still falling backward.

I spun away and lost track of up and down as my feet pounded concrete trying to use up the momentum that remained. I tipped over and started to fall.

Ethan took the brunt of the impact on his bound arms. Something, maybe an elbow or one of the bones in his hands, made a sound like cracking ice. There was another crack, louder and more final, as his neck whipped back and slammed his head against the concrete.

I slowed and regained control just a hair too slowly to avoid a painful face-first encounter with the wall. I felt the cartilage in my nose release.

Behind me, Ethan wailed through his gag, making sounds that could have been words and could have been inarticulate cries of pain. They sounded the same. When he tried to pull his leg out of the drain, something razored ground against something obstinate, and he wailed again, in a voice suddenly gone as high as a baby's.

Still dizzied from my collision with the wall, and freshly sickened by the taste of blood, I lurched away, tripped over an invisible Ethan, came far too close to another potentially deadly pratfall, then regained my balance and approached Ethan again, triangulating his position from his moans of pain. When I was sure I knew where his head was, I spun like a top and drove my heel into the side of his face. I felt his jaw leave its track. His cry went wet and bubbling, with a nasty undercurrent of fresh rage, all the shared understanding between us forgotten as I became nothing more than an enemy, beating him to death in the dark.

I couldn't see his eyes but I knew they had to be reproaching me.

We owed each other more than this. This may have been the only currency we'd been empowered to pay, but it wouldn't settle any of the debts that really mattered. Those would stay on the books forever.

The Bitch yelled, "Ethan! Oh, please, honey! Get up!"

Another voice, all but drowning her out, swelled with pride: "Show him who's boss, Jen!"

The blood bubbled in Ethan's throat. His mouth must have been full of it, but there was no place for it to go but down, filling his windpipe and cutting him off from what he needed to live. He would have been fine without the gag, but with it, he was just a man in a noose, struggling for breath a mere layer of skin from all the air he could ever need or want. He was still strong enough. If I left him alone with his will to live he might even manage to keep snatching breath for hours.

I circled him again, exhausted, unwilling to take the logical next step.

The Bitch cried, "Ethan! Baby!"

Daddy yelled, "Jenny!"

I needed a drink of water so very much.

"Ethan! Get up! Do something!"

"Jenny! Finish him! Now!"

Their voices ran over one another, melding, becoming a single shrill command in a voice that sank knives into the base of my spine.

Had I been able to say anything intelligible, I might have apologized to my brother.

Instead, I prodded him with my toe, determining his position, figuring out the most efficient way of doing what needed to be done. He lay on his back, his spine arched because of the bound arms that prevented him from lying entirely flat. His head hung backward, his spasming throat as exposed to me as that of a defeated dog offering itself to the mercies of its pack leader. When he felt the weight of my knee, resting without any particular pressure on his neck, before I made the commitment to bear down, he whipped his head to the right in a final, instinctive attempt to shake me off. I shushed him with a sound my gag transformed into a reptilian hiss, tried to send him the silent message to the effect that what I did now was being done with all possible respect, and bore down, wishing that the knee was his and the crushed windpipe mine.

The next few days passed in a delirium of shifting light, moist compresses dripping cold water into my eyes, fevers so brutal that I came out of them astonished at being alive, the agony of every glancing touch, and the uncertain comfort of female hands spreading ointment on my face, shoulders, breasts, belly, and legs.

It must have been two or three wakings before I grew used to the realization that I was in a bed with sheets, and maybe another couple after that before I registered that my arms, while restrained, were no longer drawn behind my back and were instead chained by the wrists to the bed frame.

Sometimes I heard canned laughter from a nearby low-volume television, other times I heard whispers saturated in venom. Sometimes I vomited. Sometimes, out of sheer malice, I soiled the bed and exulted in silent triumph when the soft, caring hands had to deal with my filth. Sometimes I dreamed I was still in the Deep End with Ethan. Some of the dreams bordered on the erotic, allowing me to have my way with him in every possible position despite a disapproving inner voice that insisted on reminding me that this would now be necrophilia as well as incest. Sometimes, when I told myself that, the dreams compensated by giving him Daddy's face instead, but I hated when that happened. I'd been there, and much preferred nonsensical fantasies about Ethan, even when those fantasies faded into detailed replays of the battle's final moments.

Sometimes, I returned to rationality long enough to understand that both my Mommy and Daddy were with me, whispering that I'd been a good girl, and that they loved me. I cried when Mommy kissed my forehead and told me I was beautiful. I cried harder when my Daddy told me about Ethan's burial in the desert, and of the words they'd written on notebook paper and interred with him, as of course there could not be a stone. The paper read, *Beloved Son, Beloved Brother.* Had I been consulted, I might have added, *Warrior.*

When, after a couple of days, I came back to myself long enough to realize that the restraints had been removed, I sat up, reeled from the worst dizzy spell I'd ever known, and somehow managed to focus. The tiny bedroom had faux-wood paneling, aluminum trim, shelving bolted to the faux-wood panel of the walls, and a miniature pop-down vanity complete with a perimeter of tiny light bulbs. The space between the single bed I occupied and that vanity was a narrow strip of floor just large enough to stand in. There were no photos, no personal items anywhere in sight. There was a gallon jug of water. Daylight, though sealed off by the aluminum blinds covering the only window, rested on the opposite wall in a single glowing sliver. The air was warm, but cooler than it had a right to be.

I looked down at the bed and saw a sheet liberally peppered with flakes of skin.

I swung my legs over the edge of the mattress, winced at flesh that insisted on complaining from every move, and hauled myself from the bed to the chair adjoining the vanity.

The mirror depicted a patchwork girl. Some patches of skin were still lobster-red, or tanned to near-blackness, but the worst of the burns had peeled, revealing irregular patches of pale new skin behind the dried flaps and healing blisters. Two even paler bands, reflecting the places where the leather straps of my gag had protected my skin from the sun, extended from the chapped corners of my lips, across my cheeks, and around as far back as I could see. My jaw was a mass of faded gray bruises. My eyes were red and underlined with a pair of gray half-moons. My cheeks seemed gaunt. My hair had started to grow back, though it hadn't established itself as more than a transparent blonde down, establishing the places where a full head of hair would appear once time and biology had done its work. Right now some of the bristles impaled loose flakes of skin, displaying them like butterflies on pins.

It could have been worse.

I drank some water from the jug. Slept. Then drank some more. Then slept.

After a while, I drifted back to consciousness and heard a woman laughing, somewhere right outside.

A few seconds of searching and I found the clothes they'd left for me, neatly folded on the dresser, with a note to the effect that I could come outside if I felt up to the walk. In addition to one of my bras and one of my pairs of panties, there was also an oversized white t-shirt that must have belonged to Ethan, an oversized Hawaiian shirt I also identified as his to wear over it, an ankle-length skirt with belt to cinch them tight, the sun bonnet my father had bought for me, and a pair of flip-flop sandals. The gestalt may have been random as fashion but it was all loose, all selected for maximum sun protection while offering the greatest degree of comfort for skin still so sensitive that it hated glancing contact with cotton sheets. This struck me as uncommonly thoughtful. I eschewed the bra out of reluctance to feel those shoulder straps but otherwise accepted the rest of the suggested outfit, dressing gingerly and some four times slower than I was used to.

The screen door slammed as I bopped down the steps of the mobile home. It was still hot outside, but not sweltering: maybe somewhere in the upper eighties, not all that much warmer than that. My parents, who were about twenty feet away occupying a pair of chaise lounges under a huge beach umbrella angled to catch the morning sun, both looked tanned and happy to see me. Both wore oversized amber sunglasses and big floppy straw hats. The Bitch was reading something by Carole Nelson Douglas, Daddy something by John Grisham. Both seemed delighted to see me. They waved.

"There's the sleepyhead," said Daddy.

"She looks better already," said the Bitch. To me, she added: "Better hurry up and get under the umbrella. You don't want to overdo."

There was a mesh folding chair just inside the umbrella's oval shadow.

I winced as I sat down, winced again as I edged the chair a few inches closer to my parents.

"You want something to eat?" inquired the Bitch. "I can fix something. You've been off solids for a bit, but you look like you're ready to keep something down."

My stomach bubbled dangerously. "Maybe later."

"Don't wait too long," she advised.

"I won't."

"You have to keep up your strength."

"Why?" I asked. "The fight's over."

"Just to take care of yourself," the Bitch said. "We care about these things, even if you don't."

Daddy winked at me, retrieved his own mimosa from the gutter between their lounges, and sucked a single dainty sip through a bent straw before returning the glass to its resting place. "You listen to your Mom," he advised. "She knows what's best."

I swallowed, wincing at the sudden surge of pain from a throat still too dry and raw. "Does she?"

The Bitch looked away, her right hand covering the fresh scowl twisting her lips. Daddy sighed, sat up, and removed his sunglasses so I could see his eyes, which were very pale and very blue and so very much like Ethan's that everything since my birth took hold of my heart and twisted hard. "Now, pumpkin," he said. "I thought you knew better than that. Your mother and I did need to settle our differences. We couldn't do it by ourselves. We know that because we tried, again and again, and the more we argued the more we kept going over the same patches of ground. We couldn't move on without settling who was right and who was wrong. It's too bad about Ethan, of course, but now that everything's resolved, there's no reason for any more pointless animosity. We can get along. We can even be a family again, if you'd like. We could move your Mom out of this place and get a nice house somewhere with trees and a lake. We could even get a dog. You like golden retrievers, don't you? I thought so. Just like I always promised you, I'll get you anything you want. We'll make it work."

The impossible fantasy loomed before me, beautiful and horrifying and irresistible and repugnant all at the same time, drawing me in with a gravity greater than my own capacity to resist it. I'd missed so many things, but I still had a couple of years left before I turned eighteen. Maybe it wasn't too late for me, to have the things other kids had.

I couldn't help it. I wanted to cry. Daddy had been rough on me during my training, but if he'd been less demanding I might not have survived. And Mommy might not be such a Bitch anymore, now that Daddy and I had established the order of things. I could love them and they could love me. It could happen. Stranger things had.

Thirsting for more than just water, I licked my lips and felt the sting as they cracked. "What if you two have another fight?"

Daddy winced as if stung. "We've taken that into account."

Mommy retrieved her mimosa and treated herself to another dainty sip, before returning the glass to the paving-stone by her side. "I went through the change already," she said, with what seemed infinite regret at the lost opportunities of her youth. "But you can still bear children. And twins run in the family."

I didn't know I'd risen from my chair with enough force to tip it backward, until Daddy said, "What?"

Then I moved.

Seven hours later, with the afternoon dying, the desert far behind me, and the approach of night turning the sky a shade of indigo, I pulled the rental up to a diner marked by a twenty-foot neon cowboy whose right arm wobbled to and fro in perpetual friendly wave. I would have preferred to drive still further, putting even more distance between myself and the struggle now taking place in the swimming pool, but the hunger I'd denied all day long had just settled in for good. I had to feed it or risk going off the road.

The waitress must have gotten her hair and her lipstick out of the same bottle. "I'm sorry to ask, honey, but what happened to you?"

"My ATV broke down in the desert," I said. "I couldn't get a signal on my cell, so I had to walk about twenty miles for the nearest tow truck."

She clucked. "People have died that way. You should have taken cover under the vehicle and done your walking at night."

"Yeah, well, that's what they told me at the Emergency Room."

"Are you sure you're all right to travel?"

"They said I was fine when they released me," I said. "Won't be winning any beauty pageants for a while, but I'll be good as new in a week or two."

She shook her head. "I gotta hand it to you. You're one tough kid."

"Believe me, not as tough as some."

She brought me a turkey sandwich and threw in a slice of apple pie out of sympathy.

I didn't need the charity. Between what I'd taken from Daddy's wallet, and the cache I'd found in Mommy's underwear drawer, I had a couple of thousand to fool around with. The burns, the buzz-cut, and my physique would help, too. They made me look older than I was, which would free me of any embarrassing questions about family.

I'd been better than them, in the end. I'd shown enough mercy to leave them the umbrella, and five one-gallon bottles of water. I'd also left them ungagged, with one free arm apiece, so they could drink as much as they wanted for as long as their supply held out. Of course, that gesture had been less about indulging their thirst than respecting their right to therapeutic communication. Now that they were speaking again for the first time in almost sixteen years, it would be a shame to deny them the time and voice they needed to catch up. There would be some awfully entertaining discussions going on between now and however long it would take for their voices to fall silent, and since I'd taken care to secure each of them well out of reach of the other, those conversations would all have a chance to play themselves out at proper length. It would have been interesting to stick around and listen, just to hear how often my own name was mentioned, and in what context, but I reasoned that they'd be more likely to release their inhibitions without me around. I was sure the privacy would lead to any number of fruitful epiphanies, some appreciated and some not.

I wished them well. At least, in the short term.

In the long term I hoped they fried.

Midway through my second cup of coffee, a family of four came in. Daddy was a scrawny thing with a prominent chin and weary blue eyes. Mommy, who was shorter, with frizzy blonde hair and a pointed nose, bore the grimace of any woman who had endured too many complaints for too many years. The boy and girl, who were six and five, didn't want to eat anything but french fries and had to be seated on opposite sides of their booth when the boy persisted in tapping his sister on the shoulder, again and again, a crime she found unbearable and which made her screech, "Mo-OMMM! He's *touching* me!" Daddy ended up slapping the boy and Mommy ended up informing both kids that were in big trouble if they dared make another noise: a disciplinary measure that lasted all of thirty seconds before wails and spilled water escalated the warfare, and the noise, to the next level.

As soon as I could I paid the bill and drove away, the lights of nearby homes blurring in the distance.

Maybe someday I'd be done with missing them.

PIECES OF ETHAN

Ethan's condition swallowed him whole on the day of his sixth birthday. You could say that he was dead from that moment on, though he lingered for many years afterward, dragging all of us into the same black hole with him. Maybe we were entitled to hate him for what he became, and what that did to us: but how was he entitled to feel about us, the ones who would go on after he was gone?

It happened at the place on Sunny Creek where the river turned wide enough and calm enough and deep enough to become our natural playground on those days when the afternoons were more generous with hours than chores. This was of course still many years before that creek was dried to a fraction of its former glory by the dams greedy developers constructed upstream in order to turn our little valley from a refuge on the edge of wilderness to yet another overcrowded place for city folks to breed their litters of vacant-eyed suburban tots. We could splash around in our underwear or even outside of it without fear of offending neighborhood prudes or attracting neighborhood pederasts. Until that day Ethan changed we considered the site one of the great landmarks of our childhood, and I suppose we still did after Ethan, though what it meant to us had irrevocably changed by then.

I returned to the spot just once within the last couple of years, just to see if it had continued to get worse after Ethan died and our family moved away forever. I found rust on the rocks, stagnant water that stank of sewage, and abandoned crack pipes in the dirt. Highway traffic was audible over the trickle that remained of the waterfall. The ruination of our childhood playground made the lives we had lived before Ethan's transformation look even more like what it was: an idyll we had known but lost.

But back then, it was still a family refuge beloved by all of us. And so Mom had felt no misgivings over asking me to take him there and keep him occupied until it was time to get him dressed for his party. He'd been driving her crazy for hours with his constant talk of the presents to come, and she needed him taken out of the house as acceptable alternative to strangling him. It was a choice between watching him or helping her clean the living room, so I agreed. She packed some sandwiches and sodas, and let me take Ethan and our middle sister Jean out to where the water was cold and white.

We enjoyed a few hours of innocent fun going over the falls and dunking each other under the water, before taking a break on the flat rocks that overlooked the pool so we could feel the droplets tingle as they turned to vapor on our skin. During those hours, the last unspoiled hours of our lives, I'd dared Ethan to jump from the highest cliff, something he hadn't ever worked up the nerve to do before and might actually be able to steel himself to attempt some visit soon. I'd splashed Jean in the face and endured her promises to go running to Mom. I'd endured the inevitable payback in the form of the fistful of mud she'd mined from the pond bottom. We teased and played and pretended that time wasn't passing at all as the sun rose high in the sky and started to sink again, changing only the pattern of the light that shone like diamonds on the rippled surface.

Many years later, I think about the first part of the day and reflect that if the bad thing hadn't come along to ruin it we would now remember it as one of the perfect, transcendent moments of our lives; one of those days that we all keep as permanent snapshots in our heads, when we define what was best about our childhoods.

But then the bad thing did happen, and form a snapshot of a different kind.

I remember having nothing in mind but scaring Ethan silly with a cannonball landing, right next to where he paddled around in circles, wondering where I had gone. Grinning, I shouted Geronimo and leaped off the rocks twenty feet above him, striking the water with the kind of concussive force that made the impact feel less like a splash and more like an explosion. The bubbles rose all around me, like a fleet of spaceships taking flight. I hit the soft ooze at the bottom and pushed off, grinning, happy, in what I now recognize as the last uncomplicated moment of my youth.

I broke surface just behind Ethan, with a fine view of the back of his head. Jean was screaming. I didn't know right away that this meant anything was wrong, as shrieking girls are just part of the fun of horseplay in water. But when I tracked the sound to Jean, who was paddling around in the water twenty strokes beyond Ethan, nothing in her face testified to play; she was pale, and wide-eyed, her lips peeled back as far as they would go in a grimace of horrified denial.

My first thought was that I'd just scared her more than I'd intended to scare Ethan. My second, more serious, was that some kind of animal had bitten her underwater and that I'd catch hell from Mom for not being sufficiently watchful.

Then she screamed, "*It's Ethan*!"

The back of Ethan's head looked the same as it had always looked. It looked like the back of any little kid's head, jug ears and all. I figured it couldn't be too bad, since he was still treading water just fine, but Jean was still screaming, so I grabbed his shoulder and pulled him toward me.

The only warning I had that I would not be seeing a human face where his should have been was a sudden shift of the bone where my palm touched his shoulder. It felt like the bulge of a rat scurrying around underneath a throw rug. It flattened and became something other than a shoulder just before Ethan completed his turn and blinked at me through the one eye that remained recognizable, an eye that had somehow migrated socket and all further down his cheek, and now blinked at me from the vicinity of his lips. That eye begged me for explanation. Then the skin on both sides of that eye rose up and swallowed it whole beneath a curtain of bubbling flesh.

I was away at University when word arrived that Ethan had taken a turn for the worse and that I needed to hurry home right away.

That was a hell of a way to put it. The phrase "taking a turn for the worse" implies that the state before it could be somehow counted as better. With Ethan, all developments were bad; some were worse than others, but every day brought a fresh nadir, a brand new visit to countries more terrible.

This was cram week, so it took me the better part of a morning negotiating with various academic offices before I could get a hardship leave that would allow me to postpone finals without flunking out or taking incompletes. I made sandwiches before I left, borrowed a junker from a friend in the dorm, and made it home in just over twenty hours, feeling like a failure as a brother whenever I had to stop to stretch my legs or fill up the gas tank or even take a shit. On the way back I got regular updates by cell phone. Ethan was awake and coherent now; he was asking for me. Then he was insane and ripping holes in the walls. Then he was flat on his back and gasping for air, unable to take in enough to feel anything but slow strangulation. Then he was expected to be dead within the hour. Then he was dead. Then he was alive again (or rather still, the half hour he'd spent mistaken as corpse now explained away as an understandable mistake, given that he'd been something nobody could bear to think of as alive).

Twenty hours, and then I pulled off the highway and into the cookie-cutter template the old neighborhood had become, rows and rows and rows of ugly houses without enough space between them to pass sunlight except as isolated stripes. As always after a long absence, I hated the families in all those houses, for what they'd done to the special place where I'd grown up. My folks might have still had a couple of dozen acres left over from the days when land was cheap, and they'd kept the original homestead inside it as pristine as possible behind stone walls crawling with ivy, but even as I pulled past the automatic gate, what I found past it no longer felt like a homey refuge on the edge of a forest, but rather the last threatened keep protecting itself from invaders who had ruined a once enchanted country.

It was a much smaller estate than it had been, once upon a time. Mother had been selling off our acreage, both to pay taxes and to support us when all her energies went to Ethan and no other form of income was possible.

I left the pavement of the hated outside, pulled onto the gravel of the family's circular drive, and after another minute or so came to a stop behind a small fleet of parked cars clustered at the base of the wraparound porch. Jean, who'd been up all night providing intermittent companionship via cell phone, slammed the screen door and came running to meet me, her waist-length scarlet hair bouncing behind her like a banner. She was hugging me tight even before I was all the way out of the car.

Her voice broke as our cheeks touched and her tears mingled with mine. "Oh, Lawrence. It's been so *long*."

I knew she wasn't talking about the months since my last visit home, but rather of these last days since Ethan started to fail. We'd lost our father to emphysema a couple of years back, and had learned back then what Jean and the rest of the family had been re-learning now; that deathbed vigils have a way of trapping time in amber, turning each passing tick of the clock into another slice of eternity.

I didn't have to ask how bad it had been. Life with our afflicted brother had always been bad, but my sister's beautiful green eyes looked like the last night, alone, had aged her twenty years. "I should have taken a plane."

Had I been anybody else, Jean might have said, *damn straight you should have taken a plane.* But Jean had been with me the one and only time I'd been a passenger on a commercial aircraft, and knew that flying with me was a nightmare. I didn't take well to enclosed places. "It wouldn't have made a difference. Most of the time he wouldn't have known you were here. You're here for the end, that's what matters."

The screen door slammed again, and Mom appeared. She was tall, slender, an older version of Jean who had aged in the way most beautiful women hope to age, becoming more golden where others just become more lined. Unlike Jean, who had come at a run, Mom came at a measured walk: calm, regal, as measured in every movement as only a woman who had discovered her own iron strength could be. She wore her own long hair, as scarlet as Jean's without a touch of dye, in a tight wrap behind her head, more for convenience than any aged dignity. Her tight-lipped, tired smile was as warm to me as any embrace. "It's good to see you, Lawrence. You made good time. I was afraid that you'd have to stop in a motel for a few hours. Do you need to sleep before you see him?"

"No, I think I had about twenty cups of coffee on the road. I'm about to jump out of my skin. You're looking good, Mom."

"Nice of you to say. But I know I look like hell."

This was both true and untrue. Physically, Mom had never come close to looking like what women mean when they say they *look like hell.* More than once, doing her grocery run in town, she'd been mistaken for Jean's older sister instead of her mother; more than once, she'd received come-ons from young men who would have been mortified to find out just how old she was; more than once, she had admitted to being lonely enough to want to take them up on their offers, if only for a night of anonymous release. It hadn't been loyalty to the memory of my father, or fear of our disapproval, that stopped her. It was the tormented presence in the upstairs room, the sense that allowing herself to take pleasure in anything outside the family, while he still lived, amounted to failing him.

As for the other part, the price taking care of a doomed boy enacts on the mother who loves him—well, in that sense, you could say that my mother looked like the hell she'd been through. She wore every moment of the last ten years on her face, and anybody with an ounce of sensitivity could see it. But again, on her, it didn't mean what women usually mean when they say they look like hell. Hell hadn't aged her. Hell had just brought out what she was. Hell became her.

She put her hands on my shoulders. "Whatever you say, I won't have you driving yourself to exhaustion. You can bring your bag inside later. You'll pay your respects to your brother, and then you'll come downstairs for a hot breakfast, and then you'll go up to your room and catch some of that sleep you've been missing. I won't take any argument on this. Is that clear?"

I nodded, and then hugged her. "It's good to be home."

I could see how close she came to contradicting me, to saying that she knew damned sure it wasn't—as it hadn't been; being home wouldn't be good as long as Ethan remained what he was—but she allowed the lie to stand, as she hugged me back and told me, as she told me out loud only in times of great celebration or sorrow, that she loved me.

There was no point in expending tears now, not with the sight of Ethan still ahead of me, and so I gave her one last squeeze and let her and Jean lead me into the house, where I nodded hello at the gathered forms of my cousins and uncles and aunts, all gathered out of grim sense of family duty for these last hours of the long vigil my mother had endured, almost without rest, for so many years. Then I went to the stairs, putting my hand on the polished banister that Ethan had once used to slide down with giggles, and holding on to it as I ascended toward the attic floor with the locked and soundproofed door that had never been able to cage the sound of splintering bones.

On the day Ethan changed, Jean had run home to get Mom and Dad while I stayed with him, watching him shift from one terrible shape to another, enduring the sounds his insides made as they fractured and reformed into new configurations. I shooed flies away from the lungs that had burst from his chest, glistening with blood and foaming with fugitive breath. I lied to him about everything going to be okay when his spine contracted like a salted slug and bent him over backwards, with the back of his head melting into the bare skin of his buttocks. I vomited with revulsion, for the first of what turned out to be many times in our relationship, when all his connective tissue dissolved and he became a mound of disembodied organs, pulsing on the rocks where a boy had been, with nothing but a boiling puddle of blood between them to identify them as parts of the same tormented body and not as separate butchered pieces of meat.

I had thought that nothing in my life could ever be as horrible as that half hour, and had gone away for a little while when Jean returned with our parents and a plastic tub to carry our brother in.

I surrendered myself to shock and catatonia as the three of them helped me collect Ethan's pieces, as we squared him away in an upstairs bathtub, and as we called the family physician, Dr. Zuvicek.

My ability to form new memories went away for a while. I know what happened intellectually. I suppose you can even say I remember it, in the way one remembers a favorite movie. But in another way it never really happened to me. It never recorded. I can't really call forth anything else until much later that day, until Dr. Zuvicek trudged down from upstairs to enter a living room still festooned with multi-colored balloons and HAPPY BIRTHDAY banners.

Zuvicek's status as our family doctor bore a double meaning, since he was related to us via some arcane spiderweb of genealogy that had always escaped me and frankly always would. I knew little else about him except that he specialized in treating members of our family, and in fact traveled throughout our region to pay house calls on those who had settled in the six closest states. He was broad-shouldered and thick-armed and wore a sculpted red beard with silvery flares at the pointed tips. Today he had pieces of bloody Ethan tissue on his sideburns and glistening patches of worse things on his conservative black suit. He looked colorless, which for him was like being another person, since Zuvicek had always been one of the ruddiest men I'd ever known.

As he entered the living room, he put his big black bag on the coffee table and faced my sister and myself with a look of almost infinite pity.

Jean, who was still young enough to seek hope even in hopeless situations, said, "Is he going to be okay?"

He rubbed at his dark eyes with one gloved hand. He always wore black gloves, even indoors: something to do with a skin condition that made his fingers sensitive. "No."

"Is he gonna die?"

"Yes," Zuvicek said, with a sharpness that surprised me. "But that's true of you and me as well. It might happen tonight and it might happen fifty years from now. Your brother, I think he'll still be with us for another few years yet."

I heard in his voice the admission that this would not be good news for us. "But what's wrong with him, exactly?"

We heard footsteps on the stairs, and Zuvicek said, "Your father will wish to speak to you on this, I think."

Unlike my mother, who would remain youthful even after years of fighting for her damaged son, my father looked like he had aged four decades in as many hours. Ethan's plight had ripped a hole in his life, one that had already leeched the color from his skin and the spark from his eyes. In the short time he had left, before daily existence in the same house as my damaged brother put him in his grave, he'd age still more, developing a stoop, a lingering wheeze, and a patina of exhaustion that turned every breath he took into a fresh burden he only shouldered out of habit. But on that day, as he came down the stairs, there was still some of the man he'd been left on his bones, and as he lowered himself into the overstuffed armchair that had always been his alone, it seemed less the attitude of a man without strength to stand than that of a father who now had to address his two undamaged children from across a common table.

Father massaged his temples with forefinger and thumb. "I am sorry. In any other family, you would have been able to live your entire lives without seeing this."

"Seeing what?"

"This . . . curse," he said, spitting the word as if he would have liked to wrap both his hands against the disease, and strangle the life from it, if he could. Then he heard himself, seemed to realize that anger at the fates would only frighten us, and softened. "This disorder. It is known to our family, from the old country, but it is very, very rare. Most of us have lived entire lifetimes without ever hearing of a case, except in old stories. A distant cousin you have likely never met had a child with the condition, about twenty years ago. Your grandmother, may she rest in peace, once told me it had happened to a grand-uncle of hers, when she was a girl even younger than Ethan is now; and a hundred years before that it happened to some other poor child, whose name and exact relationship to us have been lost to history. Records only go back so far, but it has always been the hidden devil inside us, the one that slept for generations."

I had been learning genetics in my science classes. "You're talking about a recessive trait."

My father looked blank for a moment, as if I'd just tossed a few words of quantum physics into the conversation.

Zuvicek answered for him. "You are a smart boy. Yes. That is exactly what your father is talking about."

"And . . . it only happens to our family? To no one else?"

"As far as I know," Zuvicek said. "There are rumored to be other families who suffer something like it. But they may be obscure offshoots of our own. There are, as I say, few records. In the old country, these things were always kept private."

Jean shivered and hugged herself, which was not just a fearful gesture, since she had donned her clothes while still wet and had caught a chill running back from the creek. "Why would anybody even want to be part of our family, then? Why would anybody in our family ever have children, if this could happen to us?"

I saw pain and anger flare in my father's eyes, reactions he tried to hide by looking away. Years later, I still wonder if that was the moment when death first planted its terrible seed in him. Maybe. It still feels like the moment when it was first planted in me.

But Zuvicek was patient. "I understand that you are upset. I don't expect you to take much comfort in this right away, but every family in the world has a history of increased susceptibility to one ailment or another. To compensate, they also all harbor areas of high congenital resistance. In our own family's case, the childhood cancer rate is much lower than the norm, and the same can be said of our personal incidence of epilepsy, diabetes, and degenerative muscle disease. Nor is that all we have to be thankful for. There are many things we have to worry about less, that are much more important in the scheme of things, than this one ailment that almost never happens."

Jean was not mollified. "Are we going to get it?"

My father was even more stricken by this question than he had been by her last one, but Zuvicek was firm. "Absolutely not. You are already older than you would be if you were ever going to get it. As are you, Lawrence. This ailment only attacks very young children, most of them infants or toddlers; tragically, Ethan was himself almost old enough to be considered out of danger. It is next to certain that your own children, should either of you have children, will also never have to worry about such a thing. All you have to worry about now is your poor brother . . . and how much your poor mother and father will now depend on you, to help take care of him. It—"

Ethan screamed. The inhuman sounds from upstairs, which would never stop in the long years that followed, had been audible since long before Zuvicek came down. But most of them had been cracking and grinding noises, as well as sudden exhalations, that had not sounded like anything in particular and had been almost impossible to identify as product of any particular little boy's voice.

This shriek was Ethan's voice, returned to him: a cry of almost unimaginable pain that would not have been inappropriate coming from a boy set on fire, or one swarmed by hornets, or one simply locked in a cramped black place along with the sound of vicious things scrabbling in the dark. There was no sanity in it, or hope. But it was, for a second, recognizable as Ethan's voice. I suddenly remembered that it was my little brother we were talking about, and half-stood, determined to race up the stairs to his side. But then the sound of his pain changed to something far worse, something with barbed wire and broken glass in it, and all my instinctive protectiveness fled, replaced by paralysis and shame as a stream of warm piss ran down my leg.

My father saw it. So did Jean, and so did Zuvicek. Not one of them blamed me. They had all heard the same thing I'd heard, and may have come close to the same involuntary release.

In the end, Zuvicek could only finish the sentence he had started before Ethan's scream.

"—will not be easy for any of you, I'm afraid."

Now I was an adult, home from the University my mother had insisted I leave home to attend, as inured to horror as only one who had lived his life steeped in horror could ever come to be.

I stood at the locked door of Ethan's room, gripping the deadbolt, closing my eyes when one of the wet sounds from within reminded me of rending flesh.

As always, standing at this threshold felt like facing a long drop into formless darkness. Even if I'd taken the next step on more days than I could count, even I knew from long experience that I'd survive an encounter with my brother, there was no way of quantifying how much it was going to hurt. The only certainty was that it would.

As always, I waited for the first cry that sounded recognizably human before I peered through the spy hole.

Even allowing for the distortion of the panoramic lens, Ethan's room no longer looked like the toy-strewn sanctuary decorated with spacemen and superheroes that it had been on the day of his sixth birthday. The colorful boy-sized bed frame and desk and toy chest had not long survived his illness unbroken; they had been removed, and replaced with padded walls and a steel trunk equipped with padlock and air holes, for those times when only absolute confinement would be enough. The padding covered walls that had been rebuilt to cover what had once been windows open to morning light, with a fine view of the trees at the edge of our backyard forest. Now the only light was a circular fluorescent ring within a reinforced cage. One of its segments flickered and one of the others gave off a dim glow brightest at the center, like the sun trying to break through a blanket of clouds. Stains of various colors, some recognizable as the things that come out of a human body, and some not, streaked from the ceiling and puddled on the knit seams between the padded places on the floor.

It was, I knew, impossible to keep the room looking or smelling like anything but an open sewer. By its very nature, Ethan's disorder meant that he leaked. Sometimes, when he transformed into whatever he became next, he reabsorbed whatever he'd spilled last. Sometimes he didn't. It was the only consistent way to tell the difference between what was part of Ethan and what was just his waste fluids.

It took me a second or two to find the twitching, half-melted form, like a man wrenched into a Moebius strip, that bubbled at the room's farthest corner. Even as I watched, it tried to grow spikes, but they deflated with a hiss. The shape softened, becoming as close to the shape of a human boy as Ethan ever got anymore: a lot like a plastic army man that somebody had melted on a hot stove and then allowed to cool.

I threw the bolt and entered, wincing as always at the sheer stench of the place. My mother and father had installed a state-of-the-art air-filtration system early on, using what would have been Ethan's college fund, but the atmosphere in here was always like a deep whiff of a sweaty sneaker that had been allowed to marinate in rotten bananas and then soaked in a puree made from the contents of a rancid diaper.

It was as impossible to get used to the stench as it was to get used to the things Ethan changed into, because fresher and more offensive perfumes were always being added to the soup. You can get used to living inside an open sewer, if you have to. Your sense of smell adapts, if only by turning off. But if shit is only the least offensive of all the possible things you have to wade through, and everything new that comes dribbling down the pipes attacks some remaining vulnerability in your gag reflex, then adaptation doesn't work. There's nothing to get used to.

I had lost one of my college girlfriends because our evening walk had taken us past a golden retriever who'd been split open by a passing car. It was still alive, and whining, even as its parts leaked from its flattened belly. The septic release of its split bowels made the site of its imminent death like the inside of a toilet. My girlfriend vomited out the General Tso's Chicken I'd just paid for and later called me cold and inhuman because the sight of the poor pooch had left me unaffected. I hadn't been able to explain to her that I'd long since grown used to obscene sights and smells like that, because my little brother spent most of his life as obscene sights and smells like that.

Now, fighting back the nausea I hadn't been able to feel then, that Ethan could still wrench from me, I padded across the sodden canvas to the place where the throbbing shape lay, trying to grow a face. Dark patches that could have been embryonic eyes, a nose, and mouth, as captured in a drawing by an ungifted first-grade cartoonist, appeared just below the thing's semi-liquid chest, and seemed about to congeal into something capable of speech . . . but then they faded, leaving only an oozing green patch, like a gasoline spill on a driveway.

Ethan quivered, that little failed attempt at coherence exhausting him utterly.

My vision blurred. "Hey, kid. I drove a long way to get here. Can you spare a little hello for me?"

He gurgled like an infant, and exploded.

There's a certain sight popular in Hollywood comedies: the hapless character who gets drenched by something slimy and malodorous—shit or fertilizer or paint or, in gooier fantasies, alien bodily fluids that have never been included in the usual list of substances produced by the human body. The victim's eyes always blink multiple times in the middle of a face otherwise obscured by muck, eloquently communicating an offended dignity that encourages the ticket holders in the audience to howl in disgust and delight.

Ever since Ethan turned six, my family no longer considers that kind of scene funny. We've all been through it too many times.

This time I was lucky; not only did none get inside me, but what got on me decided that it didn't want to stick. The layers of little brother flowed off my skin like quicksilver, forming another queasy puddle at my feet before pieces of him became the snout of a rat, the leg of a dog, the cock of a stallion. Two beautiful cat's eyes, with irises of green and gold, blinked on his surface, communicating a calm amazement that could have meant anything I wanted it to mean; then they disappeared and—in what I could only think of as a little miracle—the vomitous ooze congealed, forming an oversized, bodiless portrait of a little boy's face.

"Hello," he said.

It was the first coherent word my little brother had spoken to me in three years.

He looked like he would stay this way for a while, so I touched him on his oversized cheek. My hand looked like an infant's against that larger-than-life canvas.

A lump formed in my throat. "Hi, kid. How's it going?"

He gulped, a gesture more about seeming to swallow than actually swallowing, as his big face fronted no throat and no gullet. "That's a fucking . . . stupid question, Lawrence. You know . . . how I'm doing."

"I know. I'm sorry."

"Fuck your sorry." He coughed, struggled for voice, moaned with a supreme effort of will as his mouth tried to go away. Several seconds later he managed to bring it back, but by then his eyes had dropped several sizes and assumed normal human dimensions, which made them comical on that oversized face already beginning to run like wax at the edges. "Fuck you. Fuck Mom. Fuck Dad. Fuck Jean. Fuck all of those fucking vultures downstairs. Fuck your pity in your fucking ass. I hope your fucking kids get what I fucking have. I hope you have to fucking watch them live with this. I hope you have to fucking hope for them to die. I fucking wish it had been you all along. I fucking wish I could look down at you the way you're looking down at me. I fucking wish I could piss on you. I fucking wish you'd get cancer. Fuck you. Fuck you. Fuck you. Fuck you. Fuck you."

He tried to say more, but his moment of coherency was done. His body was too busy becoming a succession of specific things, all of them terrible. A bloody Jesus, writhing on the cross. A burned man, crawling across an expanse of broken glass, his trail marked by the pieces of himself he left behind. A little girl having her eyes gouged out by hooks. A dog trying to crawl on the bleeding stumps of amputated legs. A pregnant woman giving birth to a spiked asterisk of a thing, all bristling needles and barbs, that crawled from her bloody womb only to sink its claws into her flesh and drag itself up her body, so it could force itself down her throat and enjoy being born a second time. A little boy paddling around a favorite swimming hole on his birthday, and beaming with an innocent delight that was about to be ruined, forever, by the terrible fatal flaw that cruel nature had built into him.

None of them surprised me.

They were all things that I'd seen him become before.

I left Ethan's cell after another half an hour, feeling as unclean as I always felt, whenever I visited my little brother. It never mattered whether I'd managed to avoid getting any of him on me. I was contaminated by the sight of him, sometimes the very idea of him.

I took a shower with the water hot just a sliver short of scalding. I let it burn. There was no stain of Ethan on me—that quicksilver retreat of his flesh from my skin a measure of insufficient kindness in a visit that had otherwise afforded a full measure of his condition's cruelty—but I still stayed beneath the spray, enduring its punishment, until I was reddened and raw and able to feel scoured of every part of him.

I crawled into bed and slept, enduring the usual Ethan dreams of my bones twisting into razored shapes inside me.

When I woke, the afternoon light was fading. I got dressed and went downstairs, finding much the same assortment of cousins and aunts and uncles, their positions on the family couches unchanged. I endured the usual questions about anything but Ethan, questions that ranged from whether I was seeing anybody special to whether I'd decided what I was going to do after graduation but somehow never touched on how much I was suffocating. I asked where my mother was, and was informed that she and Dr. Zuvicek were both upstairs with Ethan, who had taken yet another in a long series of turns for the worse and was hardly changing at all, which an elderly aunt who had researched the condition told me was a sign that his remaining lifespan could now be measured in hours.

After that I endured the usual half hour of well-meaning family blather about everything but the crisis at hand; the cousin who had gotten married, the uncle who had moved to another state, the relative of uncertain provenance who had done something even more uninteresting that I was expected to note and file away as vital genetic intelligence. Somebody was doing well in business, somebody else was failing, a third had had fallen out of touch, and a fourth had committed sins that the aunt reporting them considered scandalous enough to impart in shocked whispers. I nodded and pretended to care and then watched as the subject inevitably circled back to Ethan, and how sweet a little boy he had been.

When I finally made my escape I stepped out into the afternoon's fading light and found Jean on the porch swing, smoking a cigarette. I hadn't suspected her of picking up the habit, but she didn't know I had either, and as I sat down she just handed me the butt without making eye contact. I took a single drag deep enough to make the paper sizzle, then put it out and sat down beside her, watching the sun turn to bright red shrapnel behind the sheltering trees.

"So?" she said, without looking at me. "Ready to leave yet?"

I nudged the porch with my toe to make the seat rock. "Pretty much."

"And you've only been back for a few hours. Try it when it's just you and Mom sitting on opposite ends of the same couch, night after night, trying to find things to talk about in between Ethan noises."

I held up my hands in a gesture of abject surrender. "You win."

She glanced at me out of the corners of her eye, searching for signs of mockery. After a second or two she came to the reluctant decision that I wasn't offering any, and looked away, her anger still burning but unsatisfied by any fit place to put it. "I'm sorry. You offered to stay, too."

That I had; though I'd offered only token resistance when Mom insisted that I had a life to live, that I needed to see to my own future while my poor brother burned through what little was left of his. Give her credit, she hadn't tried to inflict any guilt when I let her win that argument . . . or when I chose a faraway school that would keep me from having to come home and help out on evenings and weekends.

I just hadn't considered the pressure my absence would put on Jean during her own last two years of high school. Two years of always having to rush straight home to help Mom with Ethan. Two years of never being able to spend time with friends, of never being able to go to parties, of never being able to fumble in back seats with boys. Two years until graduation and then two more years of putting her own future on hold, so Mom would not have to deal with our family nightmare alone.

And I had to admit to myself: that was bullshit, too. I mean, that I hadn't considered it. Of course I'd considered it. I'd considered it, taken the offer of freedom from Ethan, and fled while there was still something left of me to flee with.

I wanted to say I was sorry, but that would have been an insult, so I said nothing.

She studied the fading light. "It's not even you I'm mad at. It's them. All those sanctimonious assholes in there. All those covered casseroles and cold cut platters; everybody bringing the same things, every day. Making a big show of being there for Mom, when for all these years it was hell getting any one of them to spare an afternoon or an hour to watch him so I could take her out of the house for a while. When Ethan was just this *thing* that was never going to end, they were all just fine with letting her live like somebody who had to be chained to one spot. They wanted nothing to do with us. But now that's he's almost gone, they're back, wanting back into our lives. It's like . . . Ethan was never anything but a stigma. And once he dies, we'll all be clean again."

"Maybe we will," I said.

I expected anger, but got something worse, a pathetic little half-smile of the sort an adult offers to a child who has not yet learned the ways of the world and who has said something adorable and precocious and sad and naïve. "Will we? Is that even possible now? After everything we've seen?"

"Of course it is. I promise you: when this is all over, we'll all go somewhere for a while and figure out how."

A terrible warbling sound erupted from the house. It was less a scream than a chorus of them, all erupting from a throat that now came equipped with a multitude of voices. They all cut off in mid-howl, replaced with something bubbling and liquid that invoked the image of a room of bound captives trying to breathe through slit throats.

One of the distant cousins, a stranger to me, burst from the house, fell to his knees, and vomited on our front lawn. It took him several minutes to empty, and even once he did, he remained on hands and knees, trembling, preferring that spot and the view of his own stomach's contents to the prospect of returning to the house inhabited by the family obscenity.

Jean rested her head on my shoulder. "You better keep that promise, bro. I've never even been to Disney World."

• • •

It was five hours later. We were back inside, drowning in more premature condolences, when the low hubbub of empty conversation went away all at once. At first I thought it was just one of those awkward conversational lulls endured by all families who have ever endured an extended death watch, but then I registered the gaze of an aunt frozen in the act of dipping a cracker into a bowl of salsa, the identical look on the face of her fat husband who'd been napping on and off between forced reminders of her own deep empathy, and the relief on the faces of almost everybody else, as they reacted to something over my shoulder. I turned around and saw Dr. Zuvicek, who had stopped midway down the stairs and now faced us all, looking grim and professorial and older than his years. He had washed up and changed into a new black suit, one unsullied by the various explosive effluents of time spent with Ethan; he had slicked back his hair and resculpted the flared lines of his beard and transformed himself back into the buttoned-down man of medicine, but the ordeal of the last few hours had still taken a lot out of him, and he wore the pain of it on his face and on the shoulders.

He faced us all, and announced, "Ethan's gone."

One of the distant aunts broke the silence with a tremulous, "Are you sure?"

"He is dead now," Zuvicek said, putting a slight emphasis on the word *now.* "There is no respiration, no movement, no reaction to stimulus, no sign of additional transformation. For the last four hours he has done nothing but cool. It is safe, as safe and as decent as it ever could be, to now declare him gone and go on with our lives. We may say goodbye to him."

Our distant aunt valued being part of the drama too much to do the sensible thing and just keep her mouth shut. "But are you *sure*?"

Zuvicek just raised an eyebrow at her and let the silence grow teeth.

I hugged Jean and considered how easy and how terrible it would have been for Ethan's disorder to strike either one of us instead.

"Almost free," she whispered.

"Just a little bit longer," I assured her.

I endured a shoulder squeeze from one of the many cousins jingling car keys and thanked the handful of others who offered spoken condolences. Most couldn't wait to rush outside, to retrieve the funeral urns they had brought. Jean and I were not so lucky. We had to follow Zuvicek upstairs, and aid my mother in parceling out Ethan's pieces.

This was the last necessary duty we'd spent so many years dreading. The very nature of Ethan's curse is that he changed. He changed without purpose and he changed without limit and he changed without end. It had taken him years of changing from one foul thing into another to finally change into something without breath, without heart, without voice, without any signs of whatever life meant if you were talking about something like Ethan: something that seemed content to remain what it was and could therefore be considered dead enough for a funeral.

But we couldn't afford to just bury, or even cremate, him. Unlike the more limited shape-changers of the old horror pictures, Ethan had not been granted the dignity of being restored to humanity as he lay dying. He'd remained whatever he was at the moment he stopped moving, and there was no way to know for sure that his corpse was anything but another cruel transformation, one that wouldn't decide, an hour or day or a decade later, that it was just another transition state to be abandoned as soon as it could change back to something alive.

Nor would it have helped to cremate him. After all, so many of the things he'd turned into, over his tormented lifetime, had been on fire. He'd been ashes several times, and had always turned back to living tissue.

There *was* no way to be sure. There never would be.

So his only funeral was a diaspora. His pallbearers all climbed our stairs bearing empty urns and all descended with full ones, each heavier than its mere weight could account for. They piled into their respective cars and made their way back to homes in fourteen states and three foreign countries, burying his pieces in desert sands or sinking them in wetland ooze. They fed pieces of him into raging furnaces and tossed other pieces of him over the railings of cruise ships. They left pieces of him in landfills and in the concrete foundations of office buildings, pieces of him broiling in the world's sun-blasted deserts or forming ice crystals beneath permafrost.

Nobody was going to be half-assed enough to dispose of their pieces of Ethan in any location too close to anybody else's; they'd all heard the terrible sounds from upstairs, and knew that they did not want to be responsible for the pieces of Ethan ever finding each other, congealing, and coming back. So notes had been compared, and maps consulted.

Sometime in the hours between midnight and dawn, they were all gone: all except Dr. Zuvicek, who sat with us on the living room, his own piece of Ethan sealed in a little jar beside his chair.

The house seemed emptier than the mere departure of our extended family could account for; it was as if the great family grief that had laid claim to our home for so long, so vast in its scope that the walls had seemed to creak and warp with the strain of containing it, had left only a void. Mom sat holding a teacup in both hands, staring at the tepid drink as if expecting to find some answers there; Jean and I shared the opposite couch, looking anywhere but at the sealed jar containing our own last piece of our doomed little brother.

Zuvicek had just finished saying that he was going to bring his own piece of Ethan back to the old country, where the farmland once owned by our great-grandparents and still likely our property—that being difficult to determine, so many wars and governments later—had grown wild and been reclaimed by forest primeval; he believed he could identify the spot where the old mansion had stood, and bury his piece of Ethan there. "After I'm done," he said, his eyes far away, "I think I'll do a little wandering before my return to these shores. I know I will never again have another patient quite as difficult as this one, but I have still had enough of sickbeds and death vigils for the time being; it is time to . . . re-grow myself."

"Good luck with that," Mother said.

Zuvicek must have detected the bitterness in her voice. "You should do the same thing. It is a shame that your dear husband," he hesitated, and looked at us, "your father, did not live to enter this time of healing. And a shame that the rest of the family can only help you so much, that the final step can only be completed by parents and blood siblings. But once you are done with that duty, you should not be afraid to embrace life again. As soon as it is decent, go somewhere fun and do something stupid. Remind yourselves who you are, when you don't have such a terrible thing hanging over you."

Mother covered her eyes. "I'm not sure I remember anymore."

"I understand. But you are still a young woman, with many years of life left to you. And you have two fine healthy children who will help you remember, with their own lives, and someday with the blessing of healthy grandchildren. Remember that." He grabbed his hat and his bag and his piece of Ethan, and stood before us hesitating, searching for the words that would define the moment with as much gravity as it deserved. "You should all move away, when you are done. This has become a bad place for you."

"I know," she said.

Zuvicek bade farewell, accepted our thanks, and departed.

The three remaining members of our immediate family sat in silence for several seconds, neither enjoying nor understanding the sudden emptiness of a home that had until now been driven by the engine of unrelenting pain.

For lack of anything better to do, Jean surveyed the detritus of Ethan's deathwatch: the dirty glasses on their coasters, the plates stained with the remnants of condiments or cake, the extra chairs hauled up from the basement that would need to be folded up and put away. "We'll help you clean up."

"That can wait until morning," Mom said. "We have to say our own goodbyes."

I said, "I'm not sure I'm ready for that."

"Neither am I. But he was your brother, my child, our blood. We owe him our strength."

Mom meant that, of course, but we all knew the other thought that had to cower behind the one she could bear to speak out loud. *And besides, this needs to be over. He needs to be gone. This house needs to be quit of him.*

I grabbed the vase. "Right. Might as well get this over with."

The three of us went outside, the screen door slamming behind us. The driveway, all but abandoned by the cars of family members, now only bore my borrowed junker and Jean's secondhand Yaris, each resting part on gravel and part on lawn. The stars above us were few, thanks to light pollution from the new houses that had come to crowd our beleaguered estate, but the few I could see were bright, distant points of fire that still seemed sharp enough to burn.

The moon was just a waning crescent, points curving upward like the grin of the Cheshire cat. It might have been more appropriate full, of course, but if Ethan's life story had any moral at all in the context of our family, it was that nobody can control everything, and that some of us are damned to control less than others.

We went together into the backyard, which was still enclosed by the stone wall and protected by what remaining forest the advancing suburbs had left.

Just before I took the stopper off the urn, its contents shifted with a perverse suddenness that startled me and almost made me drop it. The ceramic rang like a bell, and the grisly contents shifted again: willful, insistent, helpless, defiant, and angry.

My voice cracked. "Oh my God, he's *still moving*—"

Then the jar lurched again. This time I dropped it, enduring the century and a half it took to hit the ground, feeling myself break even as it broke, releasing what was left of Ethan to explode like a balloon of blood. In the moonlight it looked black and shiny, a lot like an afterbirth. Something like an eye floated to the surface and then popped, leaving ripples that smoothed over and became a surface as placid as any mirror.

I said. "He's alive—"

Mom put a hand on my wrist. "Lawrence. Stop putting this off."

"Mom, it's not over, he's moving –"

Her fingernails dug into my flesh, drawing blood.

I gasped and looked her in the face, expecting anger but seeing only an ethereal calm.

"It's over," she said.

Behind me, Jean had already taken off all her clothes, her breasts hanging pale and white beneath the slivered light. It wasn't just the change. Even before the fur started to sprout from her cheeks, she looked taller than she had in years, more beautiful, more at peace, and more defiantly free.

"Like you said inside," she reminded me, her soft voice turning coarse as her jaw began its transformation to elongated snout. "Let's get this over with."

By then Mom was midway through her own change; not into

the common vulpine creature my sister could become, but into the thing that had never borne a name in any human tongue, the thing that had drawn my father to her in the old-country revels. Our extended family has a saying that we each choose our other skins, and what Mom had chosen, in her youth, was broad and powerful and wrapped in a snow-white mantle that glowed with inner fire.

Watching, I could only wonder how many years this self had been lost to her; how many years she'd been condemned to a life of nothing but dull humanity, as she cared for the child whose body had been incapable of making the permanent choice all of our bodies had made.

I decided. Mom and Jean were right. It was time.

I peeled off my shirt, before it could be damaged by the emergence of my girdle of arms. Then we dropped to all fours, lowered ourselves to our departed blood, and began to feed.

THE BOY AND THE BOX

The boy looked like any other boy his age, except that, thanks to him, there had been for some time now no other boys his age, or of any other age. The elimination of all others had transformed him into the entirety of a subset that had once numbered billions. He was now the platonic ideal of his type, not just a boy but *the* boy.

As the last of his kind currently existing in what he had allowed to remain of the world, he had soft downy cheeks, a pug nose, a fan of freckles across both cheeks, and hazel eyes that went well with lips arrested in a permanent affronted pout. He hadn't had any means of washing up since he'd made everything go away, so he smelled unclean and wore permanent smudges on his palms and cheeks. His once-short sandy hair now formed a rat's nest . . . though that was a meaningless statement as well, as rats were one of the things he'd gotten rid of and there was no longer any need for their nests.

The boy had not only put all the people away in his box, but also all the animals, and all the trees, and all the buildings, and all the surface detail that made the world even at its most unbearable interesting to look at. Had the boy needed water he would have died of thirst. Had he needed food he would have starved. Had the temperature been anything but neutral he would have frozen or sweltered. But he'd put away all these concerns as well. He was self-contained, invulnerable, immortal, and free.

He had been wandering around doing nothing for longer than we have the capacity to measure when he got tired of looking at a horizon that offered nothing but a single unbroken flat line and paused in his endless wandering to take out some toys.

First he pulled a favorite squat rock, now *the* rock, out of the box and placed it on the ground, in order to sit on it. It was a comfortable rock, the best of a number he'd tested and approved for squatting purposes. He rested his weight on it and found it just as superlative as it had been during his previous indulgences, then pulled his box from the pocket of his jacket and regarded it the same way any boy would have regarded any familiar but important possession.

There was nothing special about the box. It was not some cosmic vault, glowing with portent, surrounded by a crackle of blinding energy. It was just a jewelry box, lined with soft blue velvet and embossed with the trademark of a well-known retail establishment that, like the ring it had once contained and the store that had once sold it, were now safely stored inside. In the world now stored away, the gift had been removed to be placed on a woman's finger, and the box seized in delight by the toddler the boy then was. He'd loved the soft texture of that crushed velvet, and the way a line drawn on that fabric with a fingertip caught the light differently from the unmarked material around it. He had taken a deep childish pleasure in the popping noise the lid made when shut, which he'd imagined to be a lot like the snapping of some hungry monster's jaws. Sometimes, even now, he opened the box and ignored all the panicked cacophony of billions so he could hear that snap again on shutting it . . . but this was not the diversion he wanted right now, not the kind of game he wanted to play.

The boy did not find it difficult to reach into a space that should have been too small to admit his entire hand, let alone his full arm up to the shoulder. Nor was it any strain to pull out a grown man who should have been far too large to pass through the opening or too heavy for the boy to lift. The boy didn't worry about it. He just *did.*

The grown man the boy had selected tumbled out, rolling as if tossed onto the hard baked surface that was now the universe's only landscape. He pulled himself to his hands and knees and wept, heaving if denied air for so long that he now found its weight hard to stomach. After long minutes, he peered up and faced the boy, cowering as was only appropriate for him to do, before a creature of such infinite power and limited empathy.

"You can get up if you want," the boy said.

The man remained on his knees longer than he should have after that instruction but found the strength to rise, though he didn't draw any closer to the boy than he had to. He was a stoop-shouldered, pale figure with a high forehead, crooked nose, and weak chin, wearing a blue button-down shirt that had come undone from his khaki pants; and even as he stood he didn't look at the boy, instead facing some neutral spot between his tasseled brown loafers.

The boy asked, "What's your name?"

The man resisted answering, but after a few seconds said, "Lyle Danton."

"I didn't ask you for your last name. I don't need to know your last name. Last names are stupid."

"I'm sorry."

"That doesn't help now," the boy said. "You still wasted my time with it. I think I'm going to make it go away so you won't bother me with it again. What's your name now?"

"Lyle . . . " the man began, his voice rising at the end as if something else would tagged at the end of it. Nothing arrived. "Lyle."
"Lyle," the boy repeated, as if weighing it on his tongue. "No. Come to think of it, I think that's a stupid name, too."

"I'm sorry?"

"It sounds too much like liar."

"No," said the man, who winced upon realizing who he'd just corrected. "It's Lyle. Lyle. With another L."

"It's a stupid name, Lyle. You can't use it anymore. What's your name now?"

The man whose name had been Lyle opened his mouth, then closed it again, lost for answers. "I d-don't think I have one."

"You'll need one if we're going to have a conversation. I think I'll call you Stupid-Face. What did you do in the world, Stupid-Face?"

"I was . . . a lawyer," said Stupid-Face. He blinked multiple times and then, very quickly, said, "It's, it's dark in there. I can hear my wife and my kids screaming. I can't get to them, but I can hear them screaming. You . . . put everybody in there, didn't you? You're not God, you're just a kid. How did you put the whole world . . . "

The boy shushed him. "I'll get back to you, Stupid-Face."

Back Stupid-Face went, into the box.

The boy rummaged around a little more, and pulled out a woman. She was in her late fifties and had the look some women have, or more accurately once had, if they reached a point in life where they gave up on youthful beauty and satisfied themselves with being presentable. The boy didn't know that the official word for this had been *matronly*, but had observed the principle in a number of maternal aunts. This one was dressed in a gray knee-length skirt, a white silk blouse with a ridiculous bow at the collar, and a gray jacket. Her lipstick was too red for her complexion. She didn't fall to her knees as quickly as Stupid-Face had, but instead swayed, dizzy at the sudden return of sound and light and space.

"Tell me how much you love me," the boy said.

The woman blinked, her eyes resisting comprehension. "What?"

"I'll save you for later," said the boy.

Back she went into the box.

The boy sat his knee supporting his elbow and his knuckles supporting his chin, contemplating the box as he flipped it over and over in his hand. The bridge of his nose wrinkled. He reached into the box again and this time pulled out a very big man in an orange prison jumpsuit. The big man had a shaved head, a handlebar moustache, and a swastika tattoo on his neck. His arms bulged like great stones under his sleeves. Another tattoo, a snake's head which may have been some other color once but was now faded to a dull purple, emerged from his right sleeve and sat displayed on the back of his hand, spitting a forked tongue. He didn't fall to his knees as Stupid-Face had, but instead tumbled onto his back, butt-crawling as far away from the boy as he could before his initial panic failed him and he stopped moving, his eyes black dots floating in wide white circles.

The boy asked him, "What's your name?"

"F-foley."

"Say it without stuttering."

It took several false starts. "Foley."

"You just pissed yourself, Foley."

The big man's eyes widened a sliver further as he registered this terrible truth.

"It's okay," the boy said. "I think it's funny. Are you evil?"

"What the fuck are you talking about?"

"It's a simple question, and you don't have to lie to me. I need somebody evil for a job. Are you evil?"

Foley's expression relaxed a little, and became something else: crafty and knowing. "Will it keep out of that box?"

"Yes."

"Then, yeah, I'm bad."

"How bad are you, exactly?"

"I've killed a couple of fuckers in my time. Did one piece of shit with an iron pipe, first his hole and then his face. Did another with my fists. Left a third piece of shit so messed up he's been lying around on his back for ten years, broken below the neck and shitting through a tube. Not even brain-dead, neither. Awake so he knows every day what I done to him. I ain't one of those sick serial killing shits who does that kind of thing for fun, but I got no trouble taking care of business if business got to be done. Some people got it coming. You need somebody for that kind of work, someone who won't talk back or argue, someone who won't forget who's in charge now, I'm your guy a hundred percent. I'll make you proud."

The boy spent several seconds absorbing this before offering a slight nod and pointing toward a spot on the horizon, chosen at random. He said, "All right, Foley. Walk in that direction until I look like a dot in the distance. Then sit down and keep an eye on me. When I wave, run back and kill the man I'm with."

The big man nodded, because when one was trapped with an omnipotent being it was always best to be offered an opportunity to prove one's worth. He got up and ambled off into the distance, shaking his leg a little to wring his pants as dry as the circumstances allowed him.

The boy waited for Foley to travel the prescribed distance, and sit on the cold featureless earth. It was clear that the big man would sit there for hours or days or years, had such things still existed, and not move until summoned. All things being equal, it would not be much of an improvement over the environment in the box. It would only be lighter, more peaceful, and less crowded. That struck the boy as all the incentive he needed to trouble himself with offering.

Next step. He pulled Stupid-Face from the box.

Stupid-Face shrieked and fell back to his knees, tears rolling down his face in waves. "Oh, please. Don't put me in there again. I promise, I won't ask any more questions. Just let me stay out here, I beg you."

"You were right, before," the boy said. "I am just a kid. I don't think I'm a freak or a mutant or any of those other things from the movies. I'm not even particularly smart. At least, I wasn't ever all that good in school. I was just sitting around one day, thinking, when I suddenly figured out how to do something nobody ever knew how to do before. I was just lucky to be the first one to ever have the idea. But really, it was easy. Even you could have done it. You can ask me a question now, if you want."

Stupid-Face cast about in a mind close to bursting, and after three or four visible false starts, managed, "B-but even if you *could* . . . why would you . . . ?"

The boy picked his nose. "I didn't like my Dad."

"What?"

"Don't get me wrong. He didn't beat me or anything like that. He wasn't a bully or a drunk or a perve. He was just, you know, a guy like you, going to his job in the morning and coming home to his family at night. I'll give him credit for trying to be a good Dad, for making sure we were fed and stuff, and for spending time with us when he could, but every once in a while it was hard to look at him and not know that when he got tired from trying all the time, he looked at me and my Mom and my two sisters and my Dog and kind of wished we weren't there, because life would have been so much easier for him if we weren't. When I figured out how to do what I could do, I first made him forget all of us and then put him in the box. Then I did my sisters and my Mom, because I liked them even less. It wasn't hard."

Stupid-Face fell to all fours, and shook his head, addressing the dirt because it was solid and beneath him and no less reasonable or empathetic than the boy before him. His shoulders trembled, and he too released urine, the way the big man in the orange jumpsuit had. He muttered, "Oh God, Oh God . . . "

"Now I have a question for you. Were you a good man?"

"What?"

"I'm gonna get really bored if you just keep saying *what* whenever I ask you anything. If you bore me there's no point in not just putting you back in the box. So that was the last time I want to hear the word *what* from you. In fact, just to be sure you don't say it by accident, I'm gonna make you forget it right now." The boy shifted the box. "There. You can't say that word ever again. That's not too bad, because it's only one word, but if you keep wasting my time I'm gonna also make you forget *and* and *the* and *is*, and that's gonna make it really hard for you to say anything at all. So you might as well answer me. Were you a good man?"

Stupid-Face's mouth moved, providing a moment of silence where he normally would have uttered another what to underline his lack of understanding. It was as if the one key word removed from him had shifted everything that remained, and placed them on unfamiliar shelves, requiring vast internal adjustments until he was able to provide a response. "I think so."

"But were you really?" the boy asked. "I could have asked the same question of my Dad, and he would have said the same thing, even though he was like most people, just doing what he was taught to do, without ever understanding why. I don't think he was ever really good or evil, because he was never really asked to do anything but what he was. At least, he was no hero. So I ask you again. Were you a good man?"

Stupid-Face's mouth continued to work silently, as his mind churned through any number of possible responses and rejected every single one for being attached to too many possible causes for offense. "I'm sorry. I don't know."

The boy's shoulders fell in disappointment. "That's what I thought."

He stood up and waved at the distant dot on the horizon, which stirred from its chosen spot and began to grow in size.

Stupid-Face followed his gaze and noticed the other distant

figure for the first time. His eyes clouded with dread. His jaw fell, and chewed air for long seconds as the right words were pulled from their shelves. "Who's that?"

"That," the boy said, "is an *evil* man."

The hulking figure in the orange jumpsuit approached in no special hurry, his clenched fists hanging from arms like coiled springs. His eyebrows were knit over slitted eyes, and his mouth was a lipless grimace. Together they made the kind of expression that drew a straight line between the impulse to murder and the target of that impulse, a straight line that ended in the same spot where Stupid-Face began.

There was no way for Stupid-Face to interpret the still distant figure's approach as anything but what it was. He said, "No," and whirled toward the boy, hoping for mercy, but finding nothing in those placid features but detached curiosity. He rose, stumbled, and said, "No," again, but mere denial of his circumstances accomplished nothing at all, and so he said, "You can't, I'm no fighter, look at the *size* of him," but that made no difference either. He spun in a circle, searching for havens in a world that no longer had any shelters or bolt-holes or doors to close or trees to climb or authorities to summon, that in fact had nothing at all but the killer coming for him and the boy who could summon more killers any time he wanted. He took a couple of steps back, but then stopped, paralyzed by the awareness that he could run a thousand miles if he wanted and never step outside the reach of what was coming for him. At long last, the only remaining reaction available to him burst from him in a cry so primal that it cracked in his throat. "*I loved my children, you little shit!*"

Foley arrived just in time for Stupid-Face to throw a wild punch at his jaw. It would be nice to report now that the fury of a good man, or at least a not very bad one, fighting for his life and the lives of his children, lent so much power to his swing that it struck the killer down and forever redeemed the world for all innocent men like himself. But Stupid-Face had never been a fighter, not since childhood, and the man in the orange jumpsuit had something broken in him that allowed him to hurt other people as easily as he could breathe. Stupid-Face's wild punch landed on the bad man's jaw, to no real effect, and the blow Foley threw in return knocked Stupid-Face flat on his back, to beg and plead as the bad man loomed near, filling his sky.

There was no moment, in the seven minutes the murder required where the man who had lived as Lyle but was fated to die as Stupid-Face stood even a passing chance of turning the tide of battle. He was half conscious and breathing through a smashed nose after only three, battered past the point of brain damage after only four, and likely already dead after five. A professional assassin might have done a cleaner job of it. But Foley was no professional assassin, merely a gifted and enthusiastic amateur.

After seven minutes, the boy said, "Okay. You can stop now."

Foley stood and watched, his knuckles dripping, while the boy put the corpse back into the box.

"That's it?" the big man asked. "I done good?"

"I didn't ask you to do good. But you did what I asked. Thank you."

"So, umm. What happens now?"

"What do you want to happen now?"

"I sure as shit don't want to go back in that box, I know that. If you're the only game in town I'd just as soon work for you. Be your, like, angel of death or whatever. Maybe get myself a little crew, a bitch or two, if you eventually decide that's okay. Better than nothing."

"Angel of Death?"

"That don't have to be my title if you don't want it to be. Up to you, man. I just figured, you know, if I'm taking the big job, you might as well call it what it is."

The boy considered all this. "I don't know if I'll get you a crew or any bitches, but I'll think about it. In the meantime, yeah, why not. You can be my angel of death. Go wait where you waited last time, and don't bother me unless I wave you over again."

The boy watched Foley amble off, the increasing distance transforming him from big man to smaller man to tiny receding figure to motionless seated speck.

As of this moment, the boy didn't think he'd ever have reason to call Foley over again. The man had completely fulfilled all purpose the boy had in mind for him. But promises were promises. Foley would never go back in the box. Nor would he ever flee any further, for fear of losing what he had, or approach any closer, for fear of incurring the boy's wrath. He would just remain in place, in that spot with nothing worth looking at or doing, as aware of the passage of time as any man.

The boy took out a puppy, small and big-eyed and pleased beyond whatever reason it had to be away from the cold darkness of the box. He played with it for a few minutes. It was a very young puppy and soon it grew tired enough to fall asleep with its chin on his foot. This bored the boy. He picked the puppy up by the scruff of the neck and asked, "That's all you can do?" It yawned. He dropped it back in the box.

In short order he pulled out, played with, and tired of, a paddle-ball, a yo-yo, a snow-globe, and a wailing infant, whose senses of sight and hearing he removed at a whim just before he dropped the screaming thing back in the box.

Then he pulled out the same matronly woman from before. She'd been weeping since her last emergence, and she spent the next few minutes on her hands and knees, regressed to some first language the boy failed to recognize. The funny talk amused him at first, and gave him reason to leave her be, but it then began to pall, as it had nothing to do with him and failed to surprise him after the initial novelty of the unfamiliar combination of consonants and vowels.

He made the foreign tongue go away in mid-sentence—prompting a sudden shriek of loss from the figure prostrated on the ground—and waited for her to work up enough nerve to look at him again.

He repeated his past demand. “Tell me how much you love me.”

“What?”

He sighed. “I really don’t like that word. From now on, I’m going to take it away from people before I ask them any questions. There. It’s gone. Try to say it now.“

She choked on empty breath.

“Now tell me how much you love me.”

She cringed for a moment, but then something very interesting, something the boy had not seen before, happened to her face. It sloughed off all the fear and all the hopelessness and all her concern over what the boy was going to do to her, and replaced it with something built of iron. She used the back of her hand to brush the tears from eyes that had banished fear by recognizing that she had nothing left to lose, and said, “No.”

“You have to. Look around you. There’s pretty much nothing, anywhere, not as far as the eyes can see. You could walk away if you wanted to but you’d find nothing out there, and I could bring you back any time I wanted. There’s just the two of us. Tell me how much you love me.”

“Nothing could love you.”

He shook his head. “I’m a boy. I’m a boy who lived in a four bedroom house in a nice neighborhood with lawns and trees. I was loved then, I think, even if my Mom and Dad weren't very good at it. I need somebody to love me. Tell me how much you love me."

The woman spit on the ground. "No."

"You don't have to mean it. You just have to say it like you mean it. You have to say it in as many ways as you can think of saying it, and not stop until I tell you to stop."

"No. You're an evil little shit."

The boy tilted his head, and chewed on this at length, like it was a flavor he didn't recognize. "But this is the part that doesn't make sense to me. How come you're the one who gets to say what's good and what's evil? I'm the one who took you out of the box and I'm the one who can put you back. I'm in charge. I'm the only one who matters. I should be the one who gets to decide."

"Go to hell."

He said, "There is no such place. I haven't built it yet."

The woman was about to curse him again, this time with words so passionate and so blistering that they might have given even the boy pause. They fled with her ability to speak, leaving her before him, a silent figure whose loathing of everything he stood for continuing to rage behind eyes that conceded her abject helplessness but refused to surrender to it.

There was no doubt in the boy's mind that had he permitted her to place her hands around his throat, she would have continued to force strength into her fingers long hours after all life had left him. It was a beautiful hatred, the kind that was only possible when its owner had been robbed of everything else. In a way, it was downright beautiful, and the boy spent long minutes admiring it, the way he would have regarded a jewel that sparkled from every facet.

"I have an angel of death," he said, at long last. "I could bring him over here and make him beat you until you agreed to say you loved me. But that wouldn't be you, loving me. That would just be you not wanting to be beaten. You could say you loved me forever and I'd still see that look in your eyes. That wouldn't be satisfying at all.

"But I get to decide what's good and what's evil, now. So I'll just say that from now on, it's good to love me and evil to feel any other way. If you don't tell me how much you love me until I get tired of hearing it, you'll be a bad person who deserves to have bad things happen to her. Whenever you stop, you'll be more ashamed of yourself than you've ever been and you won't want to live with what you've done. The only way to feel better, for even a little while, will be to go back to telling me you love me. As long as you do that, you can stay. But if you have any bad thoughts, you go back in the box. I think that's fair, and since I decide what's right here from now on, it *is* fair. I don't ever want you to think, even for a moment, that I've been less than generous. Okay?"

The woman's eyes went glazed, tears of pure joy forming at the corners. "Yes."

"You can start now."

And of course, as instructed, she began to tell him how much she loved him. She dwelled on her love for him. She exulted in it, and labored at it, rattling off metaphors of astonishing poetic beauty that didn't even begin to capture the infinite depths of her adoration for him, the perfect kind boy who deserved all her love because he had in his uncanny generosity given her the commandment to love. She grew so fervent that before her long her praise blossomed into song.

He listened, found satisfaction in it for a little while, and then frowned as he realized that it was still not even close to enough.

It was the worst of all sins in his own personal universe, in that it was boring.

Of course, she was only one woman. He supposed that he could take other people from the box if he wanted to; lining them up in rows, if he had to; forming armies of them, if he needed to; directing their praises until they all spoke in a unified voice millions or billions strong, shaking the empty ground with the force of their single-minded adoration. He could have them cry out for him, at a volume that could shake loose the very sky. But what kind of being would even want such a thing, forever? What kind of creature could not only demand that, but take pleasure in the same hollow compliments sung in the same voices, for as long as it took time itself to grow cold?

His own vision blurred, as he realized that he was not now personally capable of being such a thing. He could not be such a thing without first jettisoning every part of himself that knew the love to be both forced and false. He supposed he could easily put those things away in the box . . . but what was the point then? He'd be as empty, then, as she was.

So instead he opened the box and stepped in, descending only knee-deep before he became aware that the woman had stopped in mid-sentence, her adoring eyes registering only that he was engaged in some fresh activity, and waiting to discern what it was so she could proceed with telling him how deeply she approved.

He couldn't pretend he cared enough to restore everything he'd taken from her, or to bring her down into the darkness with him. Instead, he said, "You might as well go back to what you're doing and assume I can still hear you."

She beamed with fresh ecstasy and returned to declaring her love.

He descended the rest of the way into the box, pausing just before he vanished completely, to bring the box itself into the box with him. It contracted to a point and then disappeared, all access to it eliminated.

This, of course, did not stop the singing.

EXTRO: "BAD PEOPLE DOING EVIL THINGS"

You'll find the letter, and my reply, in a May 2012 Brass Tacks, the letter column of *Analog*.

It came from a reader upset at a story you won't find here, a tale that hinged on a horrific series of events on a far-future alien planet; he felt that the story didn't jibe with his vision of science-fictional optimism, and complained, "I find Adam-Troy Castro to write uncomfortable stories. He writes about evil people doing evil things. I believe that this story is more appropriate for a horror magazine. What I want from a story is something that helps me be inspired and a science fiction escape with a happy ending."

Given the chance to respond, I pontificated at far greater length than editor Stanley Schmidt ever expected, citing a number of classically dark stories that had appeared in that venue and arguing with great self-important eloquence, about fiction's responsibility to embrace the uncomfortable . . . but, more to our current point, I also revealed my essential discomfort at being labeled an exclusive purveyor of visions nasty and reptilian with the following words: "You distort my own *Analog* record just a tad. My seven contributions to this magazine also include 'The Astronaut From Wyoming' (written with Jerry Oltion; a saga of a disfigured boy who stands up against all obstacles to defy the naysayers and join a manned mission to Mars), 'Sunday Night Yams At Minnie and Earl's' (about a friendly couple who bring warmth and a taste of home to lonely early lunar pioneers), 'Among The Tchi' (a comic piece about a human writer who stands up for the value of our race's prose), and 'Gunfight on Farside' (a tale about heroism, self-sacrifice, belief, miracles, and even redemption, whose murderous 'villain' was a fundamentally decent man suffering from madness brought on by exposure to a toxic substance, and was not only understood and forgiven but also ultimately granted a happy ending of his own). Not one of these stories hinges on authentic human evil. They all hinge on humanity's virtues, and they're so optimistic about the best of us that they're downright giddy."

Translation: whatever else I might be, I'm not *just* a sick bastard.

Further exploration of my collected short fiction will further bear out the existence of my soft side, as dedicated explorers will find oodles and oodles of gentle farces, heartfelt tributes to my writing heroes, and tales about heroes saving the day.

I'm a remarkably sweet guy. Honest. You know those TV commercials for the animal charity where that pop singer croons "Eyes of An Angel" over visuals of sad-eyed puppies and kittens in cages? The wife has taken to changing the channel upon the first few notes, to protect me. I don't just weep when actually exposed to the damn thing, I mist up even now writing about it. One viewing of *Born Free* ruins me for the whole day. Don't even think about exposing me to the soundtrack of *Les Miz*. I'm so sensitive to emotional appeals that I'm downright disgusting. You can destroy me with a manipulative McDonald's commercial.

But then we have stories like the one that roused that reader's ire, and the stories you'll find in this collection, which was originally intended as a straight science fiction collection but, as works from recent years accrued, gradually developed a darker and more disturbing tone, up to and including the inclusion of some pretty extreme horror.

Where do they come from, if I'm such a sweet guy?

Well, in part they come from the awareness that the best fiction is about testing and in the process defining human nature, and that extreme circumstances tend to provide starker definitions.

They come from the knowledge that the human race is a corrupt animal and that the worst elements in our collective nature deserve just as much examination as the best.

They come from actually having experienced close encounters with a couple of sociopaths myself and trying to work out a rational explanation in my head.

Finally, they come from just paying attention, which isn't hard in a town where, just a few days ago as I wrote this, a man achieved national tabloid headlines by going berserk and chewing off another man's face.

Don't worry. You won't find that particular scene in any story here. But I will dwell on it long enough to note that a lot of the online reaction to that particular loveliness, and a similar incident from elsewhere in the country that went viral a few days afterward, involved jokes about it being the first manifestation of the oncoming zombie apocalypse. The part of me that loves zombie fiction and has written some (none of which appears here), did find resonance in that . . . but that joke actually diminishes the horror. The guy with the strange concept of chewing gum was not an undead thing, but a living and breathing if far from rational human being, who might have been an exceptionally cute baby, once. That's a life arc, people. That's a story, even if not necessarily an edifying one.

Dark circumstances *spawn* stories.

So over the past few years, in addition to some other stuff not-quite-so-dark, I also wrote some stuff that grew from that fertile soil. So let us take a look at the stories, with the usual proviso that these notes should be read after the stories and not before:

ARVIES: This one, one of the more acclaimed and frequently-reprinted pieces from my last few years, straddles the abortion debate and has been accused of supporting both sides in that contentious conflict. Sorry, folks. I'm firmly pro-choice myself, but the tale is wholly non-polemical, taking no side either way.

The premise comes entirely from one fine engine for producing science-fictional ideas: namely, take something that is considered a given and imagine the implications of a world that turns that accepted truth on its head. In this case, my starting point was the oft-repeated argument that life begins at birth. I wondered what kind of world we'd have if life legally ended there, if only the unborn were considered alive and anybody who had ever completed life's first great passage was considered "dead." It occurred to me that such a place would only be viable, you should only excuse the expression, if fetuses held all the political and financial power. One assumption led to the next, up to and including the realization that, even in societies that offer the privileged unlimited opportunities for happiness, somebody somewhere still gets royally screwed.

My biggest fear on marketing the story was that nobody would "get" the title. The story itself makes no effort to explain the term's derivation except by providing readers with room for figuring it out by themselves.

Guess what. Pretty much everybody twigged to it.

I love smart readers.

"Arvies" was nominated for a Nebula in the short fiction category, was reprinted a half-dozen times in about a year, and won the Storysouth Million Writers Award, which came with a gift certificate I used in part to buy a remote-control helicopter in the shape of the word FUCK. My cats were nonplussed.

HER HUSBAND'S HANDS: I wrote this one after first writing a failed story called "Her Husband's Eyes," in which an accident involving a pickup truck filled with unsecured saw blades sends those sharp objects flying every which way and neatly sections the spouse in question, somehow resulting in a neat, living cake-slice as thick as a good porterhouse steak that comprises the part of his head with those two blinking orbs. It's the only part of him that remains living. His wife takes the slice home on a plate, puts it on a high shelf where it can live indefinitely as long as it's regularly fed spoonfuls of magic nutrient, and then, just because she never liked him much, blindfolds him with one of his favorite ties. The End.

That first version was roundly booed by everybody who read it. In retrospect, I don't blame them. It was stoopid, the kind of stupid that doesn't even deserve a proper "u" for first vowel.

This second version had a happier fate, receiving nominations for both the Stoker and the Nebula awards in the same year.

As with "Arvies," thematic resonances arrived by accident. People read the story as a profound meditation on the cost paid by our military families, but I had the central image of the man reduced to hands first, and added all the military stuff and post-traumatic stress disorder only because I was going for a more realistic tone than the rather silly first version and seized on the horrors of war as the most direct way to, umm, disarm my protagonist. An early draft was sheer fantasy, was set in a medieval era, and posited sorcery as the source of the medical miracle—which I did not want to discuss in any real detail—but the published version invoked just enough technological hand-waving to qualify the story as science fiction. I'm glad. I prefer it as science fiction.

OF A SWEET SLOW DANCE IN THE WAKE OF TEMPORARY DOGS: This was my 9/11 story, I'm afraid. It was born during a brief historical blip, following that terrible day, where people in my part of the country kept telling me that they'd never ever want to go to New York now, because they knew it would be attacked again. I couldn't comprehend such thinking. As an ex-New Yorker, I wanted nothing more than to revisit Manhattan as soon as possible, and the thought made me think of people living in war-torn or chaotic homelands all over the world, who are willing to endure unbearable horrors just to stay in the places they love. I decided to test that human attribute in the most extreme manner possible. My future wife saw a key flaw and induced me to add an important fix. I cannot now imagine this story, my personal favorite among everything I've ever written, shorn of her vital epiphany. So thanks, Judi.

This was another Nebula nominee, the only one I've ever had at novelette length.

OUR HUMAN: This is the only story here that belongs to "The AIsource Infection," the future history that includes all three of my Andrea Cort novels and a bunch of other short fiction. Riirgaans and Tchi are previously-established alien races from that universe, and Magrison is a previously-established much-wanted fiend and war criminal, first mentioned in passing in my Nebula nominee, "The Tangled Strings of the Marionettes."

You don't really need to know any of this to get this story in full, but if you do want to know more about Magrison and just why he's so notorious, check out my Andrea Cort novels, where he is discussed in absentia.

CHERUB: This tale, one of several snagged by anthologist extraordinaire John Skipp, is born of long recognition that people don't always have the faces they deserve. Osama Bin Laden, for instance, had a kind, avuncular face, with extraordinarily warm eyes. Shorn of personal history, and possibly beard, he looked like a guy it would have been great to know. You could imagine him as summer camp counselor. Now imagine that all his sins, past and future, rode his shoulders and could be identified at a distance. Imagine a world where every man's sins ride his shoulders and can be identified at a distance. Imagine the sad life of a blameless boy with no visible sins. Brrr.

THE SHALLOW END OF THE POOL: This out-and-out horror story was a stand-alone novella for Creeping Hemlock Press. It was nominated for the Stoker nominee for Best Long Fiction. Never be afraid to go there. Any remaining comments I have on this one should be joined to the comments on the next story.

PIECES OF ETHAN: Like the prior tale, it also involves a deadly relationship between a pair of siblings, and even another brother named Ethan. I have no explanation for why this kind of thing always comes up in my fiction. But conflict between siblings has been a recurring theme, not just here and in "Cherub" and "Shallow End" but in another Stoker Nominee, "Baby Girl Diamond," and even in my Spider-Man trilogy, where I contrived to raise the possibility that Peter Parker had a super-villain sister he never knew he had. The brother-sister relationship in my novel *The Third Claw of God* isn't quite as ugly as some of these others, but is strange, and certainly key to the action. Don't question this too closely. I get along with my own sister just fine. Sometimes the imagination just runs in well-traveled grooves, that's all.

THE BOY AND THE BOX: This one's based on several questions I happen to have about just who this supreme being thinks he is, if he requires people to spend their lives groveling before him. After all, a fragile ego is an unhealthy ego. I decided to see what would happen if the equation were rendered even more stark.

• • •

Thanks, all, for joining me on this journey. I owe thanks to John Joseph Adams, Julia Sevin, Scott Edelman, John Skipp, Sean Wallace, Paula Guran, Johnny Atomic, Brad Aiken, David Dunn, Dave Slavin, Christopher Negelein, Harlan Ellison, Jordan London, David Gerrold, my parents Saby and Joy Castro, and the love of my life, the splendiferous Judi Castro. The rest of y'all: enjoy yourselves.

Adam-Troy Castro
February 26, 2013

PUBLICATION HISTORY

"Arvies" first appeared in *Lightspeed*, August 2010. Reprinted by permission of the author.

"Her Husband's Hands" first appeared in *Lightspeed*, October 2011. Reprinted by permission of the author.

"Of a Sweet Slow Dance in the Wake of Temporary Dogs" first appeared in *Imaginings: An Anthology of Long Short Fiction,* 2003. Reprinted by permission of the author.

"Our Human" first appeared in *Tor.com*, May 2012. Reprinted by permission of the author.

"Cherub" first appeared in *Demons: Encounters with the Devil and His Minions, Fallen Angels, and the Possessed*, 2011. Reprinted by permission of the author.

"The Shallow End of the Pool" first appeared in *The Shallow End of the Pool*, 2008. Reprinted by permission of the author.

"Pieces of Ethan" first appeared in *Werewolves and Shape Shifters: Encounters with the Beasts Within*, 2010. Reprinted by permission of the author.

"The Boy and the Box" first appeared in *Lightspeed*, July 2013. Reprinted by permission of the author.

ABOUT THE AUTHOR

Adam-Troy Castro has said in interviews that he likes to jump genres and styles and has therefore refused to ever stay in place long enough to permit the unwanted existence of a creature that could be called a "typical" Adam-Troy Castro story. As a result, his short works range from the wild farce of his Vossoff and Nimmitz tales to the grim Nebula nominee "Of a Sweet Slow Dance in the Wake of Temporary Dogs." His twenty prior books include a nonfiction analysis of the Harry Potter phenomenon, four Spider-Man adventures, and three novels about his interstellar murder investigator, Andrea Cort (including a winner of the Philip K. Dick Award, *Emissaries from the Dead*). Adam's other award nominations include eight Nebulas, two Hugos, and three Stokers. Adam lives in Miami with his wife, Judi, and three insane cats named Uma Furman, Meow Farrow, and Harley Quinn.